MW01325797

My Delta Blues

5th Year Anniversary
Liberation Edition

A novel by

abidemi omowale kayode

Foreword by
Dr. Mark A. Kidd

Replete with a new novel preview

Blake, Thanks for the support!

MY DELTA BLUES

Published in the United States by Abidemi O. Kayode Publications

Third Edition
First Edition 2014

Editor: Abidemi Omowale Kayode

ISBN 978-0-578-22177-9
Paperback ISBN 978-0-578-14837-3

FOREWORD

As a longtime educator who, like the author of *My Delta Blues*, is a native Mississippian, and a male of African ancestry, and one who has spent a lifetime yearning, looking and learning what it means to be a black man in the deepest South, it has been my good fortune to come to know Abidemi Omowale Kayode, and to appreciate the perspectives from which he shares the content of this book.

Having first met Abidemi Kayode, when his name was Marques Lipsey, during his years as a young, sometimes a very vocal and witty, yet always introspective college student at the University of Mississippi, aka Ole Miss, it was immediately apparent that he had a lot to share. As with many of us who did then and continue to strive to establish a sense of identity, personal self-worth and value within our surroundings, seeking to meet the expectations of others who we are endeared to, and to those who seem to be the gatekeepers to our personal success, the author was one who seemed to always be physically present, while simultaneously in a world of inner thought, and perhaps a bit of personal turmoil.

Like many a young male of color, he has had to fight demons within, many of which were created by the expected norms of a deep-south society, steeped with the traditions and values that did not allow for much deviation from the norms of the period or place. As I recall being around him, whether in a work-related environment, social setting or perhaps with the bastion of the perceptual and real boundaries of the fraternal brotherhood's activities that we shared, it was ever obvious to me that there was something more that this author wanted and needed to be free to explore and to express.

My Delta Blues provides a first real opportunity for Abidemi to delve into the life and driving forces of one who is a son, a brother, a father, and a friend who still continues to traverse through the difficult path so many men, particularly men of the southern black male diaspora, must go. This piece of book causes me to reflect upon the powerful autobiographical writings of such early authors ranging from Langston Hughes, James Baldwin to Nathan McCall and even E. Lynn Harris. It is my hope that this seminal publication by Kayode is the first of many works to come from him that will open the hearts, minds, souls and perhaps the mouths of those who are searching for true meaning to their existence and to those others who would serve as supporters and detractors of the brothers who seek true meaning in their lives.

Written by
Mark A. Kidd, Ph.D., MBA
Educator, Brother, Friend

To my sons, Quesvon and J.C., you are my lungs. There is no breath without either of you. I live to leave both of you a legacy of which you will be proud. And to my grandchildren Elijah, Tatum, and Uri, it is my will that you will take up my torch and set a light onto this world. I would that this world improves in your lifetime in order to proffer you greatness through struggle and unconditional love and that your best versions of yourselves give each of you the strength to endure. Always remember to bless your generation even if people don't return the favor. Be a blessing henceforth and forever more.

~Dad/Baba/Buelo

PREFACE (The Liberation Edition)

It is essential that we evolve. In the last 5 years, I have liberated and shackled myself alternatively. In a short amount of time, it is very possible to forget your greatness when you are tied to a person or entity that usurps both your energy and time. Love is important, but not important enough to knock you off of your path to achieving your goals, maintaining your mental health, and prospering financially, spiritually, and universally. I allowed marriage, new relationships, and work to consume me to the point that I once again forgot who I was meant to be. I am an educator, an activist, an author, and a man of the people. While I believe I am SUPERMAN, I have to understand that I cannot be everything to other people if I am not first everything to me. Thanks to my therapist, I knew TOTAL LIBERATION in 2015. So I left a loveless, lifeless marriage. Only then to find myself in yet another relationship with someone who was more dependent on me than I was dependent on him.

I didn't need a new relationship, because I had a new one with myself. I allowed my old self to come in and create a false self that needed a false sense of security. This made me do things that I had given up like becoming someone else's escape when I had already escaped that type of bondage. Unfortunately, I met some people, particularly one person in 2015 that would alter the course of my trajectory in life because of my own insecurities. I knew better and I still participated in allowing people to use me to feel better about them. For that, I regret the time I spent focusing on other people instead of pouring into me.

Whenever I sought liberation again, it was monumentally difficult to obtain it because too many people began to bleed me dry and I was giving them blood from my turnip. Since that time, I have graduated from graduate school again, been heartbroken, broke, broken, divorced, accused on heinous atrocities, and almost died a few times, or at least that's what it felt like.

Here I am again, finding myself truest and most authentic self again. It is this space where I thrive in my element. My charisma is back. I regained my health, my strength, and my drive. The republishing of this book is a death-defying feat. I didn't think I would be here to see it published again. My health was depleting and I had no idea why until I realized it was because of stress from the job, relationships, and money issues. I will no longer be defeated by problems that I cause for myself. I will push through and always remember that only have to be remarkable for me, not for any other person on this planet including family. I will leave a legacy for my grandchildren, but even that will be on my terms. I will discontinue to take no for an answer when I know I am more than qualified to be met with yes. I will always choose me and I will tell me YES 100 times over. I deserve peace of mind, happiness, prosperity, and thanks. The rest of 2019 is my year to show myself that *I will WIN WIN WIN no matter what.*

IF YOU TRULY WANT TO FLY, YOU MUST FREE YOURSELF!

JOIN ME.

HAPPY "MY DELTA BLUES" ANNIVERSARY.

There are six essential themes here in this novel; escapism, hopelessness, the fleeting nature of peace, the necessity of love, deconstruction of religion, and the inevitability of death; all of which are the trivialities of the terminality of life. The funny thing about life is that it is hardly ever alleged, as my mentor points out, as terminal, save for disease and the gates at the airport. The wanton perception of life is there is a path meant for us, be that path straight away, vertical, or horizontal. In our individual and collective misguided perceptions, we miss opportunities to be present in the now. Instead, we dwell on a past that no longer exists and a future, which is a figment of hope considering we know not our expiry dates.

We believe that our beliefs in deities or our traditional education will somehow purpose our steps to something that we have been so indoctrinated to call "success". I'd venture to say that it's called success because we all suck at it. Success, if anything, is the real S-word, as opposed to "shit". Because *shit* is easy. Shit is tangible and can be donned like clothing. Imbibed like a latte. Even smeared like peanut butter. My good reader, you see our definitions of success require three things of which we are not usually willing to expend: tedium, timidity, and tumult. There will be mountains and valleys. Know that mountains will be easy. It's those fucking valleys, about which one has to worry. What's in the lowliness, the low places, and the darkness? I'll tell you, vile pieces of infectious, insidious macabre in all its ubiquity.

Much like the protagonist, Malachi, I too had been a loved yet unloved child, if that makes sense; in a world of nonsensical, maniacal things. No daddies lived in my world either. I can relate to the character of Malachi in many ways, in terms of his journey to nowhere.

My Delta Blues is my artistic expression that stories race, class, gender, religion, and sexuality in a way that proves that we don't know what we don't know and that as matter of fact we don't even know what we do know. As a result, I wrote this story and I tried to make it as realistic and unmistakable as possible, so as to paint vivid pictures of the aforementioned through Malachi's stream of consciousness. These ideologies become indelibly inked onto the pages, and into one's psyche; as you, my fine readers, to and through the Mississippi Delta with Malachi. I remember meeting stage, screen, and television actor Meshach Taylor after he'd so graciously agreed to read my manuscript, he said, "What I loved most about your manuscript was that there were no 'good white folks' coming to save the day". That was great confirmation that I had accomplished that which I had set forth.

My Delta Blues was total labor of love, hate, and frustration. I pushed through the negativity in order to fashion a fictitious force with which to be reckoned. This novel needed to be written, and needs to be read because it sheds light on many things, of which we, as Black people, Southern blacks, in particular, have been conditioned to be silent. Let it be a catalyst in helping you to find the strength to tell your story in your own way.

ACKNOWLEDGMENTS

The universe has conspired with me as the ultimate collaborator in all my literary efforts. I do not fool myself into thinking that without support systems that I would ever have been able to complete this project. The abundance of love and outpouring of care helped me to put pen to paper and my mind to the task. Thanks to all who assisted me in some form or fashion along the way. I give much respect to my beautiful mother, Bernice, for being a role model and for making sacrifices so that my brothers and I could have a better life than you. I want to thank my dad, Victor, for always staying in my corner through every stage of my life. To my other sons, Matthew and Arthur, thank you for being supportive of me and accepting me into your space. I would like to thank my mothers by proxy Linda Coach, Janice Howard, Deirdre Woodruff, Florence Haynes, Judy Wilson, Linnette Perry for always being loving and supportive over the years. I can't stop without thanking my grandmother, Minnie B., for being the matriarch of our family and leading us with grace and poise. I would like to thank my grandmother, Annie, for sharing her wisdom and strength throughout my life. To my granny, Jerry Butts, who is the nicest, most gracious woman who ever lived. I thank you for your tenacity and strong will.

No acknowledgments would be complete without mentioning my siblings. Thanks for my brothers, Gerald and Jaquon, for loving me and always being respectful of my individuality. To my nephews, Kameron and Kamarion (my lil old thang), thank you for allowing to be a part of your world. I love you guys. To my sisters, Lakia and Makita for being truly loving sisters even though we didn't grow up together. I know our bond will only get stronger as we age. To my sisters, Kameliah (and your gorgeous babies) and Alexandria and my brother Malcolm, continue to educate yourselves and create your own spaces for positivity. To my sister Brianna Victoria and my nephew, I hope this world offers you a voice and a place to make a difference in your life and in the lives of others.

To my nieces and nephews, Eriana, Peyton, Khamari, Reagan, Xavier, Canin, Cyan, Kenya, Chancellor (Lil old Chance), Ki, Kaemon, Jordan, Blair, and Kendra. Franchesa, my daughter-in-law whom I cherish, please continue to be a great mother and to love my son through his maturation season and know that your love isn't in vain. To my great aunts Bertha, Betty, Sallie, Clara (R.I.P), Roseanne, Adele, Sarah, and great uncles Willie J, Earl L., Earl B., and Bill, I hope that life brings you more joy and happiness than a love song. To my aunts, Ella Louise, Patricia, Carol, Valeria, Michelle, and uncles Richard, Michael A., and Michael P. (R.I.P), who helped to support and raise me up from a baby to man. I dream of a world full of love and free of evil for each of you. I give each of you my love from the bottom of my heart, the depth of my soul, and the breadth of my life. To my Aunt Paris, her husband and my cousins, whom, thanks to social media, I have gotten to know and enjoy your spirit in the last few years. To my Aunt Tammy Simmons, may your soul continue to touch others as does your smile.

Thanks for being on my side. To my other aunts, Cassandra, Vickie, Daisy, Ella, Phyllis K, Phyllis C., Erma S., Meredith, Bertha, and Wanda S., Bessie, may you continue to find beauty in all that you do. To my cousins, Lasundra, Nikki, Donald, Cleveland (J.R.), Tiffany, Yokena, Lil Michael, Rasheka, Reginald, Chauncey, Cordario, Yokeen, Darius, Laressa, Wajd, Amir, Nia, Kalvin, Weam, Wallah, Hatoun, Shemeka, Valerie, Charles, Darryl, Wanda, Annie, Wayne, Adrian, Tia, Betty, Merine, Veneko, Bernard, Kevin, Brandy, Melanie, Tina, Red, Michael P. Jr, Kisha, Dee, Eva, Terry, Jeff, Chris, Tony, Junior, Milton, Mack, Maxine, Toya, Bianca, Torris, Shamona, Pamela, and Shaquita, I hope that the world continues to revolve around the sun bringing light upon all your days..

To Dr. Omowale Akintunde , for believing in my literacy and always empowering me through positivity. You have helped me to take the edge off and lessen the rigidity. Thanks for being a mentor in every sense of the word.

To my greatest friends Rodney M., Reggie B., Bakari, Steven M., Chris C., Eddie G., LaMar, Surgio, Deirdre, Terri, Kerry, Chandrika, Greg M., Dr. Dante Daniel, Marlon F., Keith T., Troy B., Tammy C., Bernard, Owens, Lamont L., Nicole T., Courtney R., Marquita F., Kim W., Marcia S., Trenton B., Ben W., Marcus W., Brandy R., Gerald Lyrik, and Candice Daniels. I wish longevity in this life, but more so I wish for you all liberty and a spirit of tranquility. To my friends in education, Steve, Chris C., Bakari, Terri, Arlene W., Tamara S., Marquita F., Megan S., Lucretia, Tasha G., Shalontae, Teresa, Coach T., Cathy, Rahein, Tiffany, Erin G., Jackie C., Latresa, Raven, Alexcia, Davonte, Emily A., Hobson, Kevin Carter, Tracy, Gines, Victoria B., Zina, Medgar, Caressa, Burma, Jeremiah, Renata, Reggie E., Srta. Adams, and the Gawedzinskis. I hope that your days are multiplied by the giving of your hearts and minds to our future as you continue to be rooted in your benevolence, grounded by your deeds, and fastened to your dreams. I'd also like to thanks some of my biggest supporters and friends, Ms. Helen Amos, Carmen Taylor, Jada Rice, Larry Wallace, Latonya Shonta, Cindricka, Ella Nellum, Shelia Vertison, Ruby Scott, Ms. Bertha, Carol Henry, Norvetta, Amos Mays, Antonio Scott, Marcus P.,Taron Perry, Antonio Jackson, Toya and Terrell Hemphill, Richard Burks, Malcolm Morris, Corey, Joel Brown, Tarvis, Ced Lewis, Marcus Pettigrew, Arnetra, Andrew Seven Moore, Joshua Alexander, Eshaela Smith, Jaron Hall, Kevin Lytle, James Willis, and Latrice and Terrance Hamilton.

To the Greenville High and T. L. Weston classes of 1996, Prince got it wrong. When people party, they should party like it's 1996. Pump da pump da party! To the educational institutions that I have attended, Sidon Headstart, Eighth Street Headstart, Emma Boyd Elementary, Matty Akin Elementary, Irene Weddington Elementary, Coleman Junior High School, Greenville High School, University of Mississippi, Mississippi Valley State University, University of Phoenix, Walden University,Texas A&M at Commerce, and Arkansas State University.

To the educators, Dr. Silas Peyton, Ms. George, Ms. Antwine, Ms. Washington, Mrs. Overstreet, Mrs. Ingram, Miss Hodges, Mrs. Mabry-Howles, Mrs. C. Karlson, Mrs. L. Miller. Mrs. A. Percy, Mrs. H. Moore, Mrs. Netterville, Mrs. Dearman(Townsend), Mariya de la Cruz, Mrs. Parnell, Coach Parnell, Mrs. R. Rodgers, Rev. Anjohnette, Mrs. M. Foules (R.I.P), Mrs. Davis, Mr. Strange, Mr. Broome, Mrs. Mattie Williams, Mr. Lynch, Mrs. Mrs. Zanders, Majoice Thomas, Ms. Y. Foules, Mrs. R. Hayes, Mrs. Estes (R.I.P.), Coach Ward, Mrs. Striebeck, Dr. Tobias, Dr. W. Thomas, Ms. Donaldson, Rev. Dr. Carter, Ms. Love, Mr. Hawkins, Mr. Doze (R.I.P), Ms. B. Felton, Mrs. Hudson, Dr. L. Taylor, Mr. Breland, Mrs. Breland, Dr. Kidd, Dr. Trott, Doc Sennett, Michelle Mize, Dr. L. Shannon, Dr. Felton, Dr. Young-Minor, Dr. Felice Coles, Dr. P. Wirth, Dr. J. Hall, Mr. Gray, Mr. Daryle Moffett, Mr. McCollums, Mr. Chrietzberg, Dr. A. Smith, Mrs. Mendy Autry, Dr. Brooks, Dr. Richards, Dr. Ealy, Dr. R. Young, Dr. Mary Alice Jennings, Dr. Ansah (R.I.P), Dr. L. Holmes, Dr. Lowery (R.I.P), and Dr. Akintunde, who have all helped to shape my roles as an educator, facilitator, and motivator.

I would like to thank the members, families, and friends of Revels United Methodist Church. My Brothers, Al, Sheldon, Jamie, and Eddie. There aren't truer people alive. To Mark Kidd, Ben, David H., Corey W., Randy, Sovent, Montray, Chris Buford, Marcus (2-mark), Solo, Vernon, Markeeva, Tony, Marvell, Dereck, Corey P., Brad, Kenyon, Black, Eric C., Marlon B., and Robbie B., for being my favorite people of all time.

I would like to thank my sister Marquita Tenison, for being a beacon of light and inspiration in my life. You are truly a gift to the world and me. Thank you to Shirley Evans, Markeda Brown, and Mashonda Redmond for holding me down as a young professional fresh out of college. To Coaches Eugene, Hope Sanders, and Rev. J. King for keeping me encouraged as a young teacher.

I would like to send a very special thank you to Willie Davis and Beverly Wright-Smoot for the talks, texts, and lunches that got me through a very rough patch in my life. Thank you to Mrs. A. J. Hicks for reading the first few chapters of this book and encouraging me to finish. Because you believed in my craft, I forged through to completion. My mere thanks don't even begin to cover it. Thank you to Greg Mazen, a true friend, for helping me through one of the darkest periods of my life. I owe you tremendously. I would like to say thanks to Aurnell, Marlon F., Jermaine Hicks, Julius Jarrod, Larry W., Dr. D. Tanner, Kavara, LaShemia, and Jackie for showing me how to be forgiven and how to forgive. Those are qualities that I cherish more than many others.

Thanks to Drs. Sloan and Tribble, Nurses Meaghan and Brian, Erin, and Isaiah for keeping me healthy over the years. I don't know what I'd do without your medical expertise.

To my I.G.N.A.N.T Family, Surgio (Blajah), Mike, Bailey, LaMar (Rajah), Tasha, Jessica, Ashley (my loyal assistant), Manuola (Mannie Ku), Paul, Keelon, Michael, Rashad (Prajah), Ian, Samyon, Keith, Lamont, Jerome, Jordan, Kirt, and Xavier. I pray you all continue to be

Intriguing, Genuine, Noble, Ambitious, Natural, and Talented for the rest of your days. Do the work. It pays off. Fajah loves all of you. To the families that have always stimulated my sense of pride, the Coaches, Dickens, Hemphills, Primers, McClays, Scotts, Lovetts, Kings, Clarks, Lewises, Govans, Prestons, Griffins, Browns, Hudsons, Butts, Bruces, Edwards, Johnsons, Sheads, Garners, Nashes, Stewarts, Smiths, Williams, Parhams, Austins, Jacksons, Goodens, Hunleys, Wrights, Barnes, Maddoxes, Thomas, Henrys, Vertisons, Nellums, Walkers, Stranges, Carters, Gilberts, Turners, Drights, Wallaces, Rices, Sanders, Millers, Simmons, McTeers, Harrises, Legacy's, Juelz, Daze, Coutures, Diors,Royals and Bryants.

I would like to thank actor, director, and producer Mr. Bill Duke, for the dinners and advice and for just taking out time from his busy schedule to entertain us. In addition, I would like to thank television, screen, and stage actor, Mr. Meshach Taylor for his beautiful spirit and wonderful stories. It was a pleasure to meet and get to know you. Thank you for reading my story and for your tremendous feedback. I would also like to thank singer, songwriter, and producer Reggie Calloway for the keen insight and great critique of my story. Thank you for your time, candor, and presence.

To the ones I've lost, James K. Lipsey, Dr. Silas Peyton, LaTerry Lipsey, Uncle Joe, Aunt Big Tee, Aunt Geri, Uncle Roosevelt, Uncle Willie J., Merine, LouElla Quinn, Aunt BayBay, Aunt Myrtle, Michelle Clark, Connie Williams, Shonte Brown, Egina Dickens, Egina Dickerson, Mikaela Haynes, Forresta and Willie C. Brady, Aunt Emma Pitts, Lakeisha Hudson, Kim, Tyler, Mr. Swilley, Alejandro, Tommie McClendon, Randall, Marco McMillan, Darius (Miami), Alex Gibbs, Amal Omer, Uncle Willie B., Ms. H. Jones, Keith Kimmons, Ada Thompson, Mrs. Valencia Wallace-Williams, Martha Little, Gloria Blakely, Hattie Miles Burns, Mr. Redmond, Mr. Bennie Marshall, Michelle Chavez, Rev. Ralph King, Mrs. Y. Jackson, Jeanette Gooden, Mr. Maddox, Michael Howard, P.J. Howard, Y'Lupe Wallace, Rosalyn Daniels, Mr. Jamison, and Dekenric.

I would like to thank each student that I have had from Carrie Stern Elementary, Garrett Hall, Leland High School, Duncanville High School, Reed Middle School, Crowley Middle School, and KIPP Memphis Collegiate High School, and Power Center Academy High School for being my students and for showing me that imperfection is okay. Thanks for being some of the most authentically genuine teachers I have ever had. Though I can't name the hundreds of you, you know who you are and I will always hold you in my heart and mind. A special shout out to L-PsiPhi step team, The Def Poets' Society, and the Panther Voices.

To all my Facebook friends, Twitter followers, Instagram followers, former coworkers at all my schools, Sack and Save, WWISCAA, and Liberty National Life Insurance Company. Without your support, I don't know where I would have gotten the courage to move forward with this project. To every person that I may have left out, please know that it was not intentional and that I love each and every person I've ever encountered and you will forever be in my heart. Remember that this is only the first book, there will be many more books and acknowledgments to come.

I Got the Blues and I Can't Be Satisfied

I died a long time before they buried me in a plot. I was emotionally emaciated, and life's maggots had already dined on my flesh. My body had become my casket, and it grew more and more comfortable of a resting place as I continued to live a miserable existence. Internally, I had come to peace with death, and all the morbidity it entailed. Death was certainly no stranger to me. We were neighborly. It kept rearing its ugly head all around me. So, why not become bedfellows with the Reaper? At least, I was sure of his intentions towards me. There was no middle ground. No grey area. No room for ambiguity. The kinship was comprehensible. It was intangible, yet edible. My spirit had long ago loosened its grip on worldly continuation. For it was all too taxing and vexing. I surrendered to the easiest thing to do, for I had become pale from extenuating so much effort trying to outlast trouble. They say trouble don't last always. Hmmph. Trouble trumped me with its incessant, persistent force, and I had neither the substance nor sustenance, to withstand it. Sorrow impeached me. My eyes were sunken like those of Frankenstein's monster. Unlike him, I was human, and created by this GOD everyone had given so much credit. They say we were made in his image. Was I? Were the Indians? Were the Jews? Were the slaves? How can a God, with so much power, do so little to cradle the persecuted? How could he sit so high, and look down so low? No compassion for the innocent. No sympathy for the weak. No solace for the lonely. No food for the hungry. No shelter for the destitute. Only….the…blues

Chapter I

Nobody Cares for Me

"Get yo' ass out that goddamned baffroom. And you better not be in there playing wit' yo' little 15-year-old dick", she shouted, with no hint of femininity or subtlety.
Yes, ma'am". I replied. That was the only way you answered Huh (her). Huh had become the name I had so unfeelingly bestowed upon my mother's mother. I called her, Huh, because I didn't want to give Huh a name. Calling Huh, Hattie only humanized her, and she was no human, at least no human by my definition.
"Wash yo' damn hands, too, you little mongrel. I git so sick of yo' black, nappy head ass. Damn good-for-nuthin'. You jus' like yo' ass mammy," she blasted.
"Yes, ma'am", I rejoined.

She often compared me to my mama even though before my mama had been locked up, she adored her. Mama had been arrested several times for fraudulent checks unbeknownst to Huh and had finally been sentenced to 10 years mandatory in jail, without parole, for violation of probation and resisting arrest. Huh became livid at the thought of her own daughter being mixed up in any crime. After all, she had doted on her most of her life. Huh resented me because I was a reminder that her daughter had made her a grandmother and that because my mother was in jail she had to do what she never wanted to do again. Raise a child. She always referred to children in a manner of speaking as ruiners. Huh would always say, "No matter how good you raise'em, chill'un will turn on ya like week-old collard greens". I had been living with Huh for 3 years. I hated it as much as she did.

"Don't yes, ma'am me! Now get in there and hang them clothes out!"
"Yes..." I stopped midways because she would just as soon as slap my mouth, and bust my lip if she even

thought I was being mouthy or disrespectful, much less disobedient.
Gingerly, yet expeditiously, I walked into the kitchen, grabbed the basket of clothes, and proceeded to the backyard like the worker bee I had become. Ahh…but the backyard. That was my safe haven. There was a cornfield behind our house where I typically frequented and pretended to be in my own little world, devoid of Huh.
"Boy, you betta not drop nothin' out that basket or else I'mma beat yo ass so good you gonna have to shit standing up! You hear?"
Not sure how to respond, I managed to mutter, "Yes ma'am".

However, she didn't even wait to hear a response as she slammed the screen door as it always double slammed because it was, '*nigger rigged'*. A term coined by black folks meaning to fix something in such a shoddy way that even afterward said repair, it was still subject to be broken again. Behind our, 'use-to-be white' chipped wooden sided house, I would look out at the field, and oft times I'd imagine the kids from *Children of the Corn* coming out, and taking Huh into the corn, and performing some kind of sick ritual on her ass. Of course, I'd see myself participating in whatever torture they'd inflict. I cared not that we were related or that she was old. I wanted her to pay for her crimes against my humanity. That is the kind of contempt that I truly felt for this lady; who had the same blood running in her veins as I had, though hers was a much more frigid in temperature.
Smack! It was the last thing I heard as I hit the ground. I looked up to Huh cussing me out as I tasted metallic ooze in my mouth.

"Didn't I tell you not to drop my shit, you little bastard!?" she lambasted.
"But…," I stuttered.
"But, my ass. This god damned sock gonna have to be rewashed and I ain't running that washing machine for no

one sock. Now gone on in that house and wash it out on yo' hands," she ordered as she pointed the way.
"Yes, ma'am," I managed to mutter, through the hemorrhaging in my mouth.
"Oh, I know like hell, *yes, ma'am,"* she replied.

I hadn't even noticed the sock had dropped. I was too busy thinking vile thoughts, about insects and buzzards eating Huh insides. I guess the slap across the face served me right. It was probably this 'God' working through her. That "Bible" of hers does speak about honoring your mama; although she wasn't my mama proper. I guess she was somebody's mama. My mama's mama? No, better yet, Satan's mama. I finished hanging out the rest of the laundry and I ran quickly to the kitchen sink to wash the sock. I felt the dried blood in the corner of my mouth as I turned on the water on, and reached for the soap underneath the sink. As I began to wash the sock I heard Huh on the phone talking to Miss Sophia. Huh voice was reminded me of hail pelting the tops of cars, causing the most damage to the uninsured, me...

"Girl, yeah, Malachi in there washin' out a sock he done dropped on the ground after I done already washed it. He git on my goddamned nerves. Can't do shit right. I will be glad when summer over so he can care his black ass back to school. Jus' wanna lay up in here, eat, shit, and sleep. I'm tide of cookin' and cleanin' three times a day and shit", she lamented. She paused as she was obviously listening to Miss Sophia. She responded, "Girl, I don't give a damn if he kin hear me. This my damn house, and if he don't like it, he can let the door meet the crack of his ass on the way out. This ain't no prison, and I ain't no warden," she continued.

She didn't care about humiliating me in front of certain people. I was literally her whipping post. If she wasn't lashing out at me with her fists, it was with her sharp tongue. I had grown quite accustomed to hearing all kinds of derogatory, profane words. However, I still had not become immune. I was a child, and it hurt more deeply

than she could know, or even care. Each time felt like the first time. I'd try to block the emotional damage, but my gumption wasn't mature enough. I hadn't yet possessed the shrewdness to repel her nastiness. She was a bully. I was a victim. Therefore, I could never find any safety inside her house.
"Sophie, girl, what's goin' on?" she asked, with the mentality of a high school girl.

Sophie proceeded to tell Huh that old man Jessie had been arrested again for beating the shit out of his wife, Ms. Jane. Only this time, when the police arrived, they found that Jessie had been growing more marijuana in his backyard than a Hawaiian nut farmer. Old Man Jessie was a big, tall, stocky, blue-black man with big crusty hands and hairy forearms. He had been a deacon in the church for over 20 years, but everyone knew he was as 'jackleg' as our first preacher, Reverend Isaiah, who had been a habitual gambler and womanizer, who owed more money to more bookies, and fathered more illegitimate children than any antebellum plantation owner. They both were symbolic of all the hypocrisy that existed within the same church that was set up to *save* souls.

"Girl, naw! I knew that piece of shit deacon wasn't worth a nickel in Chinese money. Jus' ain't no *good* in him. God ain't pleased! Serves Ms. Jane jus' right. He been whoopin' her ass since Jesus raised Lazarus", she said.
"Hattie! You ought be shamed of yo' self!" Sophie countered.
"Nah, you need to be shamed of tellin' other folks business. Don't call and tell me nothin' if I can't have no opinion!"

It was still astounding to me how Huh could reference her God, and then remark so *ungodly* and unconcernedly for Ms. Jane. Sophie was complicit in all of Huh foolishness. Little did Sophie and everyone else in the town know that before her second husband died, he use to beat Huh. It went on for years, until Huh decided to take my mother and leave. So, the fact that she was so cold in her speech made me as livid as a wet cat. It never ceased to amaze me how judgmental this lady had become in her old age. She had neither mellowed out any, nor had she acquired any grace. She didn't even say grace before devouring her food. It was just so disappointing to see the person who was supposed to my caretaker, take so little time to care.

"Guess I'll talk yo' ass later since you so high and mighty today. I gotta go see what this little bastard in here doing anyhow. Bye!"

She hastily hung up before Sophie could respond. Then she searched for me in order to rain down her terrorism on my head, as only *she* knew how. I sank in my diminutiveness. My smallness. I became a toddler all over again whenever she was within five feet of me. I always wished I had a bib, or a blanket, or a pacifier behind which to hide. Nothing ever came to my rescue or became my comfort. No crib for a bed. Vulnerable.

"Malachi, yo' ass betta be through washing that sock goddamn it! I'm bout to walk down here to the sto' to git some stuff to cook for supper. Wash down the counters and sweep up that damn kitchen and mop my goddamn baffroom. If I git back and it ain't done, yo' ass betta gone or dead! Either way suit me jus' fine."
"Yes ma'am!" I replied, as I turned my head and rolled my eyes.

She walked up to me with what was left of her teeth biting her bottom lip. She grabbed my shirt and yanked me toward her. In rage she blared, "Oh, you wanna roll eyes and shit. Baby, you can roll'em, but you better control 'em cause I'll knock'em out and make ya hold'em!" Huh pushed me onto the floor before she exited.

How the hell did she always know when I was defiant? I had no fucking idea. I just wanted to punch Huh in the face one good time so she'd know how it felt. After all I was stronger than she was. However, I knew that would make me no better than Huh, but I couldn't help feeling that way. I just couldn't stand Huh!! And trust me, she didn't make it very hard. Her austerity and severity were chilling. It had frozen her soul to the point that she couldn't ever muster one glimmer of warmth for me. There was neither a nook nor a cranny in her body, which harbored cordiality, because icicles hung in Huh thoracic cavities, and ice-cold blood ran through the expanse of her extremities. To say she was cold-hearted would be tantamount to a compliment because that would mean she actually had a goddamned heart.

The neighborhood in which we lived was no different than Huh. A failed attempt at getting antiquity to survive in modernity. Seemingly harmless, the true nature of the area was mundane, dry, and unforgiving. The deeper you entered, the less obvious were the secrets, lies, and duplicity. It was all masked by gravel driveways, perfectly upright mailboxes, and neatly manicured lawns. Nevertheless, it was decent living for the Delta, but very subtly uninviting. Every house was *lived in;* with modest amenities and accommodations. They were mostly wooden houses. With the occasional sprinkling of brick domiciles for those who could afford them, or those who had inherited them.

Most of the yards were similarly landscaped with bushes around the fronts and the sides, with a tree or two in the front and or the back yard. There were cemented driveways and gravel driveways; depending on your socioeconomic status. But what all houses had in common, were the black mailboxes that rarely saw a friendly letter so much as they had been accustomed to the common bill or check, again, depending upon the rung of the economic ladder of which persons fell. The most unwelcoming aspects were the windows. It seemed that each window was filled with watchful eyes, spying on everything and everyone that passed. I felt like I was under a microscope each time I walked outside. Especially Ms. Johnson. She'd be in that window so much that it was said that she often fell asleep standing upright with her fingers clutching the drapes, which bedecked the cloudy panes.

The people were generally decent, but they were all just a bit too conformed to the monotony of rural life. The banality of the Mississippi Delta affected many of its inhabitants psychologically. There was no escaping the triviality that came with living here. Huh was definitely no exception, and that mere fact adversely affected me. From sunrise to sunset, the phonograph in my head played the slow '*da dump da dump da dump'* blues rhythm, which was to become the soundtrack of my life. The steady bass line paralleled the offbeat of my longing heart. My soul sang the lyrics of a beaten down boy who just wanted to fit in where there seemed to be no fit. A boy who just wanted to be loved in a place where love didn't live. This song was a testimony to my displacement in the Mississippi Delta. I hoped for happier times and positivity, but I positively knew that happiness was not a thing. In fact, it was a nonentity. It was a fantasy that only played out in books and perpetuated in movies. This blues I had come to know couldn't be played by B.B. King or Howlin' Wolf. Because I lived the blues, I knew *these* blues were much too complicated to score.

Chapter 2

Salty Dog

Huh always wore this gaudy ass straw hat, carried that ugly fucking wicker pocketbook, and never left the house without slamming the goddamn screen door like a crazy person, leaving me to bear the noise of the rusty ass springs and they compressed and extended. I walked over to the window as I imagine Ms. Johnson, the snoop did daily, and I watched through the window as she walked through the front gate. I had to see her close it before I could do anything else, just to be sure she was gone. I always felt less anxiety in her absence. To be absent from Huh is to be present with one's sanity. I loathed her. But what I loathed, even more, was Huh posture and silhouette as she made that stroll to Bubba's Market. Bubba's Market was Sidon's only means of acquiring essentials such as foodstuffs, cleaning supplies, and such. It mainly served the poor families with no cars or the lazy inhabitants who didn't want to make the trek 15 miles to Greenwood, the neighboring city, full of white folks and good old brainwashed blacks.

You know the kind; the ones who believed they have arrived just because they lived near and broke bread with white folks. Or the ones who have their fancy college degrees and drive foreign cars with expensive car notes they couldn't really afford. Bubba was the opposite of all that. He was humble. Even though he had money, he resided in the town of Sidon and drove a modest vehicle. Huh and Bubba had been classmates, and apparently he had a little soft spot for her, seeing as though she was a single, elderly lady with a grandchild in tow. On occasion, he'd allow Huh to put things on credit, or not pay at all.

It was said that Huh and Bubba had a thing back in the day before he married Esther, the town's *only* female drunk, but it was never verified. I didn't care to know because it was just a nasty sight to me, just thinking about it. Bubba was an eggplant-colored, hen-pecked, portly fellow, and drawing close to retirement age. Huh, was already 65 years old and had never worked so she never had anything from which to retire. Yet and still somehow she thought she had sex appeal; even considered herself a young tender as it were. It was ridiculous how she twisted up and down the street just like any old streetwalker, while her titties hung so low, it was a wonder she didn't step on them. Then her ass was as flat as a soybean field. Even her belly poked out like a bulging eye. None of that was evident to Huh, for when she walked the down the street, it was a shameful display of sass that she conveyed through her higgledy-piggledy body movement. She swayed like willow trees did when it was windy, displaying that pithy air of, "I am more than you", that she had neither the qualities nor resources for which to flaunt.

"Hey, Hattie!" Sally bellowed.

She waved and spoke to Ms. Sally. To call Sally the biggest flirt in Sidon was an understatement. She was nothing short of a man chaser. No, a man-eater. Sally was a tall, slender woman in her early thirties. It had been storied that she collected men like most women collected perfumes or porcelain figurines. She was an aficionado of the male species, so to speak. Nevertheless, she was one of Huh acquaintances. I would hesitate to say that they were friends, because Huh could hardly fathom what it meant to be a friend.

Sally had been married twice. The first time was when she was 16, and trying to get out of her mama's house. She married her high school boyfriend, Norris, Bubba's nephew, who was 18 and had more dick than brains. He had been worth his weight in foolishness. She had the marriage annulled within a few months' time. The second time, she married her grandfather's best friend, who was 50 years her senior. The septuagenarian had actually wooed Sally since she was a girl, but she had been too naïve to recognize his advances. He meticulously observed her maturation and knew exactly when to strike, just as she turned 22, had a stable job, and had developed a more womanly body. They married one beautiful June evening. He died of a stroke on the honeymoon minutes after they consummated their nuptials. It didn't work out too well for Sally financially, as all of his estates went to his first wife because the old man never changed the will and policies. Actually, Sally had to go into her own empty pockets to help bury him because the former wife was too vindictive to share the loot. Just the same, Sally was a humble gal. So she hoped that she'd be rewarded for the benevolence she had shown to a dead man who had no one else. After all, he was her husband.

"You comin' over later? *Hope you don't, hoe*," Huh called then whispered to herself.
"Yeah, see you then!" Sally yelled back.
Huh smiled and waved to everybody on the street, but talked under her breath about each of them, as if she had any room to do so.
"How you doing, Ms. Jane?" she yelled across the way while mumbling, *You stupid bitch.*
"I am blessed and highly favored, baby. You?"
"I can't complain. Just on my way to Bubba's to pick up some neck bones to go in my pinto beans."
"Sound good, girl!"
"Well, you know I try! Gotta feed Malachi!

Huh said. As if to imply that she really cared about me. Most folks in town revered her for being some kind of saint for taking me in as if she had rescued a dog or something. Those dusty ass niggers would always go on about how good of a grandmother she was for raising me while my mother was locked up. She fed off of these ineffectual compliments in much the same way worms feed off the corn in the cornfield. Just because she could.

"How is Malachi?" Jane inquired.
"He good. I swear dat boy is growing like a weed. Can't hardly keep'em in clothes and shoes. I guess my cookin' is holpin' him some too!" She snickered, as she walked away. "I gotta get over to this sto'. You be good Ms. Jane. *You*

dumb broad!" she muttered between her teeth as she smiled.

Just as she turned and stepped into the street to cross over to the sidewalk in front of the store, a car not going very fast spanked her on her right thigh. From what people reported, she threw herself to the ground with more theatrical flair than those over-the-top white Hollywood actresses. The histrionics were unflattering and just plain embarrassing.

"Oh, Lawd, I'm dead!" She bellowed, sounding like a wounded hyena.
Bubba asked his clerk to call the ambulance, as he ran out to check on Huh.
"Ms. Hattie, is you okay?" Bubba asked.
"Oh, my leg!" she shouted, as she panted.
"I had Henry to call the ambulance, so don't move, and try not to talk." Bubba said benignly, and with as much care as he could scramble.
"God damn it. You try not to talk. Try to git da hell up out my face! My damn leg hurtin'! Where the bastard at that hit me?"
"He right over there", Bubba said with hesitation.
"You was trying to kill me," she yelled and pointed at him accusingly.
"Ma'am, I didn't even see you. You came out of nowhere," the older, distinguished, well dressed, articulate Cadillac-driving man professed in slight distress as he hesitated to get closer to the wild woman.
"Oh yeah, you saw me!" she blared, in an accusatory manner.
"Calm down, Ms. Hattie," Bubba pleaded with her as he saw her blood was reaching the boiling point in Fahrenheit.
"You calm down. This here is my leg. Not yours." It was all Bubba could do to try to help Huh calm herself; however, Huh was still cussing and fussing. She was hell-bent on making this strange man feel worse than he already did.

“Ma’am is there anything I can do?” the man inquired, as the paramedics, who got to Sidon from Greenwood on two wheels, loaded Huh into the wagon.
“As a matter of fact, there is, sir! You can git the hell up out my face, call yo’ lawyer ‘cause I’m suing yo’ ass.” She quipped, and then rolled her eyes.

It was astonishing to see how ornery she could be, even after getting hit by a goddamn car. The neighbors stood around, gawking at her like she was a sideshow act. Only she had been more entertaining, and the performance was free of charge. Bubba waited with Huh as the sheriff deputy took a report while she lay in the back of the bus. By that time, Sally and Jane had gathered at the corner talking and debating their next move.

“Sally, did you see Hattie get hit by that car?” Jane asked.
“Girl, yeah. She was actin’ a complete mess over there,” replied Sally as she tried not to notice Jane’s eye.
“Girl, yeah, it was shameful.” Backbiting was indicative of the Delta. All of its residents were so close, yet so far apart. Yet it didn’t stop any of them, especially the women, from inviting one another to card parties, get-togethers, and dinners. Most friendships were nothing more than unmitigated farces, and my grandmother helped in every way she could to steadily perpetuate the old belief that black women just couldn’t be true friends. The two-facedness was a staple in the Delta. The duplicity was rich and flourished by the day. The women would as soon as plaster a smile in the faces of their so-called friends as they would talk about them behind their backs.

“I was gon’ go over there and console her but seem like everybody who tried Hattie just lit into ‘em like a wasp. She was lettin’ em have it up one side and down the other.” Jane began again.
“Guh, I knew I wasn’t gon’ subject myself to her wraff!” Sally said, as she impishly rolled her neck.
“ Wraff? I think that word got a “th” on the end”, Jane rejoined snickering.

“Oh shit, you know what I mean,” Sally reacted.
“Hmmph”, Jane countered.
“So, is we going down to the hospital?” Sally reluctantly asked.
“Girl, I reckon so. You know ain’t nobody else gonna go check on her triflin’ ass!” Ms. Jane responded.
“Now you done said a mouthful. You can pass a collection plate after that *sermon,* Reverend Jane!” Sally approved. They laughed.
“Girl, you a mess,” Jane retorted.
“Jane, we need to go get Malachi and take him wit’ us”, said Sally.
“Yeah, you right. Poor child got to deal with Hattie old tired ass,” Jane replied.

Sally and Ms. Jane pulled up in the yard in Old Man Jessie’s Buick LeSabre. It was the nicest kept car in the neighborhood. Rightfully so, considering Old Man Jessie washed and detailed it twice a week. He had rebuilt the entire car to look like it had just rolled off the assembly line. Ms. Jane had a black eye, and a bruise on her left arm, but she still held her head high. I assumed there was no other way to be, considering everyone had seen the police escort Old Man Jessie away. There was no need for discourse about the obvious. Jane was a classy looking lady in her late 50’s. She was a light-skinned, thick lady with curly hair and Asian slit eyes. Her eyes were mesmerizing to men because it subconsciously harkened to something they knew they’d never have. Jane was a sharp dresser too, she had the hair texture and skin color that was hated outwardly, but coveted inwardly, by so many self-loathing black women. Nonetheless, anyone could tell Jane could probably have had any man she wanted back in the day, but she settled for Old Man Jessie. Ms. Jane and Miss Sally knocked. I answered with caution because not many people visited other than Sally, Jane, and Sophie, but all of them knew Huh had gone out to the store.

“Hey Malachi.” Miss Sally and Ms. Jane said in unison.

“Hey Miss Sally and Ms. Jane. Grandma’s not here. She hadn’t made it back from the store yet,” I said, as diminutively as I always did; with little to no eye contact.
“We know baby. How you doing? You look good. Gittin’ taller ain’t you?” asked Miss Sally.
“Yes ma’am. I’m pretty close to six feet,” I said, proudly considering.

I was really shaping up to be a nice size at 15. I was already 150 lbs and not an ounce of fat, even though my diet consisted of lethal doses of sugar, pork, and grease. Since my mama and Huh were both a little on the plump side, I can only assume I had my absentee father’s good genetics and high metabolism.

“Well, baby, we came to pick you up. Your grandmama been in a little accident,” Ms. Jane declared.
“Is she okay?’” I asked, trying to sound as concerned as I possibly could. I really wanted to ask if she was dead. As bad as that sounds, it would have suited me either way.
“Yeah baby we think so. But we all gonna go over to the hospital, so put your shoes on and lock up, and we will wait on you in the car.
“Okay!” I replied, in a pseudo-worried voice.

I was in no hurry to go see Huh, and I am sure the feeling was mutual. When I thought of having to visit Huh, the guitar inside my mind was being plucked, and a death march began. My theme song. As we got closer and closer to the hospital, my blues got bluer, and so did I. The low tones turtled though my corpuscles, and the musicality of it all stopped short of ruining my immune system. During that short ride, a whole 64 measures of blues played in my soul. My slow thumping heart struggled to release enough blood to my brain to care about Huh. The guitar faded along with my good spirits as I prepared to breathe in the cold air of the hospital, and the frost that Huh breathed out instead of carbon dioxide. I needed something more than the blues because Huh was the blues, which always reminded me of what my mama going to jail took away from me. My voice.

Chapter 3

Big Leg Blues

When we arrived at the Delta Regional Medical Hospital, we were directed to the Third floor. Huh had already been giving the nurses hell. She was complaining about the food and the temperature of the room. As we walked in she was ordering the nurse around like a maid.

"I need more cover up in here. It's cold. What ya'll tryin' to do? Freeze a helpless old woman?" Huh carried on.
"No, ma'am. I will get you some more covers. Please calm down." The nurse implored.
"You calm down. I am sick of everybody tellin' me to calm down. Hell, I am calm. Like to see how calm ya'll'd be if ya'll was laid up in here," Huh growled, as we entered.
"Hattie, girl hush yo fuss up in here. Now these nurses are only doing their jobs," admonished Ms. Jane.
"Job? Hmmph! Some kinda job; if you call hasslin' me a job. I ain't been in this here hospital for forty minutes and they go the nerve to be complaining 'bout me. I'm a customer, and the customer is always right," Huh stated, as arrogantly and ignorantly as she did most things. Nothing, or no one, was ever good enough for her. However, I was a bit shocked at her behavior in front of Ms. Jane and Sally.
"Hey!" I said to Huh.
"Hey baby, come gimme a hug!" I was afraid to go near her. She hadn't hugged me in years, and even then, I am not sure how sincere it had been. I eased over close to her and she loosely gripped me like one might grip an uncooked egg. I stood there lifelessly, with a half grimace. There was no way I was going to put on a performance. I didn't feel anything from that hug but the transference of distance. We both knew it.
"Girl, so what the doctor say wrong wit' yo' leg?" asked Sally.
"He said I got me a hairline fraction or some 'nother. I got to git a cast on my whole leg."

“So how long you gone have to have the cast?” asked Ms Jane.
“He said about 6 weeks. I get it tomorrow. I sho’ hate it too!” Huh lamented.
“Well girl, I am just glad you alright, because you carried out ridiculous in front on Bubba’s sto’!” Sally reminded Huh, as they all laughed on cue. I turned my head and smirked a bit, as I imagined Huh being hit by that car.
“Girl, I ain’t stud’n’ you! Some friends ya’ll is. Didn’t even come see bout a defenseless old lady”.
“Hattie please, you ain’t hardly defenseless.” Sally quipped.
“Whatever! they all laughed. Anyhow, I’m gon’ need y’all to call my brother Roosevelt from Cleveland to come see ‘bout my house and watch after Malachi since I’m gon’ be off my foots for a while”, Huh proceeded.

My body tingled with glee. I had dreamed many times that someone else would live with us to act as a buffer to minimize the inhumane cruelty that I endured under the Huh rule. Uncle Roosevelt was just the guy too. He was everything a boy could ask for in an uncle. He didn’t mind spending time with me, talking about life, or cooking for me. The latter being the main thing, because he didn’t cook all that soul food foolishness that had become the misery in my life, not to mention in my stomach. I couldn’t wait for his arrival. I felt like a kid anticipating Santa, except Uncle Roosevelt was black and was only bearing the gifts of sanity, kindness, and peace of mind.

“Okay. Gimme his number?” I’ll call as soon as we leave here”, Sally acquiesced.
“Thank you! You’s a lifesaver!” Huh replied.

Just as we were preparing to leave, a pain shot up through Huh leg. She screamed loud enough to wake the dead. She writhed in pain and gripped the leg with the arm that contained the I.V, as the leg with no cast flailed without restrictions. The nurses rushed into the room

almost knocking us over. Their quick response was actually quite impressive.
"What's wrong Ms. Dixon?" One nursed queried.
"My leg. The pain is killing me", Huh said, breathing hard, as if she were in labor.
"Okay, we will give you something for the pain!" the other nurse responded.
"Can y'all please hurr' up?" she asked more sincerely, and without the incessant attitude as the nurses prepped the I.V. filled with morphine to release relatively small doses.

It almost made me feel sorry for the old battle-ax. I could see she was in a tremendous amount of pain, and at that moment, she had almost seemed human to me for the first time. I hated her. Often, I had thought of her being tortured and maimed, but seeing her flinch in pain softened me a bit. I knew at that point that I didn't want her to die, but maybe this pain would soften her some too. It could have possibly been her reaction to the pain medicine that made her human to me. I just wondered what it would take to make her feel for me and make her care for me.

"Ms. Dixon, you will feel more relaxed in a few minutes", the nurse said lovingly, as she stroked Huh's bangs back out of her face.

Her eyes rolled back into her head, and she drifted off to sleep. She almost looked peaceful and sweet. I imagined that it would be how she might appear in her casket. Seeing her there again made me feel bad about ever having any thought of her dying. She was just really unreasonably mean to me. I was just a child, and she treated me no differently than a stray cat that wouldn't leave just because she fed it! The nurses asked us to allow her to rest so the three of us left. Miss Sally and Ms. Jane gossiped the whole ride. Finally, Ms. Jane addressed me.

"Malachi, you hungry?" she asked.
"Yes, ma'am", I returned.

"Well, you in luck. I got some cabbage, yams, pig's feet, and cornbread on the stove at home", she rambled on.

I thought "YUCK" in my head, but I smiled, then I rolled my eyes when she turned her head. I really didn't want to go to her house because of the turmoil with which she had been dealing, but I knew she was lonely since the deacon was in jail. Even though she was just as lonely when the deacon was there with her, she was probably glad I was there instead. I could only imagine the sadness that she endured not being close with her children and grandchildren. I didn't mind eating her *slop,* and being a substitute for what she lacked; if only for one evening.
"Sally girl, you comin' ova to eat?" Jane asked.
"Naw girl, I gotta go home and git ready for bingo. I feel lucky, plus my friend Joe is gon' be there!" Sally said, as she girlishly slung her head to one side and played with her hair.
"Girl, that don't make no damn sense. You been playing bingo for 3 years and ain't won yet. And every week you have a different man on the menu," Jane smirked afterward.
"Well hell, until I can order some'n that will fill me up, I will continue to sample the appetizers!" she said haughtily, as she jerked her neck sassily then turned to the passenger window.
"You a mess!" they both laughed. So did I, even though then I didn't really realize Jane was *actually* calling Sally a loose woman, and Sally pretty much agreed.
"Malachi you be good now! I'm gon' call yo' Uncle before I leave. If you need me call me." It was at the point that it dawned on me, that until Uncle Roosevelt arrived, I would have to stay with someone. I then realized that it would be Jane. "Damn!" I thought.

The last place on Earth I wanted to be was around Ms. Jane and her abusive husband. Her situation was tragic. We all pretended not to notice the black eye, which stuck out like a white shoe after Labor Day.

"He gon' be wit' me! He will be all right"! Jane shouted.

"Well, I will see you girl! Call me later!" Sally replied.
"How bout I let you call me, Miss Thang!!" Jane retorted.
"Yeah, that might be better because you know how I get down!" Sally responded.
"Um Hmm!! I do!" Jane pursed her lips and rolled her eyes in jest.

They laughed in unison and we drove off. We were off to Ms. Jane's where I was to be held captive until Uncle Roosevelt, my Moses, would come to free me from the chains of my Delta blues. To add insult to injury, I would be forced to clog my arteries with all Ms. Jane's food. Mama and I had moved from Mississippi when I was 3, so I had gotten used to the city routine of eating foods out of boxes and cans, fast food, and the one occasional healthy meal of fish, rice, and veggies. My mother certainly hadn't picked up the traditional habit of cooking soul food every night of the week. I was grateful because I would have died in those 10 years after eating baked macaroni, neck bones, rutabaga, pig ears, fatbacks, mustard greens, candied yams, and pinto beans all the damn time.

During the years I had lived with Huh, I had more than made up for those previous ten years. She cooked that shit, all day every day. The summers were the worst. Her church members would bring over buckets of snap beans, purple hull peas, and butter beans. Not only did I have to eat one or the other every day, but, I was also charged with the task of snapping or shelling. My thumbs stayed purple for the remainder of the summer months.

The key was to look as if I liked doing it, or otherwise, I would have been nailed to the cross for being ungrateful. We would end up with two or three buckets full of peas and beans each time Mr. Buck or Mr. McGee came. The beans had to be blanched and then put away into the deep freezer. From that point, we ate peas and beans clear up until New Year's.

When we arrived at Ms. Jane's house, I could smell the food she had cooked. It made me nauseous. I was dry heaving at the pure stench of cabbage greens steeped in pork parts and fat. I took short breaths for a while until I had become immune to the smell. I was hungry, so really, no matter how much I abhorred the food, I had to eat. That was the life of the Delta. Either you ate what was offered up, or you starved. There was not a preponderance of food as it were, so you ate regardless of your finicky nature.

"Malachi, go wash ya hands baby! I am bout to warm this food up for yo supper!" Jane admonished.
"Yes, ma'am! I answered as I traipsed over to the bathroom.

As I proceeded to the bathroom, I noticed all the antiques and nice bric-a-brac Ms. Jane and the deacon possessed. They had one of the nicest homes in Sidon. I am sure the property value was about $4.00 or less, considering all of the other worn-down dwellings that existed in the vicinity. I always wondered why they continued to live there. I found out much later, that the Deacon had been willed the house by his grandfather, and with all the renovations over the last 20 years, it was worth more than anyone was willing to buy in that area.

Therefore, they were doomed to dwell in a No Man's Land, forced to live in a place of poverty. They lived miserably among people who had nothing for which to live or to die. The longer they stayed, the more complacent they became. The more desperate Jane became. The more violent Old Man Jessie became. The Delta was their prison, and they had been sentenced to life.

When I returned from the bathroom, she was setting the table for two. She was humming some church ditty that I came to realize much later was "How I Got Over!" I am sure it was a testament to her strong wills to survive in a time and place that was unkind, and harsh, and she knew she didn't deserve it. However, after so long, there was no leaving. I watched her place each glass, plate, fork, spoon, knife, and napkin with such intricacy. It was routine, it was how she learned to not fight back. She was like a soldier who had better make his bed correctly, or shine his shoes properly, or there'd be consequences. Even though Old Man Jessie wasn't there, she still did things in this way, so as to meet a certain aesthetic for his approval. I was saddened by her need to make others content, as she forsook her own joy.

"Come on in and sit down right here while I fix your plate!" She politely ushered me to the chair and pushed it up to the table.

That felt good. No one had treated me with that motherly instinct in quite some time. I think it felt even better to Ms. Jane than it had to me. She liked doting over me as if I were her own. Since her children were grown, and hardly ever visited because they knew that their father wasn't worth a quarter. They had tried to get Ms. Jane to leave on many an occasion, but she refused, holding fast to her marriage vows; for better or for worse. Outside, she was a mess, but she had it covered inside.

The day that Jane's children abandoned her was the same day that I had arrived in Sidon, March 3, 1989. I remembered it like it was yesterday, for it was two years prior to the Rodney King beating, the Billy clubs heard all around the world. Jane and Jessie's children lived with them, so Jane was particularly happy during that period. The deacon had made many attempts to get Jane to ask the children to leave the house. The deacon felt as though the children were much too old to still be living at home. Jane knew this was the case, but she also knew that once they left, she would have no purpose.

The children were not at home when Old Man Jessie took it upon himself to have one final conversation about the children moving out. Jane was not amenable. She fought him every step of the way with words. When Jessie saw that his wife was not being agreeable, he struck her. Jane wailed in pain and tried to escape her husband's fury. He reached out and grabbed her and held her down, and began to impact her with punches. As she screamed, her children were arriving. They ran into the house with all intentions to fight for their mother. Old Man Jessie was awaiting them with a double-barreled shotgun, and he dared any one of them to come closer. He gave them a week's notice of their eviction. The children consoled their mother as Jessie backed out of the room still pointing the gun at the people he was supposed to love and protect. Their children had been pleading with Jane to leave their abusive daddy. She refused. They told her that if she didn't leave with them, she'd never see them again. She lovingly looked at each of them in the eyes got up from the floor, hung her head and trailed behind her husband. She retreated into her room. Her children left.

Jane's life was much like my Delta blues song chorus. It was a repetitive refrain over blue notes that played over and over again, speaking of the woes that she had endured since she had been married to Old Man Jessie. Freedom wasn't something that one could earn, but it was definitely something that one could lose. She had lost her freedom long before she even had a space in which to sit in her truth. Ms. Jane's blues had usurped her freedom. The blues had bought her liberty and literally stole her peace. She was a slave to the blues. The blues were the only thing Ms. Jane had left to call her own. Only now, the call and response of her blues were different. Freedom called, but her soul wouldn't respond.

Chapter 4

Waiting for You

Ms. Sally had called Uncle Roosevelt that night before Bingo. Uncle Roosevelt had agreed to come as soon as he could. Although Uncle Roosevelt was retired, he did some sideline landscaping to keep himself from being bored to death, so he had to finish up the jobs he had started first before coming. It was amazing that at the age of 70, he still had the energy and agility to ride lawn mowers and bend at the knees frequently. Until he arrived, we had gone to Huh house to retrieve some of my personal effects. I ended up staying with Ms. Jane for a few days.

Huh came home the same day that Uncle Roosevelt arrived in Sidon from Cleveland, Mississippi. Ms. Jane, Ms. Sally, and I had gone to collect her from the hospital earlier that day. They talked about how she complained the whole way home about the stay, and the nurses, and the doctors, and the food. We all knew that even if she had been in heaven, she would find something about which to complain. Ms. Jane and Ms. Sally made sure that she was comfortable in bed and had enough cushion to keep her leg elevated. As they were preparing to make things accessible to her, considering she would be laid up for a while, we heard someone entering through the front door.

It was Uncle Roosevelt. "Unc" was a big robust guy of 6'3 with a graying head of thick hair and surprising boyishly good looks. He had become something of a ladies' man in his later years, as his wife of 20 years had passed away before he retired. Ms. Sally lay eyes on him as if she had never met him before. She literally drooled down the front of her dress as he spread his friendliness and spirited disposition around like marmalade. His weatherman personality was refreshing, and just what the doctor ordered, to combat the stormy emptiness I had come to know while living with Huh.

"Hey! Hey! Hey!" Unc said jovially.
"Hey Roosevelt!" we all said collectively, almost in unison.
"Where is Mama Broke Leg?" Unc joked. As we laughed, he put me in a headlock and playfully dragged me from the hallway into Huh room.
"What is ya'll doing in there?" Huh questioned rudely, as we incited much ruckus.
"What you doin' in here?" Unc opposed.
"Velt, that you?" Huh asked, in an anticipatory manner.
"Yeah, ole girl. It's me in the flesh! With my big ole fine self!" he said, as he hugged and kissed Huh. It was still miraculous to me that anyone could embrace Huh with anything other than the enmity with which she served me, along with a tall glass of chilled disgust. Nevertheless, it was good having Unc there.
"And who you calling old?" she asked with a smugness, as she patted her hair and coyly rolled her eyes.
"You too damn old to still thank you cute!" Unc said, as he let out a laugh that shook the room. I wanted to laugh, but I didn't know how she would receive that, so I opted to cover my mouth and snicker to myself.
"Boy! I don't know what you talkin' bout. I'm as fine as I was 30 years ago!" she replied, with a little harmless venom while sneering at Uncle Roosevelt before she burst into laughter.
"Who said you was fine then?" Roosevelt asked, in a none too subtle way.
"Don't play! I had all yo' little friends runnin' up in behine me!" Huh retorted.
"That's cause they knew they could get you to pay for stuff!" he said, and doubled over with laughter.
"If I could get out this here bed, I would be buying yo' casket you old goat!!" Huh recoiled easily.
"I might be old, but you old and you a cripple!" they laughed and went back and forth until Huh had to take her pain pills, which made her drowsy. Unc took us all in the kitchen and rustled up some ground beef and potatoes, and made the best homemade hamburgers and French fries.

In the Delta, we didn't eat a hamburger on a bun. We ate it on white bread. It was a cholesterol nightmare waiting to clog every artery in the body, but it was good. Two pieces of Wonder bread, mayonnaise, mustard, onions, pickles, lettuce. The sheer mass of the burger was way too much for the greasy bread to sustain, but that is what made a homemade hamburger a burger.

Ms. Jane, Ms. Sally, and I ate until we nearly burst open. However, it didn't matter how full Ms. Sally had gotten, she was still hungry for Roosevelt. Sally was still bent on throwing herself on Unc. He ate it up too. He was an older chap who could still attract younger women, and he knew it. While Ms. Sally was certainly neither a spring chicken nor virginal, she was forty years Uncle Roosevelt's junior. It was no secret she had an affinity for older men.

Eventually, Ms. Jane and Ms. Sally left. Unc and I sat in the living room and talked well into the night. We had some interesting conversations about Huh, and when she was younger. The days before my grandfather, and others helped to make her the bitter person she had become over the years. It was then that I started to understand that she had evolved into the terror that I endured on a daily basis, and it was not indeed I who had catalyzed the inhumane way she treated me. I wanted to discuss with Unc how horribly she behaved when no one was around, but he talked about her with so much affection that I couldn't bring myself to tear down this inner shrine he had built in honor of his only living sibling.

Unc fell asleep in the lounge chair in mid-conversation. I covered him up and I slept on the love seat perpendicular to him. I pined for some kind of peek into her past, or even an inkling of how she may have turned out had she not become a bitter old, unfeeling spinster. I would even have accepted a dream of what it was like to know a kinder, gentler Hattie Lee Dixon. To know what she used to be, or even what she could have been. All I had been privy to was that she was a sea marred by a painful past, in which she was reluctant to allow me to take a swim.

Ms. Hattie's blues. Huh blues had become the bane of my existence. The songs sung by her soul haunted mine. I couldn't find a space to dwell devoid of Huh agony. The ghosts of her past, the ghouls of her present, had alienated me. Huh blues played in the radio of my heart, causing a murmur that was detrimental to my life. The notes had gone from blue to deep mauve, symbolizing the inner wounds that had birthed her antagonism. They were tantamount to insufferable pain, and insurmountable unrest that tainted her spirit. Living and breathing were labored for her and me. It was almost as if I had to grieve because she refused to grieve. I had to suffer because she had lived for my future sins, and until her crucifixion was over, it was my lot in life to bear Ms. Hattie's blues. If only I were not the sole audience to her many blues concerts, then maybe, maybe I'd find peace, and we would find one another.

Chapter 5

Funky Butt

Huh had lain up for about a week before her crony Miss Sophia decided to come over for a visit. She hadn't even called once. She was the truest definition of a busy body. One who only calls or come by to gossip. Her colossally big, messy mouth was only minimized her short, fat frame. They nicknamed Miss Sophia, Channel 12 news because she could spit back the trivial goings-on in town, save for her own business of course. Trust me; she had more skeletons in her closet than the graveyard behind Mt. Pisgah Missionary Baptist church, literally.

Miss Sophia had been born an only child; therefore, we assumed that she grew up possibly having to make things up so much that she never grew out of it. If Miss Sophia didn't know the truth about something, she would intricately fabricate a truth as she went along, so as to make the story juicier by embellishing. I never understood why she and Huh were so close. Miss Sophia had lied on Huh so many times. They had even almost come to blows once. She had gone around the town and spread that Huh was sleeping with a married man. We later found out that she had spread this because she indeed was the one sleeping with the man and his wife was hot on her trail. Huh cussed Sophia out so badly and shouted the kind of obscenities that would have made Lucifer blush. Sally and Jane were Sophie's only saving grace.

They physically held Huh back from giving Sophie one good ass whooping. I haven't liked her since then. Whenever Sophie was in earshot, I always felt a sweltering gust of air that reeked of the most diabolical stench. Her aura spat dark colors, and striated hues, that just didn't sit well with me. The day she came over to see Huh, she was wearing a turquoise and pink flowered housedress, and some dusty, run over pink house slippers. Her hair was very coarse, you know the kind of hair black folks call 'bad hair', and beyond that, it was badly dyed red. It was hidden underneath a blue bandana, which made me shiver, as she looked very much like an obese voodoo woman. To make things worse, she always stank of bleach and old pinto beans, a smell very specific to the Mississippi Delta.

I held my nose and rolled my eyes as she pinched me on the cheek and rubbed my head. I hated that. I was too damned old for her to be violating my personal space. She was just too damned country to know any better. There was nothing in the least sophisticated about her. She waddled to Huh room and started yapping soon as she walked in.

"Hattie! Is you up?" she bawled, in that mammy, from *Gone with the Wind, I don't know nothin' bout birthin' no babies* way she had about herself.

"Yeah Sophie, Girl! That you?" Huh questioned.

"You know it!" Sophia belted.

"Well, it took yo' fat ass long enough to come see me! You triflin' heifer you!" Huh rolled her eyes.

"That aint no way to talk about your dearest and bestest friend!" Sophia lamented, hoping for sympathy. However, the only way she'd get it would be to look it up in a dictionary between shit and symphony.

"Girl, whatever! Onlyest friend I got is in Jesus! They that wait on the Lord shall renew they strength. They that wait on Sophia shall renew they burial insurance! That's straight out the book of Ephesiastes 30 and 4!" Huh retorted haughtily.

"Ephesiastes? Girl, that ain't no book in da Bible! And it's Isaiah 40 and 31."

"Uh huh! I need a beer. Go git me one out the Frigidaire. That's Colt 40 and 5." They laughed simultaneously. "Girl, hurrup! Don't let Velt see you. He don't like when I drank! Sophia wobbled her barren hips down the hall about as inconspicuous as an invalid hippopotamus. Somehow, she managed to make it back without Unc noticing her glistening, sweaty forehead.

"Girl, thank you! I needed this here!" she averred, as she took positively animalistic gulps.

“So how you really doin’?” Miss Sophia asked as she tried to sound sincere.
“I am doin’ good, but you don’t give a shit!” Huh barked.
“Don’t act like that Hattie! You know I be busy workin’ at Mr. Cholly them house!”
“Uh huh! Mr.Cholly them got phones too!”
“Um sorry Hattie. Ain’t no excuse! I just didn’t call, and I ain’t even got a good reason.”
“I’m over it! Now, gone back in there and git me another beer! I might forgive you.” She hurried into the kitchen, and as soon as she was headed out, Uncle Roosevelt caught her.
“Sophia!” Velt scowled.
“Oh, hey Roosevelt!” Sophie flinched.
“What you got in yo hands?” he asked, in his rather avuncular way.
“Jus’ a little some’n to wet my *thoat*! It’s hot out there!”
“When you start drankin’ beer?” Velt inquired.
“I do ev’ry now and den to settle my stomach!” Sophie replied.
“You think I am a fool, don’t you? You standing yo’ pickaninny lookin’ ass over there lyin’ through yo’ teeth. If you take that beer to my susta I’mma bust yo’ ass!” Velt warned.
“I wasn’t finna give dis to her! I promise!” Sophie winced.
“Like hell you wasn’t! And I am Sandy Clause!” He had walked over and snatched the beer from her, in this rather scolding manner as Sophia stood there looking like a raccoon.
“You can gone on back in there and tell her all we got is water for cripples!” Velt demanded.

“You so crazy!” she said, with an awkward half smile and chuckle as she turned to walk away. Uncle Roosevelt rolled his eyes and looked at her billowy body and dimpled posterior. He shook his head in pure disgust as Sophia meandered down the hall back to Huh room.

“Girl, where da beer is?” Huh probed.
“Velt caught me gittin’ it fah you!” Sophie rebounded.

"I shoulda known not to sen' yo' ass in there! You ain't neva been able to be 'screet bout nothin'!" Huh rebuked.

"It ain't my fault yo' brother nosey as hell!" Sophie recoiled.

"I know yo' ass ain't callin nobody nosey! Cause you so damn nosey you keep your eyes open when you is sayin' grace," Huh bantered.

"Guh I ain't stud'n you! But did you hear bout Willie B. and Ro Lee?"

"What done hap'ned?" Huh sat up and listened intently for the foolishness that was about to spew from Sophia's mouth.

"Well, girl, they say Willie B. come home and caught Ro Lee in the bed wit' another woman! They said he went got his shotgun and started shootin' and Ro Lee and da other bulldagger scattered like ants. They said they was nekkid as jaybirds and haulin' ass down the street." She said, as they laughed ferociously. It always amazed me that when people gossip, they always preface their statements with "they said". Why can't they just say from whom they got the gossip? I never trusted people who said that.

"Guh naw! I know Rosie Lee ain't lapping all up tween no dyke's legs is she?" Huh asked, with hopes that it was just a rumor.

Huh and Ro Lee used to be as thick as thieves back in the day. They were like partners in crime until she married Willie B. Willie B. was a man's man. He drank a glass of whiskey every morning before breakfast, and every night before bed. He watched every sport, played spades, bid whist and poker, fished, hunted, bowled, and shot pool recreationally. Before he dropped out of high school to take care of his family, he had been the star quarterback and something of a player with women. He was like a town icon, and still even as old as he had become. His thick, black curly hair was still as plush as it had always been. The only things that disclosed his age were his infinite wisdom, salt and pepper mustache, beard, and sideburns. Over the years he had always done some type of construction work, which kept his body pretty muscular. After all of his brothers and sisters had graduated and gone on to college, he met Ro Lee. Ro Lee was 15 years Willie B's senior. She still had very youthful looks and a beauty queen figure that she had managed to keep even in her sixties. So it was terribly hard for Huh to believe that Ro Lee would play for the other team, so to speak.

"That's what they say now! I am jes' reportin' what I done heard!" Sophie said.
"Yeah, but dat use to be my ace boon coon!" Huh replied.
"Hmmph!" Miss Sophia said in an attempt to imply the unthinkable about Huh.
"Hmmph hell! I know you ain't tryin' to say nuttin' 'bout me…cause I likes strict dick!" Huh replied vulgarly.
"You know I wouldn't thank nothing like that 'bout you guh! Where all dese nice flowers and plants come from?" Sophia quickly changed the subject.
"I don't know. Don't none of 'em got no name on 'em! Far as I am concerned, they coulda kep'em all. Got it looking like a damn jungle up in here!"
"Well, it fits 'cause they say you acted a monkey when that man hit you!" Sophia laughed heartily.
"Girl, git somewhere and sat down wit' that foolishness! You let somebody hit you on yo' hip and see you feel. But den again you might do mo' damage to the vehicle den it would do to yo' big ass!" Huh teased.
"You always tryin' to call somebody fat! You ain't missin' no meals neither you know!" Sophie cracked.
"Bitch, I am barely a size 10 good now, you need to go home and put yo' bifocals on if you can't see that!" Huh admonished.
"I will go home, cause I ain't gon' be too many mo' bitches up in here!" Sophie replied.
"Bitch! Bitch! Bitch! Bitch! Bitch!" Huh said in a mocking sing-songy manner. "Now how many mo' bitches ain't you gon' be?" Huh mocked.
"You need to grow yo' cripple ass up!" Sophie chided.
"And you need to wash your fat ass up!" Huh responded childishly.

"I ain't gone sit here and be insulted by the likes of you Hattie Mae Dixon." Miss Sophia said as she stormed out!
"Well, don't let the do' get stuck in yo' fat ass! And it's Hattie Lee, bitch!" Huh yelled, as Miss Sophia left. Uncle Velt hurried in to see why they had been talking so loudly.
"Hattie? What the hell wrong wit' you?"
"Ain't shit wrong wit' me! What da hell wrong wit' you?" She asked, with an air of ill-conceived confidence as she cocked her head to one side.
"Hattie, Go to sleep! I know I shouldn'ta let her raccoon lookin' ass up in this house. She done gone and got yo pressure all up, and I ain't got time to deal wit' yo' ass when you like this." Unc said as he turned to leave.

Huh eventually went to sleep. She tossed and turned as I heard her calling Sophia's name over and over, so it was obvious that she had been dreaming about Sophia. Huh woke up screaming and sweating profusely. We ran into the room and she told us about the dream she had had about Sophie. She said she dreamed she had killed her with by pounding her in the head over and over with a beer bottle. We all had a much-needed laugh in the house that was slowly becoming a home thanks to Uncle Roosevelt.

The notes of my blues song had become much less blue. Its darkness had seemed to fade away, and the repetition took a new turn, if only for the moment. I could hear a progression in the chord. The laughter in the air seemed to straighten out the bent notes, and my blues song had become more graceful. In that instant, the melodic fall was merely a memory. My blues were light blue, like the midday skies in the summertime. Although the refrain was much less familiar, I didn't mind it playing in my head, in my heart, in my soul. Uncle Roosevelt had become my musical director. I was no longer an audience of one. He populated my soul with his laugh, his benevolence, and his strength. My Delta blues faded a bit by the day, but more than anything, I no longer had to face the music alone. This was a musical feat. There was no more trepidation in my song. Unc was now the bandleader and I could now listen to the blues without crying in a silo.

Chapter 6

Fired a Shot, Missed Him

For weeks, we had been trying to figure out where all of the anonymous cards came, flowers, plants, and balloons had been coming. We thought we had narrowed it down to two men that use to be sweet on Huh back in the day, but we weren't able to confirm it. One day, I was sitting in the back porch making a stick gun. It was one of the rites of passage for a young country boy. Even though I was urban as hell, some rural experiences grounded and humbled my city slick ass. A stick gun required a few items that one could usually find if he was resourceful enough. I needed a chunk of wood, about 2 and a half feet long and about 4 inches wide, a couple of two 2-3 inch nails, rubber bands, a clothespin, and soda pop can tabs. To be able to make a functional stick gun was a true coming-of-age ritual in the Delta. In order to do it right, I had to make sure my rubber bands were taut enough to send those tabs flying like real bullets.

We use to have stick gun wars and try to shoot birds. Luckily, we never actually hit the birds. How inhumane would that be? As I was putting the finishing touches on my gun, I heard a car pull up. I walked around front, and much to my surprise was a big bright white 1988 Fleetwood Cadillac, replete with classic whitewall spit shine tires, and an added v-shaped spoiler on the back. To try to get a good look before I approached the car, I used my hand as an awning because I was temporarily blinded by the shine the sun reflected off of this big-bodied automobile. As the engine cut off, a tall, older gentleman got out; clad in a 3-piece white suit, and a bowtie. I kept blinking my eyes, thinking maybe I was hallucinating from the day's triple-digit temperature that enveloped me as the sun leaned on my shoulder. As sweat beaded across my brow, the man walked closer and began to talk. But in my heat-induced stupor, I hadn't heard a word.

"Hey! Can you hear boy?" I heard the words, but still thinking I was dreaming there was no need to respond. Then he finally shook me.

"What?" I shouted. Partially out of fear, but mostly out of shock.

"Does Mrs. Hattie Dixon live here?" He said in an accent certainly not indigenous to these parts.

"Yes, sir!" I managed to utter.

"Will you tell her she has a visitor?" he asked.

"Okay," I responded. Right at that time, I opened the front screen door to go into to our lukewarm house; I ran smack dab into Unc. He grabbed me playfully by the shoulders.

"Do you need glasses?" he chuckled. He then looked out on the front porch and eyed this oddly handsome older guy with his big cliché white cowboy hat atop his graying head. The black Boss Hog was literally standing outside our house. He carried an unlit pipe like one of those smoked by plantation owners and black great-grandfathers and great-uncles. His wrinkleless face was vexingly clean-shaven, giving him a babyish profile, definitely not indicative of the gruff Delta standard. He was very lean.

"Who is that?" Unc asked concernedly.

"He didn't say! He said he came to visit H…I mean grandma!" I had to catch myself. I had almost called her Huh in front of someone and that would have ruined my long-running secret in an epic way. Unc walked out onto the porch to greet the stranger in white.

"Yes sir, may I help you?" I looked on as Unc walked out with his chest stuck out like a chocolate Labrador retriever, protecting the henhouse from the foxes.

"I am Billy Ray Bonds. Unfortunately, I am the man who accidentally hit your…uh," he anticipated the nomenclature for Unc's relationship to Huh.

"Susta, she is my susta!" Unc completed his sentence assertively.

"Good to meet you…" Billy Ray extended his hand.

"Roosevelt, Roosevelt Lipsey!" Unc grabbed his hand assuredly and shook it with a firmness that insinuated a hint of dubiousness.

"So is Mrs. Dixon up to having visitors?" Billy Ray asked.

"I'll ask her. Come on in and have a seat! Can I get you a drank or some 'nother?"
"No, sir! Thanks!"

He sat on our plastic covered couch, with a snooty air, as if our furniture was beneath him. He looked around with his nose in the air like he smelled a chitlin' stench. I stood at the door and watched him as if he were my favorite TV show. Fixedly, I met his gaze, for I had always been told the eyes were the windows to the soul. If they indeed were, his windows must have been shut, because I could discern nothing about him or his soul. All I could see was a seemingly rich man in elegant regalia who looked very uncomfortable surrounded by our impoverished living conditions, and semi-dilapidated furnishings, in our less than humble abode. Uncle Roosevelt cleared things with Huh and ushered Billy Ray to the back room where she had been bed-ridden for weeks.

"Hello."
"I know got damn well Velt ain't let this nigger *in my house*." She said in distress.
"How are you Mrs. Dixon?" Billy Ray queried.
"It's Ms. Dixon thank you!" She said, with all the impudence she could muster. I knew then this was about to be a battle royal, so, I hid just outside the door in order that I could witness firsthand the knock-down-drag-out blow by blow.
"Sorry, *Ms*. Dixon!" He said, overemphasizing the *Ms.* as his eyebrows rose slightly, and his eyes rolled indifferently.
"What kin I do you for Mr. Cadillac-Driving Man?" Huh surveyed.
"Please call me Billy Ray," he insisted.
"Mr. Cadillac-Driving Man is fine. I don't go on first name bases wit' attempted mudderers who run over defenseless old women in the middle of the streets!" Huh quipped.
"Surely you can't call that tap on your side attempted murder. I am told your injury came from the actual fall, not the tap!" he rebuffed.
"My injury? Nigger, I am laid up in this here bed wit' my leg wrapped up like one of them damn Messican burritos. This

here, sir, ain't no injury. It's a goddamn war wound and I need a Purple Heart!" Huh maintained.
"Ms. Dixon, I apologized profuselythat day. I have sent all these flowers and things to further express my remorse!" he said.
"Remorse! I don't know what no *remorse* is. But don't thank you gon' come up in here wit' yo big fancy suit, and yo big fancy words, and impress nobody. I am not impressed easy," Huh warned.
"That is the furthest thing from my mind! I am simply a humble creature coming to offer my unabashed, heartfelt concern for your health."
"If'n you don't use some Anglish, *unabash* you over da head wit' this here cast!" Huh cautioned.
"You are a feisty little woman aren't you?" he investigated.
"I don't know about feisty, but I fights!" Huh responded.
"Well I didn't come here to fight. I came to offer any help you may need in the form of money or assistance of any kind!" Billy asserted.
"Oh no, you ain't. You ain't finna be throwin' yo money all around up and through here, like this no hoehouse. I told yo ass I was gon' sue and dat's what I aims to do!" she upheld.
"Ms. Dixon, I can offer you far much more than a judge will award you in a court of law. Trust me; I know my way around these kinds of situations." Billy Ray said, with the poise and coolness of true gentleman, but with the shrewdness of a politician. Huh just laid there with a deer-caught-in-the-headlights look on her face as she planned her quick-tongued retort.
"Look here, Mr. Cadillac-Driving Man, don't tell me what the judge gon' do? Who da hell you thank you is? Thurgood Marshall? What you kin do is take yo big wallet and yo big mouf on back to BougieVille. Take a right on *Get the hell out my house*!" She responded, as unladylike as she possibly could. But I had to give it to her, she let him have it, however uncalled for, she gave him the what for.
"Ms. Dixon, although you have made it clear how you feel, I have never backed down from a fight. I know eventually,

you will come around to seeing things my way!" Billy Ray said as a matter-of-factly, as he smirked and walked out, but not before sliding 10 crisp 100 dollar bills underneath her cast.

My eyes bucked because I had never seen that many one-dollar bills let alone 100's. I sat there mesmerized, and in a daze, looking at the money, but wondering, what she would do when she noticed the money was there. My mind danced around the thought that she would reject the money, as she had rejected his help. However, my soul wanted her to spend the money, and throw a little bit my way. But I knew better, considering I really wasn't a priority or a thought for that matter. After Billy Ray left, she indeed folded the bills up and placed them in her bra.

"Boy, what you doin' out here?" Unc asked, as he startled me unintentionally, as I had been spying in the hallway.
"I was about to ask Grandma if she needed anything." I stuttered, as I managed to finish the lie.
"Oh, okay. I got it. You gone on in there and git ready for supper. I fried some chicken and made some spaghetti. Now that was my kind of eating. I quickly forgot about the money as I prepared my taste buds for dinner. Unc had just walked Billy Ray out and was ready to get the scoop on his visit from Huh.
"Hattie, what did Mister Boss Mane sir want?" Unc teasingly asked, mocking the slave vernacular as it were.
"That sadiddy bastard come up in here flaunting his big words and money like I was sposed to be impressed! I told him where he could get off and how to do it!" she replied, in her famously country, aggressive way.
"Did he not apologize?" Roosevelt inquired.
"Hell, if'n he did, it was hiding somewhere in all of them high society words. I jes' felt like he thought he could come up in here and impress somebody wit' his *proper* speech and his leather billfold. He just didn't know that this wasn't the day and I wasn't the one!" she stated.
"Ain't the one for what?" Unc asked rather inquisitively as if he thought he would glean something intelligible from Huh.

"The one for him to be pickin' on! I'm a defenseless old lady!" Huh said, pursing her bottom lip as she pulled up the covers.
"Please! Girl, you bout as defenseless as a pit bull!" Unc replied as they both let out a burst of uproarious laughter. Unc made sure she had some food. She ate, took her medication, and eventually drifted off to sleep.

Unc and I sat at the kitchen table. We talked about the one subject that had been avoided since I moved to Mississippi. My mother. It was a pretty sensitive subject as far as I was concerned. I loved my mother, don't get me wrong, but I hated that she had left me. Not only had she left me, but she had left me with Huh! I was constantly ridiculed and put down. It was a wonder I didn't begin to wet the bed. I continually felt helpless. My suppressed emotions had begun to affect me physically, but Unc's presence had become the healing salve I needed to ameliorate a once worsening situation.

"Son, how is it living here with Hattie?"
"Grandma is cool!"
"Boy! I been knowing that woman for 65 years, and ain't nobody never called her cool! So try again!" Uncle Roosevelt said, in between bites of food. His compassionate demeanor petitioned me to spill my guts, but she was still his sister, and they had a stronger bond than he and I.
"Things are okay around here. We don't have much of a relationship though. I'm mostly in my room or out back when I am not doing any chores around the house," I lamented.
"Now that's more like it! So you miss yo' mama?" he probed.
"Yeah, every day. I wish I could see her," I said, fighting the tears that I had been holding in for 3 long years. I dropped my fork onto my plate. The clank prompted Unc to grab my arm.
"Son, it's okay to cry. As men, we got to stop tellin' our boys, 'Men don't cry!' or 'I'm gon' give you some'n to cry about!' I cry. If I am sad, frustrated, or mad, I cry dammit,

and I like to think I am more man than the next guy! So if you need to cry, let it out! It's good for yo' soul," Uncle Roosevelt held.

It was at that moment that I let the tears flow. I cried so hard that my eyes were bloodshot. It was the ugly cry, the cry that made you look demonic or diabolical. Slowly, the former rendition of my blues was returning. As much as Unc had been a rock in my weary land, the trance-like rhythm of the blues shuffled back into my soul. Its groove slashed through to my core. I didn't know who I had been or whom I had become whilst living in the Delta having to deal with the absence of my mother. Harmonicas and guitar licks traipsed through the vestibules of my soul like venom, quickening to my heart in order to stop it from beating. The blues, my mother's blues, Huh blues, and my own blues in unison, da dow, da dow, da dow, da ...

Chapter 7

I Shall not be Moved

A few days after I had had my breakdown, I decided to venture outside my comfort zone and actually interact with people my age. I had read somewhere that life begins beyond your comfort zone. It had to be true; even though I had left my genuine comfort zone back in the streets of Detroit. I had acquaintances at school, but after 3 years of school in Mississippi, I was still a social outcast of sorts. No *real* friends. I half-heartedly associated with kids at school; however, I never spent any real time with anyone outside of school. I neither talked on the phone nor did I have people over for visits.

It just wasn't my practice. But this particular day, I felt a catharsis after that long cry with Unc, and I needed to change if I were going to finally embrace the Mississippi Delta in all its dreariness.

I began my promenade through the park down the street from our house. It was actually a vacant lot with a decent sized slab of concrete, a few benches, and a tree or two. On one of the big trees that hung over the slab of concrete is where the kids in the neighborhood had fashioned a makeshift basketball goal. Therefore, this park had become known as: "The Goal"! As I got closer, I recognized many of the beige, brown, dark brown, caramel, and mocha colored faces. Although I had never been there before, it was just as I imagined a breeding ground for machismo in its most raw form.

All of the guys were playing or sweating, waiting to play again. The girls were all vying for the attention of the guys. Dressing garishly, or talking loudly, and some even pretended to be cheerleaders for their favorite guys. As I approached the perimeter of the actual playing surface, a very unfamiliar face ambled over to talk to me. I immediately clammed up. My fists were soggy and damp from being packed inside the pockets of my cut off jean shorts. Perspiration dripped from my brow down my nose like tears. I unstuffed one fist and redistributed the sweat.

Then, I looked away demurely, so as not to be conspicuous, hoping she was not venturing for a conversation with me.
"Hey!" the bizarrely appealing girl said, as she sucked on her BlowPop.

"Hey!" I replied, as coolly as I could. My eyes scrambled searching for a spot to avert themselves, so as not to make me appear unaware of myself. I stood there with dry mouth and wet armpits.
"I am Andrea," she spoke.
"Malachi," I said, trying not to look at her with obvious anxiety in my eyes.
"You're not a man of many words are you Malachi?" she examined, in an intonation incontrovertibly not of the Delta.
"Nah, I don't talk much," I returned.
"Well I guess I will have to talk enough for the both of us." She said, as she giggled diffidently.
"How will you do that?" I queried.
"Stick around and you will see! So Malachi! You are obviously not from Mississippi. Where did the wind pick you up and blow you from?" she probed.

"Detroit, and you?"
"KANSAS!!" she squealed, as she dodged the basketball and fell into my arms as some of the players clambered in our direction.
"You okay?" I scowled out of concern. I noticed that she smelled like cocoa butter and bubblegum. Oddly enough, the smell aroused my sex and she piqued my interest.

"Yeah, I am good. Don't let all this beauty fool you. I am a tomboy by nature, this makeup and perfume is just my superheroine costume!" she exclaimed, as she moved away to straighten her clothes and collect herself.
"Are you serious?" I asked, with laughter breaking up my speech.
"As serious as a heart attack!" She smiled.

Her perfectly white yet imperfectly set teeth glimmered in the midday sun. This was the first time I had had an actual physicalized presence stimulate a remote sexual thought. I watched in amazement how much self-confidence this girl exuded. Her legs seemed to keep going like run-on sentences in paragraphs. The most seamless and inarguably supple skin I had ever seen covered them. Her long flowing locks were kept in a ponytail adorned with a matching bow. Though she was black, she would be what we in the black community considered "*mixed*". The word mixed was an unequivocal indicator of the racism within our race or more specifically, *colorism* and our insensible ability to devalue blackness by cleaving to whiteness. We had all learned to put stock into *race* as an ideology versus a social construct. Somehow, 'mixed' just didn't define Andrea. To me, she was more like the result of an ice cream cone with one scoop of vanilla and one scoop of chocolate, melting into one another. Sweet.

"Well, I won't fight it!" I reacted.
"Would you like to go for a walk?" she asked.
"Only if I am allowed to buy you a soda on the way?" I said, trying to sound polished, like a true gentleman.

The truth was, I only had enough to buy one soda, and it was hot as peppers and piss in the Delta around noontime.

"It's the least you can do!" She fired back.
"You *are* something else!" I lobbed.
"So I've been told," she volleyed back cleverly, as she flung her ponytail back behind her in a way that I had only seen white women do on television shows.

It was at this time that I could see that this maneuver was clearly not just germane to one faction of women. It was an awakening for me, from the narrow scope to which I'd relegated myself. Moisture beaded down my face like condensation on car windows in the mornings. My heart sprinted like a jackrabbit, and not to mention, sweat poured over me even in the shade, so I knew it had to be a neophyte emotion I had never emanated.

"What kind do you like?" I asked Andrea, as we walked closer to Miss Mary's house. Miss Mary was the old lady over on the next street who sold penny candy, cookies, sodas, booze, and cigarettes to everybody in the neighborhood. Miss Mary was only about 60 or so, but she looked and smelled every bit like a nonagenarian; due to the bad eating, drinking, and smoking she had done over the years. Miss Mary was about 5'7 with a hump from obvious osteoporosis. Her skin was paper bag brown and wrinkled, like a Chinese Shar Pei. She had a house full of cats, and yard full of dogs which included, Mr. Johnny, the blackest, meanest, most cantankerous one-legged husband this side of the Mason Dixon Line. The dogs outside barked, but not as well as ferociously as Mr. Johnny could, with a stogie dangling from his toothless orifice. He was a true curmudgeon. It wasn't our fault that leg was chopped off. He only had himself and diabetes to blame.

"I like Coke!" Andrea indicated.
"One Coca Cola for the lady please," I declared.
"50 cent!" said Miss Mary, as dryly as she had always spoken. I handed her the two quarters.

She turtled over to the refrigerator where she stored the sodas and the bootleg alcohol that she had been selling to the neighborhood drunks for years that included Ms. Bobbie, who lived behind her, and who drank nothing less than two glasses of cognac with a beer chaser for breakfast, lunch, supper, and snack. She gave me the bottle of coke, and like always, never uttered a word of thanks for my patronage. Miss Mary was such a witch; however, I was never disrespectful to her. I didn't want a reenactment of Hansel and Gretel; besides, Miss Mary's oven wasn't large enough.

"Thank you too!" Andrea said.

She shockingly addressed Miss Mary and the rudeness that had become commonplace with those of us who frequented her kitchen of goodies and contraband. Miss Mary frowned before her rude reply.

"Why you little hussy!" Miss Mary redeemed.
"Hussy? Let me tell you one thing Methuselah…" I covered Andrea's mouth and dragged her out of the house before she continued to read Miss Mary her rights or Mr. Johnny could upright himself. "Let me go Malachi! Somebody needs to teach her some manners," Andrea yelped.
"I think she may be a little too old for etiquette classes!" I exclaimed.
"Well, if you had let me finish what I was saying, I would have given her the crash course!" Andrea bellowed. I managed to calm her down by the time we got to the end of the carport. It was no easy feat. She was out for blood; however, I knew Miss Mary's was mostly alcohol and plasma.
"You are something serious. You pack a little punch in that little body of yours," I said obsequiously.
"I know!" as she twisted the cap on the Coke to unleash the effervescence into the ozone and sipped more seductively than I think I had ever seen anyone do.

Though It may not have been all that seductive. I think since my manhood had surfaced, I may have been seeing things a lot differently than I had prior to my meeting Andrea. But everything she did put a smile on my face.
"So Andrea, what tornado brings you to Mississippi?" I asked, with a hackneyed Oz reference, as we stopped under a shaded area just down from Miss Mary's.

We sat on the curb of the sidewalk where people hardly passed through. Sitting on the curb was a thing we'd never do in Detroit. Just as soon as you'd sit, something was bound to happen. A drug deal or bust gone wrong, high-speed chase, you name it. There was none of that casual haphazardness that played like a symphony orchestra in the Delta. Detroit was a hotbed of violence, poverty, and desperation. Though I didn't want to remain a part of it, I didn't necessarily want the cold buffet of spitefulness, nonchalance, and pretense that Mississippi was serving either. However, being able to sit on the curb and chat with Andrea made being here less of an imposition.

"I have been coming here every summer since I was 8. My grandmother lives here in Sidon. It's like my home away from home. This summer, my dad came with me. He is working on some business deal in Greenwood. I just enjoy the simple things about Mississippi," she verbally perambulated.

She was endowed with beauty and I was in awe of her entire package. I sat in veneration of her. She was not only beautiful, but also smart, and buoyant. I wondered what she had been given that I hadn't, that kept her bubbly and exuberant. Was it because she had a dad and I didn't? Was it because she was born a girl? I couldn't put my finger on it, but it troubled me at the moment.

"Oh yeah?" I said, hoping it was an apt question, seeing as though I wasn't really listening because her looks and my curiosity drowned out her speaking in that time continuum.

"Yeah! My dad is all about business. He lives and breathes it," Andrea held.
"What does he do?" I probed.
"He is in land development. He owns acres and acres of land that my grandfather left him here in Mississippi, and even more in Kansas where we live now. So he is back and forth between here and there all the time," she indicated.
"What about your mother?" I asked before I realized she would probably ask about my family next. Then I wished I had not brought up the subject.
"My mother's dead. She died after giving birth to me. From what I know, she wasn't especially young when they had me, but she had what's called gestational diabetes that complicated her pregnancy and her life. They couldn't

save her, so they saved me," she said, with obvious despondency in her tone.
"I am sorry to hear that!" I said, as I hesitantly put my hand on her leg. This was a huge step for me. I didn't touch people. I didn't feel for people. Yet in that space, I touched and felt deeply for her. I was her. We were if just only for one moment, the same.
"Now, what brings you to the Delta?"
"Unfortunately, I live here now. I have lived here for 3 years." I concluded, hoping she wouldn't autopsy that body of information if you will.
"Why is it unfortunate? Do you live here with your mom and dad?" She hit me with the double whammy. At that very moment, my chin dropped and my eyes lowered. Looking down at my clasped hands, I deliberated how I'd respond. She took a sip of her Coke and looked at me curiously, yet unassumingly. Then, she placed her hand on my knee. Much like when Uncle Roosevelt comforted me, it felt good; but I felt vulnerable.
"My mom's in prison, and I don't even know my dad. I live down the street from The Goal with my grandma who hates that I was ever born." I found myself summing my existence up in two sentences still hoping the conversation wouldn't necessitate much more information than I had already articulated. Her spirit was so unalloyed, beauty so salient, and conversation so entrancing that I really didn't mind being an open book for her if needed.
"I didn't mean to pry and make things hard for you. I just want to know you. I get this feeling…this vibe from you. And before you think I am a psycho, I am not trying to marry you or nothing. But I do feel a bond between us," she said, with more sincerity and clarity than anyone I had ever chanced upon.

At that moment, I began to experience a balance, a kind of homeostasis I had never known. I was completely grounded. All seemed well with my soul. We just sat there for another two hours in silence. By allowing our kindred spirits to intertwine, our souls meshed and were marinated in strength that was birthed from travail. Sitting there on the curb we had taken journeys to each other's worlds without uttering a word.

At that time, I heard a saxophone composing a jazz tune in my mind. A drubbing pulse I'd never heard, theretofore, accompanied the rhythm section. This new melody made my heart become a metronome, which marked time. While trumpets mollified my soul, trombones quelled my hormones. I was the drummer in the band of my soul. I played a solo. The trumpets faded. There were no more trombones. My saxophone subsided. All that remained were the wildly staccato flams, paradiddles, and triplets that ruminated from my drumsticks of my soul. For the first time, I felt alive. My blues now had a new cadence. In a matter of hours, my blues became jazz and I was Count Basie.

Chapter 8

Let the Lady Flirt with Me

Meeting Andrea was the best thing for which I could have hoped. After I walked her home to her grandmother's house, a house I'd passed a million times walking home from school, I went back by The Goal and I played a couple of games. I hadn't played in so long; I had forgotten how good I had been back in Motown. My jump shots, vertical leaps, dribbling ability, and crossovers slew those Mississippi corn-fed country boys. Looking back on it, I don't know if I was having amazing games, or if I was just high from the quintessence of Andrea. Nevertheless, I had to practically run away from the guys at The Goal who had nicknamed me T-Pot, because I was steaming people on the court. They didn't want me to leave, but it was getting darker, and I knew I needed to get home to help Unc around the house.

When I entered the house I heard some strange noises. I immediately went in to check on Huh. She was sound asleep. I went into the kitchen and saw food on the stove. Then I checked the living room. Uncle Roosevelt was nowhere in sight. The noises became more and more distinct, and more familiar as I grew closer to the source, so I stopped and let my ears lead me to them. My body stopped in front of Unc's room. I leaned in closer to the cracked door and the noises became more audible. I still couldn't see so I pushed the door. That's when I saw Unc on top of Miss Sally.

"Close that door boy!" Unc yelled, in an out of breath pitch. I stood there in disbelief.

My body had virtually transmuted into a statue. My brain said move, but my feet wouldn't obey. I had heard about sex and had seen it on feigned on television, but to witness it live and in action rendered me inimitably rapt. Suddenly, I shook my head like a wet puppy. I ran outside onto the back porch. I sat there for about 15 minutes with my face in my sweaty palms. The aroma from the fresh corn blew into my airways as the slight warm wind flagellated through the field. The fragrance of the corn jogged my memory, and I realized that I would hear similar noises at night coming from my mama's room back in Detroit. That really sickened me. To think that some man had done the same things that Uncle Roosevelt was doing to Miss Sally. I couldn't regain my bearing for the life of me. I just wallowed in my naiveté until I felt a hand on my shoulder. I looked up and it was Unc.

"You okay Malachi?" Uncle Roosevelt questioned.
"Y..yeah…I guess." I muttered.
"I'm sorry you saw us like that. I didn't know you was gon' be back so soon." He said, ruefully yet unapologetically, if that was even conceivable.
"It's okay Unc," I released.
"No, it was irresponsible! I gotta be mo' careful," he said woefully.
"Unc, I aint no baby!" I returned.
"I know you ain't. But I don't need you learning no bad habits from old Unc," Roosevelt conveyed compassionately.
"I'm good Unc!" I tried to convince him without very much conviction. I really wanted to sidestep a talk about sex as much as I could.
"We'll talk later. Come on in and freshen up! I will warm up supper. Sally's gonna be eating with us," he noted.

Sally was a sweet woman. I had always thought she was one of Huh least convoluted friends. However, after seeing her in the buff, I wasn't sure I would be able to look her in the eyes anymore. It became increasingly difficult. All I could picture were her breasts swinging back and forth with her face in the pillow, and her ass in the air, as Uncle Roosevelt dug into her from behind. The image just wouldn't leave my mind. As I finished washing up for dinner, I hesitantly entered the kitchen where Unc and Sally were having a small talk as she smoked a cigarette, and Unc gathered plates. I braved it even so. With false bravado, I pasted on a smile.

"Hey, Malachi!" Sally spoke cheerfully, with a just a soupçon of embarrassment.
"Hey, Miss Sally! You been to Bingo lately?" I asked. It was my feeble attempt at trying to cut the tension in the room with a butter knife.
"Yeah, I was there last night. I won $500 too. I been playin' for a long time and ain't never won befo'! It was a good idea taking yo' Uncle Roosevelt wit' me. Even though I ain't superstitious, he was like my big ol' rabbit's foot," she said, looking over at Unc fluttering her eyelashes.
"I don't know 'bout all that! I just sat there. But I do know people take Bingo seriously. I ain't never seen so many people act so ign'ant over some damn game boards and ink bottles!" Unc decried.
"Roosevelt stop!" Sally admonished, as she playfully hit Unc.
"You know I'm just kidding!" he said, as he set the table. "*No I am not*!" he mouthed when Miss Sally wasn't looking.
"You ready for school to start back Malachi?" Sally inquired.
"No!" I said emphatically.

I knew that once school started my Dorothy would be back in Kansas. I shuddered to think of her having to leave. I needed her to help me find my courage, mind, heart, and home. I had been useless to do so, or even think I could before meeting her. In just one day, she'd given me more for which to be hopeful than I had ever thought imaginable.

"Boy, why not? I know you ain't trying to be here all day wit' Hattie grouchy ass too much longer!" Unc thundered.
"It ain't all that bad!" I wanted to say, I could brave anything after meeting Andrea, but it was too soon to alert the family about a girl I just met.
"So Malachi, any little ladies got yo' eye?" It was as if she read my mind. "You are a handsome young man, and I know these young gals can see that!"

I had never really thought of myself as handsome. I grew up around thugs. I was too rugged and rough around the edges to think of myself in any other way. The streets of Detroit didn't raise pretty boys. Its products were survivors, with a *get-it-how-you-live* mentality.

"I don't think so," I said guilelessly.
"Boy, don't never sell yo'self short! You come from good stock!" Unc said, as he instinctively stuck his chest out.
"I'm gon' have to agree wit' yo' uncle on that!" Sally said, as she pursed her lips.
"I am sure that you'll someday find that confidence us Lipsey men got. It ain't arrogance or nothing. It's pure self-assuredness. Any successful man should have him some of tha! I guarantee you will you find it, and get rid of some that modesty you holdin' on to. You will see many doors open up for you!" Unc professed.
"And legs!" Sally said out of nowhere.
"What you mean Sally?" I dared to inquire.
"Pussy! You will have pussy thrown at you like baseballs in the World Series!"

She said, as cavalierly as she wanted. I certainly wasn't ready to discuss the female body parts and reproduction with a friend of the family. It made me feel way more uncomfortable than having seen her in the buck with Uncle Roosevelt just 30 minutes prior.

"Sally, that boy ain't ready for all that just yet! Let me handle that okay baby!" Unc pleaded, ultimately coming to my rescue.
"I am just saying the boy could be gittin' some on a regular. If he got anythang like what you workin' wit'!" Miss Sally bluntly stated, as she rubbed Unc on his thigh as we attempted to eat.
"Sally, I said let me handle it!" Unc roared quietly.
"Okay Cat Daddy!" she acquiesced.
"Malachi gone on finish yo' supper so you can bath!" Unc said, as he nodded.

I doggedly ate my food so as to avoid any more talk about *legs and pussy*. I went to the bathroom. I drew my bath water and disrobed. I began to look at myself in the mirror. What I saw was a handsome young man. I was still basically *baby-faced*, save for a little peach fuzz over my lip, and a string or two of hair dangling from my chin. I noticed I really did look a lot like my mother. She was beautiful. I had always heard boys who looked like their mothers were generally more attractive. As I stood there stark naked in the mirror, I heard the door open. I turned in astonishment. It was Sally, and I was standing there with my *dick* hanging, and nothing to cover myself with. So I stood there with my eyebrows raised nervously, looking side to side with quick glances at Sally as I made an X over myself so as to cover my dangling appendage.

"I knew you had some meat down there!" She said, with her index fingernail between her teeth. "Don't be shy. I ain't gonna bother you, but I do wanna help you. I want you to come by the house tomorrow afternoon before I go to work. Your Uncle don't want me to talk about sex wit' you, but I'm here to offer you some help in the lady department that yo Uncle can't help wit'!" Sally said, as she turned and walked away, but not before getting one more glance at pubic region.

I scurried to lock the door. Thoughts ambushed my mind. I was in a whirlwind of confusion, so much so that I almost forgot to turn the water off in the tub. I finally got in and bathed while wondering if I would take Sally up on her offer, or just pretend she'd never cornered me in the bathroom. As I dried myself off I remembered that Unc said we'd talk later. I wondered if he remembered. My soul needed for him to forget in order that I could go to my room and ponder my decision. When I walked out of the bathroom, I heard Unc snoring. Fortunately for me, he had fallen asleep. I didn't have to have the dreaded sex talk at least for another 24 hours.

The blues was back it seemed, and its repetitive chord was never-ending, and not progressive at all. The refrain kept playing over and over, but I intended to draw it to an abrupt close by going to bed. I lay there longing for a new chord. My eyes were blinking in modified succession, trying to find a new rhythm. I yearned for either a new ditty, or a dream, neither came, just the slow blues, some mo' blues, not yo' blues...*Mine*...

Chapter 9

Make me a Pallet on the Floor Baby

That night while I slept, Sidon had started to get smaller unbeknownst to most people. Old Man Jessie had been bonded out of jail two days prior to my meeting Andrea. To this day, we still don't know how Miss Sophia missed that tidbit of information. It was revealed that Ms. Jane had given into Old Man Jessie's phone calls and apologies, and had gone to pay his bail. When he got home, they picked right up where they left off. The tradition argumentative noise of their fights ventilated through their home as unfailingly as their central air and heat. The next-door neighbors shook their heads and turned up their televisions and radios to muffle the screams, shouts, and sounds of things breaking.

"Why didn't you come to see me when I was in jail?" he demanded to know.
"Why should I have? You the one who put you in there!" Jane resounded.
"So you sat up here and spent my money while I was locked up!" Jessie pointed out.
"I just paid the bills and bought groceries. It's what you woulda done if you was out!" she reminded him.
"But it's my money to spend! I make the money 'round here!" Jessie reverberated.
"The only thing you make is me sick! Now, I wish I woulda let yo ass stay in there until ya court date!" Jane lamented.
"Bitch you tryin' make me whoop yo ass?" he said, as he moved in closer.
"Seem to me, you the bitch! Keep comin' up in here hittin' on a woman!" she returned.
"I'll…"Jessie hissed.
"You'll what? Punch me? Kick me? I'm used to it all. Can't nuthin' you do hurt me no mo"!" Ms. Jane said, as she turned and walked to the kitchen where she began to wash dishes. Old Man Jessie followed her into the kitchen.

"Who da hell you thank you is? You don't walk away from me. As long as you black, and you live in this here house, you will stand there until I say you leave!" he reprimanded.
"Yo chirren is grown and out yo house. You wanted it that way. You don't run me!" Jane said unmoved, as she continued to wash dishes.
"Turn around and look at me!" he warned.
"For what? I know what you look like!" Ms. Jane replied stoically.

Old Man Jessie reached to grab her to turn her around to face him and before he knew it, she had lodged the 10-inch serrated knife into his abdominal section. The blood trickled down the base of the knife onto her hand. Something wouldn't allow her to let go of the knife. He uttered, "You yella bitch!". She leaned in and gave it a twist and pushed it in deeper as she began to cry inconsolably. Tears surged from her eyes as the mass of his bleeding body slumped over on her, and she slid to the ground. Her hand loosed the knife. She ended up seated on the floor. The heaviness of his body lay gutted across her lap. Her blood-soaked hand lay lifeless on top of him. He was still breathing sporadically as blood escaped his mouth. He was losing so much blood, and she couldn't pull herself together enough to care or to call for help. He slipped into unconsciousness while lying on the woman who had loved him through sickness and through health. Now death indeed did they had finally parted. He took his last piss, shit, and finally his last breath.

She felt his last sigh, and Ms. Jane fainted. A dream of killing Old Man Jessie woke her. Much to her surprise, it hadn't been a dream. Hours had passed, the sun was shining again. The birds were chirping and she was still seated on the floor with her dead husband lying on her. She panicked and pushed him off her. Jane realized that the night before was a reality. It rendered her voiceless and helpless. She paced the room pulling at her hair and clothes. Suddenly, her mind shuffled to the bales of hay that were in the backyard. She didn't know how they could help her in this situation, but it didn't stop her from going outside to drag the three bales that had garnished their backyard since the church's Harvest Festival of the preceding year. After she reentered the house, she flipped Old Man Jessie over and removed the knife. She threw it into the sink. Instinctively, she lined the 3 bales of hay next to his body. With a shot of adrenaline and some remarkable strength, she was able to lay Old Man Jessie on top of the bales like a crude hospital gurney and makeshift gauze, to soak the remainder of the dark magenta spillage. She then cleaned up the blood, washed the knife, and bleached the house from corner to corner.

The phone rang and rang, but she didn't answer. She showered, made up her face, put own her favorite nighgown, her pearl necklace, and pearl earrings, and lay in bed. The body of her slain husband lay in an area near the kitchen and living room.

Ms. Jane felt nothing. Neither warmth nor emotion circulated through her body. She was at peace. Her body had become a harsh environment of unfeeling. Dangerously, she drifted off to sleep where she would continuously be plagued by morbid nightmares. She endured each and every gruesome scene because she refused to wake up to face the inevitable consequences and judgment that awaited her.

When I heard what had happened, I knew what would it all would cost Jane. The music that we both had gotten use to would keep playing. An organ churned out her funeral dirge as she lay in her bed, which may as well had been her tomb. We all knew she had been dead inside for years. Her soul was the only thing she had left. It died with Old Man Jessie. She steeled herself. Then Jane readied herself for heaven, hell, and nowhere. She had her own peace. Her unrest was finally requited. Jane settled in for the most tranquil slumber for the first time in over thirty years. Her blues began to fade away as she closed her eyes. She now owned the chords, and she let the music lull her into a state of unresponsiveness. She drifted into a serendipitous serenity for her life after death.

Chapter 10

Nobody's Business

I skipped breakfast. I decided to stay in bed. The time on the alarm clock in my room appeared to pass by the hour instead of the second. Noon was fast approaching. I got out of the bed and freshened up. As I got dressed, my mind darted to different recesses in my head trying to figure out how Miss Sally intended to help me. I was scared and anxious simultaneously. Once I finished dressing, I swung by the kitchen to grab an apple. I let Unc know I would be back later. He was still resting in the same spot as the night before. It was only a 5-minute walk to Miss Sally's, but it took me 15 minutes due to my initial reluctance. When I arrived, the door was open and the screen door unlocked. Miss Sally must have seen me walk up.

"The door is open Malachi!" Miss Sally called from the inside.

I walked in to find her lying on the couch clad in a revealing satin robe. Her skin glistened like glass, as she had moisturized her body to perfection.

"Come on sit next to me," she motioned, then patted on the couch cushion. "Don't be shy. You want anything to drink?"
"No ma'am!" I said, rather unsure how to respond.
"Stop all that ma'am stuff! I am Sally! You can call me Sally!" She insisted as she moved closer to me looking me dead in the eyes.
"Ok…S.S.Sally…" I stuttered profusely, as I often did when I felt anxious.
"Relax!" She said as she placed my hand on her thigh.

There that touching was again. First Uncle, then Andrea, now Sally, but this touch was much different. The warmth that radiated from her touch was stimulating. It was awkward, but it felt good at the same time. It was inexplicably confounding to my 15-year-old mind. Especially since Sally and Uncle Roosevelt had a thing, but I liked it.

"Have you ever kissed a girl?" she asked salaciously.
"No ma'…I mean…no!" I answered.
"Well, sweetie the first thing a man gotta know how to do is to kiss! A woman needs to know in a man's kiss how he feels about her!" she chided.
"What do you mean?" I asked.
"Well, if a man kisses a woman soft and meaningful it gives her a warm feelin' that makes her moist!" Sally rejoined.
"Moist?" I queried.
"Yeah! That's when a woman's inside parts become wet and ready for passion!" she explained.
"Passion? Is that sex?" I questioned.
"It's makin' love! So the kiss is important! The first thing is to grab the woman by her head with yo fingers behind her ears and the palms of yo hands resting gently on her cheeks! Let me show you!"

She said, as she began to grip my head and moved closer to me while slanting her head with her eyes closed.

"W...w...wait!"
"Just relax Malachi. Close yo' eyes and relax your mouth!"
She moved in and again repeated her actions. It was very sensual. It was like she really loved me. I was so overwhelmed by her seriousness. She was very passionate in her tutelage. This was better than any tutorial theretofore. I don't know how good of pupil I had been, but I relished the study.
This time, as she moved closer, I opened my eyes. Her breath smelled of Juicy Fruit gum and it was kindred mix with the peppermint on my breath. When her lips touched mine, I begin to feel her wet tongue protrude between my lips. I jumped back. I was confused as to why she had stuck her tongue into my mouth. I had definitely never seen that on TV.

"What's wrong?" Sally queried.
"Nothing!" I replied.
"I told you, you gotta relax!" she maintained.

I did as she instructed. I relaxed and allowed her to kiss me. After a while, I got the hang of it and I kissed back, even using my tongue. I obviously did a good job because she didn't stop. We massaged one another's tongues in a manner that had actually really started to feel good, and my penis hardened with each lash of her tongue. She leaned back and pulled me on top of her as she gripped my face. While our lips were still locked, she took my arm to place one of my hands on her breasts and helped me give it a yielding squeeze. Then, she moved my hand down to undo the knot that secured her robe. Underneath the robe, she was butt ass naked. I never realized sexy and supple Ms. Sally's body was. My view from the door of Unc's room hadn't made me privy to what she had to offer. My eyes bucked. Her breasts sat up without a bra as if they were balanced on a shelf. They were as round and juicy like the grapefruit Huh ate for breakfast. Her midsection was flat, not athletically flat, but there was just the right amount of softness around her abdominals, which complimented her femininity. She had a light fuzzy trial from her navel that lead to her vagina, which was practically clean-shaven.

"Damn Miss Sally! I mean Sally!" I corrected myself.
"You like what you see?" Sally asked.
"Yes, ma'am...I mean yeah," I said, sounding like a virgin, even to myself.
"Now, you gotta use your lips and tongue to find the sensitive spots on my body!" She directed breathlessly.
"How do I do that?" I inquired.
"Lick slowly, with long strokes!" Sally said, rather confoundedly. "You should start at my neck and work yo' way down! The most important thing is not to use yo' teeth!" she admonished.
"Okay!" I said in agreement, but I had no idea what she meant.

I began to do as she had instructed. I switched sides of the neck then I started to lick and munch softly. I began to hear her moan. That was my signal that I was doing something right. I worked my way down to her clavicle where I licked just ever so slightly. I felt her tingle and jerk delicately. Then, I motioned my way to her breast where I tasted her flesh as I cupped her mounds and buried my face between them. I took her nipples into my mouth as if something would pour from them. She could barely catch her breath with every stroke of my tongue. I made one long journey with the wetness of my tongue to the bottom of her torso. I licked her pelvic region, saturating the crevasses of her v shape. I began to feel her hand push my head down further and further. Finally, I was between her legs with my nose in her faint pubic hair. It was the most awkward moment of my life. I had no idea what to do next, so I licked the hair. The moans ended there.

"No go down further!" she beseeched.
"Your thighs?" I asked, baffled by her request.
"No the center!" she said, as she gapped her legs open wider.

I frowned as if I were looking at a bowl of chitlins. I hated chitlins, so I certainly wasn't putting my tongue in that!

"Center of what?!" I asked, with great hesitation.
"It tastes a lot better than it looks!"

She intimated, with a degree of certainty as she pushed my face into it. I licked around it. It sure smelled better than it looked. It was as aromatic as flowers and fruit. The more I licked the more it made her moan. I became brave enough to stick my tongue in. She pressed her fingers harder into my back. She then started to play with this part of herself that extended beyond the lips of her vagina. I later found out that it was a clitoris. When I saw she got pleasure from that, I began to lick and suck on it. She squirmed and moaned and it made me leak. After a few moments, she pushed me back, tore off her robe, and climbed on top of me. She voraciously undressed me. I was a bit intimidated by her animalism, but it turned me on. She was like a wild cat, and I was her prey. When she had me down to my underwear, she touched me tenderly with just the tips of her fingers.

This sent chilling shocks all over me. I began to tremble slightly. She lightly scratched the surface of my skin and I wanted more. Then, she started nibbling on my ears and licking up and down my neck. This made my penis throb and leak semen even more. She sucked on my nipples, in what I thought was a strange turn of events, but oddly, it felt good. I didn't even know the male nipple had any nerve endings until that very moment. Finally, she made her way to my penis. She put her mouth on it. I got the best weird feeling ever. Before I knew it, these warm white spillages spewed everywhere. I thought she was going to be mad.

"I'm sorry!" I apologized.
"There is nothing to be sorry about!"

She said, as she wiped her mouth and climbed on top of me. She sat on top of me. It was the warmest feeling I had ever experienced. Almost like a bowl of warm oatmeal on a school day morning. I lay my head back and she slid up and down on my dick. She rode it to the head of my shaft, but she never did get off of it. After more intense moments, she leaned back and pulled me on top. I had no idea what to do.

"Move your hips!" She instructed me. I begin moved awkwardly from side to side. "No baby…move in and out of me!"

I proceeded to do as she said, and I got a rhythm going. Once I had done that, our moans morphed into pants. After more violent thrusts causing a clapping sound from my pelvis to hers, I felt that feeling again. I let out a howl of sorts and her pants became more emphatic. I fell on top of her out of breath, releasing yet another round of warmth inside of her.

"Shit!" she said between breaths.
"Did I do something wrong?" I asked, breathing stagnantly.
"You did everything right! You keep that up, you gon' be jus' fine. Now you can't tell nobody 'bout this! This will be our little secret! Even though ain't nothing little 'bout you!" Sally suggested.
"Okay!" I replied.
"You better get goin'! I gotta get ready for work!"

She said as she kissed me on the forehead, as I got dressed. I felt used. I had just *made love* to a woman and she was kicking me out of her house; without so much as a hug or a glass of water. I didn't know whether that was how things worked, but my feelings were hurt. Again, the tides of my life were cresting only to ebb and flow out of my little soul. However, I finished dressing and left, lifeless, and with no dignity. I pulled myself together, and I went home to bathe again so I could meet up with Andrea later in the day.

Meanwhile, Miss Sally drew herself some bath water. Then she called Ms. Jane who always gave her rides to work. She didn't get an answer. Miss Sally decided to call her back once she was done bathing. Much to her dismay, she still didn't get an answer. After Miss Sally had gotten dressed, she walked over to Ms. Jane's house. She knocked until her fists turned red. Miss Sally recognized that Ms. Jane had to be inside because both cars were in the yard, and Ms. Jane never left the house walking if it wasn't necessary. Sally went around back to make sure Ms. Jane wasn't hanging out clothes or doing some yard work. When she saw that she was not back there, she noticed the back door was cracked.

Miss Sally walked inside the door, which led into the kitchen. As she maneuvered through the house, she called out Ms. Jane's name, to which there was no answer. Before she knew it, she had tripped over something. She looked down, and to her surprise, she was atop the body of Old Man Jessie; lying face up on three bales of hay. Miss Sally screamed as she struggled to get up. Once she finally managed to pry herself from Old Man Jessie's corpse, she ran through the house concerned that someone had maybe broken in on Ms. Jane and Jessie, and possibly killed the both of them. When she made her way to their bedroom she saw Ms. Jane lying on her back, as still as someone would be lying in a tomb. Miss Sally started to cry and tremble, as she traipsed over to the bed to shake Ms. Jane so as to arouse her. She became frantic and shook her more violently while shouting her name. Ms. Jane came to. Miss Sally grabbed a hold of her and held her close rocking back and forth.

"Thank God you alive!" Sally sighed with relief.
"Where am I? Who are you?" Ms. Jane asked, like someone with dementia.
"It's me Sally!" she shrieked.
"It's that you mama?" Ms. Jane replied, in a child-like manner.
"Oh my God Jane...Jane, girl it's me!" Miss Sally belted, as she began shaking her again.

The first person Miss Sally thought to call was Huh. She was still laid up in the bed taking advantage of having her every whim catered to. The phone rang and she ignored it. I was just about to leave when I heard it ring. I answered.

"Malachi!" Miss Sally said, more distressed and out-of-breath than the way she had been earlier during our rendezvous. "Put yo grandmama on the phone!" Sally demanded.
"Okay!" I obliged.

I put the phone down in the kitchen and I ran to pick up the one in Huh room. I handed it to her.

"Who this is disturbin' my rest?" Huh wondered.
"It's Miss Sally!"
"Sally, guh what you wont?" she interrogated.
"Hattie, I am at Jane and Jessie's. It's some'n bad done happened over here!" Sally reported.

"Girl, slow down and tell me what you talkin' bout!" Huh commanded.
"I came over here to Jane's for her to take me to work. I got here and saw Jessie was dead in the front. I found Jane back here stiff as a board, but she alive. But some'n ain't right 'bout her. She talkin' all slow and she don't remember me," Sally recounted.
"You got to call the police!" Huh reacted
.
In Mississippi, anybody in a patrol car was the police. In our town, the sheriff and his deputies had jurisdiction over crime. It really wasn't a misnomer considering sheriffs really did police the area, but being country as hell, that's just what everybody said.

"Hattie, what if Jane killed Jessie? Dey gon' take her!"
"Sally, you know damn well Jane ain't kilt nobody! Somebody had ta break in there and kill that man! Now you gone on call the police and I'mma send Velt 'round there to see 'bout ya'll!" Huh said, in an effort to calm Sally.
"Hattie I can't do it!" Sally responded.
"Sally, I'm fixin' to call the police! Go outside and wait on'em to come!"

Huh hung up the phone and immediately dialed 911, and reported a murder at Ms. Jane's house. Then Huh informed Uncle Roosevelt about what had happened. He hurried over to Jane's. By the time he had arrived, Miss Sally was outside talking to the deputies. Ms. Jane was seated in a chair on the front porch staring off into space. She was very detached, like a loose button of an old jacket, just dangling, hoping not to come completely unraveled.

"Sir, can I help you?" the deputy inquired of Uncle Roosevelt.
"She is my...girlfriend!" He replied, unsure of what she really was to him.
"Please let him come in here!" She begged the officer.

Miss Sally buried her head in Unc's chest as the tears began to fall again! She felt safer in his arms than she had felt in a long time. Her mind had undoubtedly blocked the events of earlier that day with me. What we shared had a been a distant memory.

"Is there any other information that you can give me about what you saw inside the house?" the deputy questioned Sally.

"I have told you all that I know? What ya'll gon' do with my friend!" Sally asked.

"Ma'am she don't seem to be coherent enough to answer any questions! The ambulance will be here in a little bit to take her to the hospital for observation!" the deputy replied.

"What you mean observation?" Sally queried.

"The doctors will run tests on her to assess her condition and mental health!" the deputy assured Sally.

"Ok!" Sally responded.

Once the ambulance arrived, Roosevelt and Sally climbed in and rode in the back with Jane to the hospital. Roosevelt held Sally and Sally held Ms. Jane's hand. In the midst of all the excitement, Sally had neglected to call into work to tell them she wasn't working that day. She had been working at the local motel, the Regal Inn, for a couple of years at the reception desk.

The tumult of the events of Sally's day played a swan song. The tune left her emotionally barren. The ravenous appetite of a bass guitar had bitten into her sense of security. Miss Sally closed her eyes and prayed for a melodious coda to the pandemonium she had experienced earlier. The blues came for Miss Sally like the Sandman, only it wasn't bringing dreams so much as it has brought a nightmare to which Miss Sally would never sleep the same again. The low-slung notes changed the beat of her heart and lessened the depth of her soul. She was no longer as whole as the notes that played in her blues song.

Chapter 11

Right Away Honey

I heard police sirens on my way to meet Andrea, but the thought of seeing her was more important than satisfying my curiosity about where the sirens were headed. We had decided the day before to meet in the spot where we had sat talking nearly 3 hours the day we met. When I arrived, she was already there, seated, and dressed in her red knee-length shorts; called *cool-lots* in the Delta, and her white halter top with red embellishments. Andrea had let her hair down. It fell midways her back and she tucked it behind her ears like white women do showcasing her huge gold hoop earrings. It was the first time I had noticed that she had the most piercing hazel eyes I had ever seen. I had never seen a black person with these eyes in person. I stared at her as she sat sucking on her signature red BlowPop.

"Are you just gonna stand there staring at me?" Andrea asked rhetorically.
"Uh…no!" I bumbled.
"Well sit down already!" she commanded playfully.
"Okay Mama!" I retorted.
"Alright now! I can have you calling me mama if that's what you like," Andrea noted.
"Oh, really!" I chuckled.
"Yes, really. Did you hear those sirens?" she quizzed.
"Yeah, I did! I am sure we will know what happened in a little while! Don't too much go on in this town that everybody don't know about!" I bemoaned.
"I have noticed that over the years," Andrea agreed.
"Yeah! People around here can't hold water!" I said.
"I know! I was at Bubba's with my grandma the other day and the cashier was filling her ear with all kinds of gossip. We didn't have but 8 things in our basket, but we were holding up the line listening to all of that foolishness. I was rolling my eyes at the lady so hard I got a headache!" Andrea held.

"You crazy!" I declared as we both laughed.
"I did! She was standing up there talking about other people's business when these people were only trying to check out and leave!" she recounted.
"I know what you mean, and it's too hot in Bubba's for all that!" I granted.
"What's with that? Not too many places in this town have good air conditioning," Andrea lamented.
"No, it's not! If it's a 100 degrees outside, it feels like 130 degrees on the inside! Being from Detroit, it took me a minute to get used to the hot weather down here! It's so hot some days my skin feels like bacon!" I said.
"Bacon? Now that's hot!" she related.
"Yeah, but you know what? People who been living here all their lives ain't bothered by the heat! Yesterday, I saw a man with a sweatshirt on mowing his lawn at one in the afternoon. I said to myself 'This man gonna combust'! But he was just a' mowing like it was 45 degrees out there!" I narrated.
"Boy stop lying!" Andrea returned.
"I promise to God!" I communicated.
"It ain't that serious for you to be promising to God now!" she said, with an air of sarcasm.
"So Malachi from Detroit, how do you function down here in No Man's Land?"
"I just do. Detroit's got its things. Mississippi's got its things. Seen a lot of stuff tho'. I deal with life like any other kid, I suppose. Do what I gotta do to survive. Don't bother nobody, cause I don't want nobody botherin' me. Things change, and I got to roll wit' it; just a matter of how hard the wind blows!" I avowed.
"Don't go getting all deep on me!" She said lightheartedly hitting me in the chest.
"Me? Deep?" I asked.
"You are a different kinda boy I must say! I knew that when you came walking up at The Goal that day. It was just somethin' about you. That's why I came over and started talking to you!" she connected.
"Oh, and all this time I thought it was because I was the finest boy out there," I volleyed.

"Boy, please!" she bantered.
"You tryin' to say I ain't fine?" I queried.
"Nah, you are pretty handsome! But that ain't what attracted me! It was what your body was sayin'," she said.
"Wow! So my body was speakin' huh? What language was it speakin'?" I laughed profusely.
"Ha Ha! You know what I mean. When I go to the goal, all of the boys have weak, disrespectful ass come on lines! You didn't see me as any different from any other girl out there!" she detailed.
"To be honest, I didn't even see you until you walked over to me!" I reminded her.
"Exactly! I hadn't been there twenty minutes and at least ten boys tried to get with me! I just went to hang out and pass time. Not waste my time on sweaty little boys trying to show whose dick is bigger on the basketball court!" she conveyed.
"Do you always speak your mind?" I inquired.
"It's the only way to be. It's the way my daddy taught me. He told me to always be myself because nobody else could do it for me!" she said.
"Oh, I see!" I replied.
"Is it a problem that I say what's on my mind?" she probed.
"Not at all! I think it's good that you do! I have always kinda had a problem doing it myself!" I lamented.
"Well, you don't seem to be the type that needs to. You are the strong, silent type. It's somethin' about your presence alone!" she countered.
"Not only are you beautiful, but you are a psychologist too!" I spoke without thinking.
"You think I am beautiful?" she asked, looking at me while she sucked on her lollipop intermittently.
"Uhh…yeah!" I stuttered.
"It's okay!" She said, as she moved closer to me putting her left hand on my leg making me overly nervous remembering how Miss Sally had touched me earlier that day.
"I didn't mean…" I said.

"Don't worry about it boy! I like you, so you don't have to think I think you are like the rest of the snotty-nosed bastards in the neighborhood." She stated as she squeezed my leg.

My penis began to harden instantaneously. In an unusually unanticipated turn of events, she took the lollipop from her mouth and rubbed it against my lips. Then, she leaned in, closed her eyes and suckled my bottom lip in the gentlest way. My mind retreated back to what Miss Sally said about the kiss 'being important to a woman'. I put on my game face and waited for my chance. She opened her eyes briefly, then licked top lip. I reciprocated. I sucked her lips and she opened her lips and then the magic happened when our tongues touched. Fireworks shot up in my mind and my dick stood erect in my pants. There we were, on the sidewalk, in a sweet embrace a lollipop's breadth away. This kiss was much more intense than the kiss I had shared with Miss Sally. I actually felt a tingling all over my body.

I didn't know what to make of it. I just knew that I liked the feeling that it was giving me. It was like sitting in front of a hearth on a winter's night. At that moment, I realized I hadn't felt that particular sense of warmth in such a long time. The mystique of this angelic girl had stolen my heart and pierce right to the core of my soul. She sensed my woes, yet she still wanted to have something to do with me. This day marked my cerebral transition from a downtrodden bastard orphan, to an uplifted youth with a freer spirit. Her gentle kiss saved me, unlike Jesus who left me to rot like maggot food. My real savior had ridden in on a cumulus cloud and I was happy to float into the stratosphere with her.

To my delight, *My Delta Blues* had a metamorphosis once again. No more sad songs that depressed and oppressed my 15-year-old soul. No low notes that played perpendicular to my spirit. No more bass guitar marking time in place of my heart. In the totality of two days, Andrea had squelched my blues. Now, I was a little bit more rock and roll. There were much more tambourine and cymbal that elevated my 15-year-old existence to a whole new plateau. I reveled in the new music that Andrea conducted. She did so effortlessly, and with more finesse than someone with classical training. She felt good, and the music felt celebratory in its prelude, interlude, and postlude. I danced on the inside. There was now a glimmer of happiness and of hope, as opposed to the myriad of misfortune to which I had become accustomed. I could breathe and I could have a sing-along with the newness in my song.

Chapter 12

Spiders and Spidermen

After I left Andrea, I stopped by The Goal. As usual, the guys were shooting hoops, and the girls were standing around watching. It was still amazing that this was the norm in the neighborhood. This routine never got old for these kids. I guess it was an indicator of how you had to adapt when there weren't many activities or options from which to choose. It spoke to the resilience of poor, black folks in the Mississippi Delta. Ain't much to brag about, but it's our "ain't much to brag about". Even I had gotten to a point where I was okay with just going to play ball, or just observe. I had turned down the opportunity to play this particular day; even though they were begging me to get in on at least one game. I declined because my knees were still a little weak from spending time with Andrea, and I knew my head wouldn't be in the game. After a while, I decided to go home. When I got home, I noticed Mr. Billy Ray was pulling up at the same time. I wasn't sure how to receive, him considering he and Huh had had their verbal sparring match the other day. I pretended not to see him as I walked into the house.

"Hey, son!" Billy Ray said.
"Sir?"
"Is your grandmother home?" he queried.
"I guess so!" I responded, with hesitance.
"Will you ask her if I may come in to speak with her?" he cross-examined.
"Yes, sir! Wait right here please!" I said as I jogged into the house to rouse Huh.
I walked to the back to Huh room. The door was open, and I could hear her on the phone. This made me scared to go in there. I braved it and went in there anyway.
"Mr. Billy Ray is out there to see you!" I said, breathing a bit laboriously.
"Who?" she demanded that I repeat what I'd said.
"The man who drives the Cadillac!" I resumed.

"What the hell he want? Me and him ain't got no business! Tell him I said care his ass home!" Huh demanded as she continued to talk on the phone.

This made me really uncomfortable as I had to do her dirty work. I had to go tell a man that I have nothing against to go home. I wasn't too sure how I would do it, so, I walked slowly, so as to plan my words carefully. I made my way to the screen door. I looked up at him.

"She said she don't feel like much company," I lied rather inconspicuously.
"Son, I heard her tell you to tell me to go home!" Billy Ray blasted.
"I..." I stuttered to find the words.
"Go tell her I am not going anywhere until she talks to me," he demanded.
"Yes, sir!" I acquiesced.

I began to feel more discomfort, as I had to go back inside to tell Huh what he said. I breathed deeply as I writhed in discomposure. I knew she wouldn't receive his message well. I had to prepare myself for a good tongue-lashing.

"He said he won't leave until you talk to him!"
"I know this nigger didn't...where my damn gun at? Sophie, girl, I'ma call you back!" she said before she hung up the phone. "Tell him to come on in! Shit!" Huh commanded.

I went to invite him in. He followed me down the hall. I felt like a jailer leading a prisoner on his last walk before the inevitable capital punishment. However, this walk may have been worse. The wrath that she rained down was nothing with which to be reckoned. We entered. I exited immediately standing outside the door in my usual spot so I could prepare to listen to the execution. I could not fathom why Billy Ray would even return to her fury after the verbal thrashing that she had given him during his first visit. He must have been some epicure of chastisement or better some glutton for punishment, because if so, she had a buffet of impudence to serve him.

"How can I help you M*r. Attempted Mudder*?" Huh inquired condescendingly.
"This again? Oh, come on now Ms. Dixon, I didn't come here to fight with you! I came to apologize for minimizing your pain and suffering by offering you money. I am a shrewd businessman who is used to using my money to solve all my problems. Indeed, I am sorry for insulting you the other day!" he conveyed repentantly.
"Look here Mr. Cadillac-Driving Man…" she began.
"No, please hear me out! I have done a lot of thinking since our *run-in*.
"Our run-in? No, Nigger, let's be clear, you run into me…" She gestured by pointing to him and back to herself."
"That's not what I meant."
"Just so we clear."
"I meant, over the years, I have made all kinds of deals and dealt with all kinds of people. I don't hear the word "no" very often. You made it clear to me how you felt, and I appreciated that more than you could ever know. You are a strong woman with values and that is to be commended!" Billy Ray spoke with a brand of humility unique to me so I know it was certainly a *new* concept to Huh.

I peeked in to see the look on Huh face. It had softened from the initial scowl that festooned her visage when he first arrived. She opened her mouth but nothing came out. I knew she wanted to slice him open like bass fish with something really abrasive, but she began to sob uncontrollably. My eyes widened to the size of half-dollars. I saw Huh display many emotions, but these tears were something I'd definitely never witnessed. They were real tears. They were indicative of sadness and fear, two emotions I never thought the woman was even capable of exhibiting. This was the second time I had countersigned humanness from Huh. I couldn't understand from where it was coming. My feelings about her were strangely

conflicted by this turn of events like it had been in the hospital that day.
"*Ms.* Dixon, did I upset you?" Billy Ray inquired with concern.
"No, it's not..." Huh tried to talk through the tears, but astonishingly, she had no words to express what she had been feeling inside. This softer side of Huh steeled me.
"What is it?" Billy Ray queried, as his concern grew more increasingly distressful.
"It's my friend." Huh managed to complete a sentence. Billy Ray handed her a handkerchief from his coat pocket in a very gallant, but caring manner.
"What about your friend?" he probed.
"She might be in some trouble," Huh said, as she shook her head helplessly.

I wondered whom she could be talking about. Huh didn't really consider many people her friend. But if I had to surmise, it had to be Sally, Jane, or Sophia.

"What kinda trouble?" Billy Ray quizzed.
"I can't say!" Huh stammered.
"You can tell me. Maybe I can help," he offered.
"Can't nobody help her but God right nah," she returned, in a melancholic tone.
"Try me and see!" he said, as he precariously reached out and touched her hand.
"Mr..." she started.
"Please call me Billy Ray," he insisted.
"Billy Ray, I don't know you. I can't be putting her business out to you. She is my friend, and I got to protect her!" Huh exclaimed
"Well, I understand!" Billy Ray disarmed.
"Maybe you can do me a favor! Can you drive me over to the hospital!" she asked.
"Sure!" He said, with more willingness than he really should have. "How do we do this?"
"I got a wheelchair over there. You can help me out this here bed and into it!" Huh instructed the handkerchief wielding man.

Billy Ray obliged Huh with all the sincerity in his heart. He helped her into the wheelchair, put on her shoes and hat for her, handed over her pocketbook, and even lifted her into the car, and folded the wheelchair to store in the trunk. I wasn't asked to ride with them. Not that I expected to be, but I might have wanted to see first-hand how the next part of their conversation would ensue. However, I stayed behind and intended to enter the cornfield as it awaited my return.

"Malachi, stay here 'til I git back!" She yelled at me from the car.

On the way to the hospital, the car was empty of words between the two but packed with awkwardness. Huh could never quite get comfortable as she twiddled her thumbs, and subsequently rummaged through her pocketbook looking for nothing. She was quite the untrained thespian. As it has been said, the mark of a great actor is not what he or she is doing when he or she is speaking, but what he or she is doing when he or she is not speaking. Neither of the two of them knew how to cut the tension, for it was as thick as forest brush.

The glacial air from the vents provided a steady hum that set the tone of the distress of their travels to the hospital. He hadn't even had the forethought to turn on the radio in all of his astuteness; temporarily enshrouded by apprehension. His mind searched for words to break the unnerving quietness, but even his extensive vocabulary couldn't show up to save him. Huh sat staring out of the windows with one arm resting on the door, and her chin resting on her fist, which clenched the handkerchief Billy Ray had so magnanimously offered her. She sat fighting the emotions that battled for first place in her head and heart.

Billy Ray reached over and grabbed her hand. Never looking at him, she appreciated the touch, for it had been so long since anyone besides Bubba, had exhibited any kind of gentlemanlike gestures toward her. He squeezed her hand, as tears began to stream down her face into her lap. Billy Ray held her hand for the remainder of the ride. It was obvious to Billy Ray that she wanted and needed his touch. At that moment was when he realized that her longing for a genuine touch is what had iced her heart. Never had she experienced authenticity from strangers. His genuine concerned showed Huh that he was more than a suit with money. More than he would ever know, Billy Ray actually had some profound calming effect on her, and to think, just days earlier, she had torn into him like a bag of chips with her hardheartedness. Hattie Lee Dixon was truly in rare form, for no one had seen her sensitive side exposed in decades, and there it was Billy Ray, the least likely person who helped her evoke it. The moment was definitely for annals of history. All of the roots of her nastiness were afoot. The *dam* and *damnation* in her heart built by outside forces that had caused the hardening of a once potentially vibrant lady had held these tears back. She had grown tired of the hatred, the sadness, the bitterness, and the loneliness, so she expressed tears like milk from teats.

When they arrived at the same hospital that she had been cooped up in, the memories of her stay quickly hastened her tears away. She wiped them with the backs of her hands. As Billy Ray shut the car off, Hattie did the same with her emotions. Her demeanor went from victim to villain within a few minutes. It was how she fortified herself. This fort was her way to block and thwart bullshit, lies, hurt, and chicanery. Luckily, Billy Ray was equipped to deal with it. He had met plenty of Hattie Lee's in his day. He rolled up his sleeves and steeled himself for someone different than the person whose hand he had just held. She snapped and demanded that he hurry to get her out and wheel her inside.

He remembered the tears from the car, he breathed, exhaled and jogged to the passenger's side of the car to comply with no reservations. Billy Ray actually smiled as he knew that Huh was only ashamed that she allowed herself to be vulnerable in front of him. It was at that point that he began to care for a woman that seemingly despised him. He gloated on the idea that he had some lasting effect on a bitter woman whose life had been a ball of deliberate misconceptions, and blatant convolutions about living and existing. As he pushed her in the wheelchair, she reached up and placed her hand on his giving it a swift, unexpected clutch. It was at this point that Billy Ray was assured of their unlikely connection. He also knew this connection would be analogous to a rollercoaster ride full of twists, turns, flips, and the possibility of throwing up. Strangely, Billy Ray was willing to take his chance. This crude, crass lady had somehow stolen his heart. There was a gravitational pull from Billy Ray's high horse that brought him crashing down to the reality of his own loneliness. He realized that in that loneliness, he'd forgotten how to be sincere and compassionate. Billy Ray had let his work strip away his sensibility, and the least likely person, Hattie Lee Dixon, clothed this nakedness, on that day.

The notes to Billy Ray's blues were just that, *notes*. They were not even a song proper, just a music staff full of bland notes forming depressing arpeggios. Mimicking musicality and mocking melody, these notes had no measures, no time signature, no dynamics, and no rests. They were without rhythm, much like the beginning of this relationship with Huh; just noisiness. This day his notes came together to form an unmelodious, unharmonious funk. Not like the fun he'd been in theretofore, but the musical funk rooted in Sub-Saharan culture and strong bass lines. It was one long chord with progressions and his heartbeat a booming, resounding bass drum. Billy Ray's spirit moved to a danceable, rhythmic groove that he hadn't felt in many years. His soul was beginning to have a cadence with an onbeat/offbeat structure full of riffs and snap back snare drums. At that moment, this alternative to his blues became blameless, honest, and natural. He welcomed and accepted the unspoken proposal to forever be betrothed to a new type of funk.

Chapter 12.5

Blessed Be the Name

Dear Andrea,

I don't even know what to write. I guess I should start by saying that it's been a joy to get to know you. I think you are a nice girl, and I am glad that I have been given the chance to meet you. You don't know what it's like in my world, and I say my world because I don't fit in this world. It's something that don't want me to be happy. I don't know what it is. I don't really care. I do care that you see something different than what other people see when you see me. I like that about you. I wish more people were like you. I would be able to face each day better. I would smile more. You make me smile. I try so hard not to look stupid while grinning like a kid when I'm with you. I don't know how to put in words what I really mean. Like right now, I am just searching for words to say. You are one of the things that makes life a little bit easier for me. It's always been hard to write down what I feel. I thought I would try to put pen to paper, and express my feelings. As I write each word, it's like I'm running out of words. I know what I want to say, but I can't explain myself in a way that makes sense to me. So I know it doesn't make any sense to you. I feel like I'm just rambling on and on, about a bunch of nothing. That's like what I feel like sometimes. Nothing. Nothing is probably just the right word to use to describe my feelings about everything, except you. I light up like a street corner when I'm near you. I know that's so stupid, but it's the only thing I could think of. I keep saying that. Am I sounding stupid? Do I make sense? Now I'm asking questions that you probably can't answer either. Then again, you might be able to. You are pretty smart. My mama always said when I start liking girls to find a smart one. I never knew why. Well, now I guess I do need one to help me make myself clear to people. I know I need some help in that area. I know I don't have a lot to offer nobody, but I got a lot to learn. I just know that when I'm around you I feel good about myself because you like being around me. I ain't never had that from somebody who ain't in my family. When I say family, I really just mean my mama when she was around and my Uncle Roosevelt. I guess I'm just writing this to myself. I could never let you see this. I would be too shameful to let you see this. You would probably not want to be around me if I did let you see this. So I'll just fold it up, put it in an envelope, seal it, and put it under my mattress in a slit in the box spring. Yeah, that sounds real good. I will start writing these letters to you and others, to help me get my thoughts across, and help me to make sense of things. See, you are helping me already. Mama was right. I do need me a smart girl. I just smiled when I wrote that thinking that you would probably smile too. I like your smile. It's nice, and you got a good set of teeth. There I go sounding all crazy again. I'm gonna end this letter now because I'm running out of things to say. Thank you for letting me know you. It's the nicest thing anyone has done for me in a long time.

Always,

Malachi

Chapter 13

Cryin' Since You Been Gone

Still reeling after penning that letter to Andrea, I waited patiently for either the phone to ring or for somebody to return. For some odd reason, I just couldn't rest until I knew what was going on. My homegrown curiosity had taken control of the steering wheel, and it was literally driving me crazy. This was the first time something had happened, and I hadn't so much as a clue to at least know whom it involved. My appetite had even been suppressed by my inner desire to ascertain the: who, what, when, where, how, and why. I tried watching TV to switch my brain waves, but it was pointless. I couldn't focus on any program, let alone stop flipping through the 10 basic channels we had.

I got up to clean my room. Something that really didn't need cleaning, because Huh made sure that our old run down house was clean even if she couldn't do it herself. That was one thing for which I had to give her credit. Our house wasn't the most aesthetically pleasing, but the walls were immaculate, and the floors could literally be eaten off of. I know because I had eaten from it before, when she knocked a sandwich out of my hand after I had rolled my eyes at Huh. I remember the day vividly. I had arrived home from school. She told me that she didn't feel like cooking, so I would have to make myself a sandwich. As I was making the sandwich, she rattled off a list of chores she needed me to complete after I did my homework. One of the chores was to wash out all of the trashcans in the house. I had already done that particular chore just three days prior to that particular day, so I felt it a truly superfluous request from Huh.

"I already did that a few days ago," I rattled off, as I was putting the finishing touches on my sandwich.
"Say what?" she demanded to know what I had just uttered.
"Nothin'," I mumbled.
She walked over to me with fire in her eyes. I braced myself, as she got closer. I gripped my plate as if it would anchor me to the floor.

"Let me tell you something goddamnit! If I tell you to spit shine the toilet, you better do it. Don't you ever talk back to me, or mumble shit else whilst you live under this roof. Or you will find yo'self living underground. You hear?" she asked, as he shoved my plate to the ground scattering potato chips and my sandwich toppings. I scurried to clean it up. I piled it all on my plate and walked over to the trashcan to discard it. She cut her eyes at me with a look I'd seen before. It was murderous.

She said, "I wish you would. You gon' eat that shit. I don't know who *thank* got money to throw away".
"Yes, maam," I replied, as I set my plate down on the table in order sweep up the mess.

After I finished cleaning up the mess, she stood and watched me eat every crumb from my plate. I was humiliated. She had treated me no different than the common canine. She was my master, and I was the mutt that she had to feed because no one else would. I fumed on the inside, but I dared not convey it outwardly, or I'd be the next thing to end up on the floor. However, as I stated, the kitchen floor was spotless, so there was no visible dirt on my sandwich because she did take pride in keeping up appearances, but the fact that we had been walking on the floor sickened me. I guess I had to appreciate that she was anal about cleanliness; the whole cleanliness was next to Godliness mantra. Her love for this old house was unmatched.

As I began to move toward my bedroom door, the phone rang. It startled me. However, I regained my composure and I ran to it. I answered. It was a collect call. I accepted it, but with reservation, because I knew as soon as Huh got the bill I would be in for an eve of reckoning.

"Malachi, is that you?" the female voice asked, sounding as if she were underwater.

"Yes, who is this?" I inquired.

"It's me baby!" My mother said in a tone like a hush before a cry.

I dropped the phone. I stood motionless as I searched for the right emotion. So much ran through my mind that I was almost too dazed to pick up the phone. It had been at least a month since she'd called. I had begun to think she no longer cared enough to call or worse, she hadn't planned to ever call again. I had taught myself not to care either way. However, as soon as I heard her voice, I knew that I did care and I cared a great deal. I loved this lady. I missed her touch, her smell, her hugs, and her just being in the next room. My mind continued to race and my heart pounded like a toothache; because it hurt both to hear her and also not be able to see her. I finally got the strength to pick up the phone.

"H...hello..." I said hesitantly.

"Hey, baby! How you feeling?" she said in that motherly way that I had missed so much.

"I'm okay ma! What about you?" I questioned.
"Baby, you know I'm good. I can survive anything! I have been worried about my baby! How are you and mama getting along?" Mama asked.
"We okay!" I started.
"You don't sound okay Malachi. You know you can tell mama anything right?" she reminded me.
"Yeah, I know." I said as I began to feel the wetness roll down my face.
"I know I was the last person you expected to hear from. We don't have that many chances to call. I know I ain't talked to you in a while!" she bemoaned.
"Yeah, it's been a while!" I echoed her sentiments.
"You miss mama?" she asked.
"I do miss you! I think about you all the time ma!" I returned.
"I miss you more baby. I think about you every day. Things just ain't the same without you," she said.

My mind raced back to times when she had said that very same thing to me when she had been locked up for shorter periods of time. I hesitated to believe her, but my heart still bled for her. She'd given birth to me, and no matter how much it hurt me that she had been imprisoned and as a consequence, so had I. Nonetheless, I could never think ill of her. I could never blame her for all the times she should've been there, but wasn't. She was my mother. I knew I still owed her a certain amount of respect for all of the things she had done right and done out of love for me.
"I know ma." I said, in a defeated tone as I let out an unconscious sigh.
"Baby, I know it's hard with me being in here. I just need you to be strong for both of us. You are all that I got, and I want you to be all you can be. I only got a couple more minutes, but there is something that I have to tell you. In the last month, I have fallen in love. I know you know that I am in a women's prison, so it is a woman. Her name is Raquel, but everybody calls her Rocky. You know that I have had many boyfriends, but none of them treated me as kind and with as much love as Rocky has. I know this

may be awkward for you, but you are my family, and I needed to share this with you. I am sad because I can't be with you, but I am happy because someone in this God awful place loves me, and I need that to survive. It's tough being without you, and not having my freedom. You mean the world to me. I promise when I get out of here, I'll never leave you again. I got seven more years to be back with you; maybe less than that if I continue good behavior. Remember, I love you more than I love me. Don't you ever forget it! I gotta go now baby," Mama lamented.
"Bye Ma. I love you t..." I was interrupted by a dial tone.

I hung up the phone. I sat in the recliner forgetting that I needed to clean up my room before Huh returned. Having remembered how much I missed my mother, my eyes welled up. I sat in a state of uncontrollable solitude. I sat trying to process the fact that my mother had become a lesbian as a result of being caged like a bird with no wings; helpless. As much as I had been confounded by her revelation, I was glad she could find a flicker of happiness; as both our lives seemed to be in flames. With a grain of salt, I respected my mother for having the courage to reveal her love of Rocky to me, but even more so, for not being afraid to find love in a hopeless place. Instead of cleaning my room, as I had been wont to do, I found myself pickled in sadness as I recalled the day my mother left, and I was bussed to Mississippi.

It was a cold, virulent winter that year in Detroit. Christmas, New Year's, and my 12th birthday had come and gone. It was the year Mama got me the Atari system and bike that I had been asking for all year long. The Atari system made me popular with the guys in our housing project. Mama would let two or three come over at a time to play Pac Man, Dig Dug, and Space Invaders. Though she was really picky about which boys I could let in the house. I would always remember her saying, "Don't let Mane Mane and Li'l Pat roguish asses in my house". She was right. Mane Mane and Li'l Pat would soon as steal your thoughts let alone your drawers off your body if they could have found a way to make it happen. Having the

Atari was great, but I loved that bike because it took me on excursions that I had theretofore been deprived.

There was no more having to wait on the bus, or for someone to drive me places that were miles away. I felt like I could go any way at any time, and nobody could prohibit my journey to freedom. That is, until the day after Valentine's Day of that year. I stopped at the store to get me a grape soda, some salt-n-vinegar chips, and a Suzie-Q. I was in the store for approximately thirty seconds, as I knew exactly what I wanted, and there was no time to tarry. I paid for my goods in single brown and beige food stamps, and I darted out of the store to find my 10-speed missing. I fell to my knees unto the ground, and my 16-ounce bottle of grape soda and goodies followed. The pool of grape soda that surrounded me was symbolic of bloodshed. I wished I were dead at that moment. I dispensed tears as would a bartender draft beer. My source of freedom had been stolen, and I was powerless to do anything about it. Not a soul was on the corner where the store was located, or on the street nearby; so there were no witnesses. I finally gathered my Suzie Q and chips and traipsed home. No bike, no feeling in my face, no soul, no anything.

When I finally arrived home, Mama and her latest boyfriend, Larry, were lying on the sofa watching TV. I passed through without emitting a word of greeting. Once I entered my room, I closed my door and crashed face down onto the bed still bundled in my parka, corduroys, and boots. I tossed my goodies to the ground on the other side of the bed nearest the only window in my room and continued my crying spell. Before I knew it, I mourned myself into a deep sleep. I had had several dreams about my bike as I lay there. At that point, I really didn't care if I woke up, because I knew my mother would be so disappointed in my carelessness. However, loud talking and shouting awakened me. I was sweating profusely as I was still clad in my outside winter apparels.

I ran out of my room almost falling, as I had arisen much too fast. I turned the doorknob to find the police forcibly subduing my mother and Larry, as they protested in a harangue of copious obscenities. I screamed, "Let my mama go," as loud as I could, in hopes that my pleas would quell the onslaught of brutality I was witnessing. To no avail, the only black officer grabbed me and slung me over his shoulder, as I kicked and pummeled his back with my fists. He carried me down the stairs behind my mother and Larry, both of whom had been handcuffed and feet shackled due to their respective resistive arrests.

I watched in horror as they were stuffed like pillows into the back of two separate police cruisers. The officer who grabbed me kept me behind. He calmed me down enough to ask me questions like how old was I? Was I afraid and were there any family who could pick me up from the police station? The officer then escorted me to the police car where I was allowed to ride in front. I surmised that he didn't want to give me any indication that I was in trouble, or being apprehended for wrongdoing. I appreciated the way that he'd handled me. Once we arrived at the station, I was allowed to sit in the police break room. It was there that I found out that Larry was arrested for armed robbery, and because my mother had interfered with the arrest, she was now being charged with resisting arrest. They then ran her profile against their database and found that she had a warrant for her arrest for check fraud. The officers were nice to me. They fed me, and each officer that came into the break room spent a little time with me.

Finally, the black officer, Sergeant Josiah Johnson came to ask me my grandmother's number. I hesitated because I knew I didn't want to have to leave my mother or Detroit. He called *Huh* and they had arranged a money wire from Mississippi to pay for a bus ticket for my departure to Mississippi. Officer Johnson took me home to pack the biggest suitcase my mother owned with as many seasonal clothing as I could stuff. I left behind all my other belongings including the Atari, all my posters and baseball cards. I left my life in Detroit. I spent the night in a hotel room; the only time I'd ever done so, right next door to the station. The Sergeant ordered room service for me and sent an officer to check on me every so often. As much as

I would have liked to relish in the experience, my heart had been shattered, and my spirit had deserted my body.

The next morning, I was allowed to say goodbye to my mother through plexi-glass and a mounted tan phone. A sight I'd seen all too many times when her other boyfriends would take me to visit when she'd be in jail for a few days or weeks. She cried which made me crumple like aluminum foil, for I knew this time had finality. I knew even as an adolescent, that this was irrevocably, and inevitably irreparable. Promising me that she'd get out soon and that she'd come to get me as soon as she could, even she didn't believe it to be true. She placed her left hand on stained barrier as she clutched the phone receiver more tightly, I followed suit as she articulated, and "I love you more than I love me. Don't ever forget it." I walked out of the jail as Sergeant Johnson held my suitcase in his left hand and my right shoulder with his right hand. He dropped me off at the bus station, gave me $10, and instructed the security guard to watch out for me. As I sat on the bench outside the station I people watched and soul searched; what little soul remained. As I stepped onto the bus, I looked straight to the back, which at the time, seemed too far to walk, so, I opted for the front. My naiveté in that instance hadn't prepared me for the realization that the 875-mile expedition would be the shortest trip of my life.

Remembering that time period made my soul sink in sorrow, for I longed for the days of life with my mother in Detroit. That life hadn't been that much better, but better nevertheless. Things were challenging there, but somehow, compared to living in the Delta, Detroit seemed like a walk in the proverbial park. The Delta was just so unpredictably unsettling, especially while dealing with an uncommonly, unconcerned grandmother, who made things unequivocally complicated. In Motor City, there was no ambiguity. Life was either really decent, or really depraved. Situations were serene, or intensified, and people were benevolent, or nefarious. Debauchery wasn't masked by secrets and deceit; it was in your face, and stamped its mark so you knew its intentions. I wanted the life back of which I had grown accustomed, but the fact that I couldn't regain the reins on that life started to make me feel empty again. The phone call from my mother had sparked some subconscious feelings that I hadn't embraced in such a long time. It had unearthed a veritable cornucopia of emotions that I just hadn't been equipped with which to contend at that juncture.

I fell asleep. I dreamed of waking up in our apartment in Detroit. My mother had gotten out of jail again. We were happy. As I turned to leave for school, the police were at the door. They were there to take her away again. I shouted "No!" as I grabbed ahold of my mother. She begged the officers not to take her away from me, but they read her rights to her and took her away anyway. I couldn't wake up inasmuch as I wanted to. It was all I could do to break the spell this nightmare had on me. In the dream, I slumped in a corner and cried; punching at the air as if I could win. I felt someone shake me. I was still fighting. Uncle Roosevelt was shaking to wake me up out of what probably looked like an exorcism in progress; while sweat rained down my skin. *Déjà vu.*

"Malachi, wake up!" Wake up boy!" Uncle Roosevelt bellowed to get my attention.

"Where is she? Where is my mama?" I awakened still delusional.

"Malachi, you was dreaming. It's alright son," he said, as he pulled me close to him, just as caring as Sergeant Johnson had been many years prior.

My sweat and tears dampened the portion of his shirt where my eyes rested. Uncle Roosevelt didn't seem to mind the moisture, as he did hold me until I stopped crying, and he stayed with me for the next few minutes to make sure that I didn't have a breakdown. I really appreciated that about him. He was such a selfless guy. I always hoped I could be half the man that he had been. *From my lips to their God's ears*.

This day had been as debilitating to me as a sudden case of the flu. My body ached, my head hurt, and all I wanted to do was sleep. But I couldn't. I dreaded dreaming of my mother yet again. These nightmares brought with them misery like that due to the grief over the loss of a loved one. And I had lost a loved one. *My mother.* I knew grief on a first name basis, and it hadn't been my pleasure to make its acquaintance. Again, I felt that agony on the inside that reminded me that I had been sentenced concurrently alongside my mother. While she had been incarcerated proper, I had been confined by bastardization and the wretchedness of the Delta, both of which had haunted me daily.

After the tears subsided and Unc had left my room, I was able to collect myself. I wiped my eyes and nose with the backs of my hands and I sat there looking like a 4-year-old. I felt like a four-year-old, too. It was times like this that made me revert back to an uncomplicated state. My esteem was profoundly fragmented, which in turn, made me volatile at best. I teetered between the extremes of mania and depression as if I were on a seesaw with myself. It was just not a good place in which to be; the ups and downs, the rocks and hard places. However, when I snapped out of sorry for myself, for it profited me none, I remembered there was another calamitous situation imminent. Who was in trouble? Who was in the hospital? Determined to put my own mind at ease, I left my room. I sought Uncle Roosevelt, my sage.

"Unc what's going on? Why was ya'll at the hospital so long?" I queried.
"Well, son, it's Ms. Jane," he responded glumly.
"Is she alright?" I asked.
"Not really," he returned with pessimism.
"Oh my goodness, is she…" I asked thinking the worst.
"Wait a minute son. Calm down. She is still alive, but she ain't doing so good," he said, in a very indulgent manner.
"What's wrong? She sick?" I probed.
"Guess you could say dat!" he construed.
"She gon' be alright?" I asked concernedly.
"We don't know!" Uncle Roosevelt exclaimed.

Unc went on to tell me what had happened to Ms. Jane. His words anesthetized me like no surgeon could duplicate. I felt myself becoming indifferent to pain. I knew this didn't bode well for me. I looked at Uncle Roosevelt wanting to say something. I couldn't regurgitate any previously used expressions that had any semblance of lucidity. I tried to find them, but my mind held them at bay. The pure shock of it all had overcome me, like an infection meticulously destroying me from the inside out. Just when things were seemingly coming together for me, in a day's time again, they were falling apart right before my eyes. I likened myself that old red arm on our decrepit mailbox. No matter how much we bent it to alert the mailman there was mail to retrieve, it failed to perform its only function. My only function was to exist, and it was clear that I wasn't up for the task.

"You don't have to say nothin'. Sometimes silence is good for you. Words can't always express what you feel in yo' soul," he comforted me.

It was those words, that unbeknownst to Uncle Roosevelt, illuminated a light inside me. Newly lambent after years, I had been freed from thinking and feeling obligated to find the right words in every situation; evidenced in my letter to Andrea. Every situation hadn't necessitated the *right* thing to say. It was Uncle Roosevelt's unpretentious message that abetted me in being cognizant of the fact that I had been spinning in circles, making myself dizzy trying to make sense of the illogical, and trying to fix the damaged. The truth of the matter was that my existence wasn't logical, and I was too damaged to fix anything. The events of that day routed me from sorrow to nowhere. A place I had lived a long time. Luckily, my citizenship hadn't been revoked.

My rock and roll had rocked and rolled, leaving me high and dry on the shore of my erstwhile blues. Pain and angst washed up and lapped at my feet. The coldness and liquescence of the two emotions wrote a loose narrative in the sand of my reality. *My Delta Blues* were back to occupy the vacancy in my soul. It took up residency where it had deserted me just days earlier. Its rhythmic melody was becoming cyclical. Every time it seemed to change, the more it stayed the same. That same guitar licks strummed by the fingers of a void. There was the same chorus sung by the caterwauling messenger of despair. The same inauspicious tune played by the mouth organist of ruin. Again, I was relegated to the place where I always end up. My ultimate destination...the point of no return...

Chapter 13.5

My Sunshine

Dear Andrea,

Here we are again. I know we've only known each other for a short period of time, but I feel I've known you forever. I think writing to you is becoming a way to counsel myself, if that makes any sense. It's just the simple things. Going to the goal always makes me think of you. I just laugh every time I think about you snapping at Ms. Mary. Nobody ever talks to her like that, but you just came in and put her in her place. I wish I could be like that. I don't know how to feel right now. One day I'm good and the next I'm down. It's like I'm riding on an elevator, but I don't have enough sense to get off before I'm realize that I am not going anywhere purposeful. You might be the only thing I have to make me think good thoughts. But then I feel bad for feeling good. It's crazy I know. You said I was different. I guess that's true. This summer wouldn't have been too great without you. You have made it easier to be here for the first time in three years. I know that sounds hard to believe, but it is how I feel. I couldn't have made it. The talks we had made me feel like I was important to somebody. I like that about you. It's like you have a certain way about you that I can't put my finger on. It's like a spirit. I hope I'm not creeping you out. I'm just trying to say things that I have never really said to a person. It's just easier to write this. Even though it's hard to find exactly what to say, even I know full well I don't have to. Old habits are hard to break. Given the fact that you will never read this, I will just keep writing until something comes to me. I am not a good writer, as you know, well you don't know 'cause I didn't give you the first letter. But I do have a good grasp of the English language. I've read so many books, plays, and poems by Maya Angelou, Alexandre Dumas, James Baldwin, Spenser, and Marquez. I have a notebook of words that I have learned while reading like ubiquitous, pervasive, tantamount, anomaly, and respite. Not that you care. That is so crazy and random right? I often think of that kiss you gave me. That was so sweet. Really sweet thanks to the lollipop. I just smiled again. It's hard to smile though, when everything around me just ain't right. It's like you cursed on me. It's like my mama 'nem say "don't eat no woman's spaghetti cause they'll put a root on you"! The only woman's spaghetti I ever ate is my grandmama's. I don't guess she put a curse on me. Now I know I sound crazy talking about roots and curses, but I know ain't no such thing. I just keep thinking about the day you kissed me. I know I mentioned that already, but it just makes me feel good to know that of all the boys you could have kissed, you chose me. That makes me feel pretty special. I got a little piece of your world that I can say is just mine. I'm not trying to say you are mine or nothing, but you know what I mean. I think. There I go again, talking out the side of my neck as they say. I am gonna hate to see the summer go, because I know you have to go back to Kansas, and I have to go back to the more of the same. I ain't looking forward to that at all. I just wish we had met earlier in the summer, and that way we could have had more time to get to know each other. I just hope when you leave we can stay in touch. I gotta keep reminding myself that I am saying all this to myself because you will never read this. Maybe I should let you read this and the other letter. I don't know. I gotta stop writing now. I am starting to scare myself because I feel like I am talking to myself. All I know is that I will miss you. I will never forget what you have brought to me in such a short time. I know I will never forget you.

Always,
Malachi

Chapter 14

Long Ways from Home

After the call from my mother and the news of Ms. Jane, Andrea came. She appeared like a purple, pink, and blue horizon. She separated my Earth from the sky. Trees, mountains, or edifices no longer obscured it. Even though I was powerless to find any refuge theretofore, Andrea had become my only source. It was in her presence that I felt vicariously invincible. I ingested her spirit and I imbibed her aura. Full and drunk, I escaped the defeat that my life served up daily like it was what was for lunch. She had become the one constant, beautiful, non-threatening, unbiased entity in my life in such a short time. I don't think Andrea had any idea how profound the effect she had on my self-worth.

We met in our usual spot. This day she was different. I could tell that her smile was a façade, and disingenuous in its inception. In my finite wisdom, I could discern something was askew. Her mannerisms had dimmed. Her stature was recessed. Her attitude mitigated. The lollipop was in her hair. We sat. Our souls separated by whatever she had brewing.

"Hey you," I spoke.
"Hey you." she replied, with a smile but her soul frowned.
"Everything good with you?" I asked.
"Yeah, why you ask?" She queried, with uneasiness in her eyes.
"Just making sure," I stated.
"So what's new with you?" she asked, with no real diction or inflection.
"Not a whole lot. Talked to my mom though," I spilled.

“How’d that go?” She said, twiddling with a twig she’d picked up from the ground in front of us.
“Alright, I guess. She’s happy and in love,” I responded, with vulnerability seeping out of my eyes and skin.
“She’s what?” she asked, startled by my revelation.
“She apologized for not calling in the last few weeks, and she rattled off that she had fallen in love with another woman in jail!”
“Wow! That is a lot to handle, especially through a phone call. Are you okay with this?” She asked as she placed her left hand on my thigh in hopes of comforting me.
“Yes it is a lot, but I can deal with it. Though I didn’t get a chance to tell her, I am very happy for her. It can’t be easy living trapped in a place with no one to love you and care about you. I love my mom. I just wish I could do more than talk to her. I haven’t seen her since the day I left Detroit 3 years ago. It’s hard,” I indicated.

“I know it’s hard, but it’s good that you can be happy for her, and not be all judgmental like people can be. At least you can still talk to her,” she said sadly.

I knew what the difference was in her after her words. I felt her pain of being a motherless child; even though she was choosing not to say it outwardly. I also knew she was sad about leaving. I was inclined to give her the time she needed to make mention of it.

“You are right, and I am thankful for that,” I sustained.
“That’s good,” she responded inertly.
“Thanks for your support. It means a lot to me,” I replied.
“You’re welcome. I appreciate that. Well, you know I will be leaving in a week or two. Summer vacation is coming to an end. No more easy livin’,” Andrea lamented.
“Don’t remind me” I said, as I heaved a sigh.
“Not like you gonna miss me!” she replied.
“Oh, but I am gonna miss you! These meetings have been the highlight of my summer. Without you, I would have been cooped up in my house, or out back reading in the cornfield. Waiting for another day of nothing, heartache, and confusion,” I returned.

"You find all of that in a cornfield?" She asked, with a slight giggle. It was real.
The color had returned to her face. Levity lit her up like lighted lanes. Her demeanor was kicking back into high gear. She was returning to normal; as if the banter with me had been her salve or her antibiotic.
"No, but I found you. I finally met someone normal in Mississippi. These country folks is crazy as hell!" I carped.
"Folks? Boy, you been here way too long!" she teased.
"You right about that! You know what they say…" I started.
"What? Country is as country does!" Andrea exclaimed.
"Ha ha! No! It's just that, when in Rome, " I said, as I met her gaze.
"Be country as hell!" she laughed uncontrollably. I was glad to see that blush in her cheeks, and that glint off the green flecks of her hazel irises.
"You just full of jokes today huh?" I asked rhetorically.
"I am sorry Mr. Malachi Dixon," she said haughtily.
"No, it's cool! I like it," I assured her.
"Well good, because I got few more jokes about watermelons and collard greens," she jested.
"Wait a minute now, I live here, but I'm a Northerner," I reminded her.

We laughed harmoniously, as she removed the lollipop from her hair, unwrapped it, and inserted it onto her tongue. She was back to her true and authentic self, the self-aware girl I met weeks ago. It did my heart well to see her cheer up underneath my sky. For once I had been a healing property for her. Somehow, I briefly usurped her energy in order to resuscitate her spirit. Although we never talked about her missing her mother, it was almost as if our souls had discoursed, and as a result, she was restored. I put my arm around her and she rested her head on my shoulder as she suckled the lollipop. I smiled.

"Did you hear about the lady who killed her husband?" she asked, with a disconcerting look on her face.
"Yeah, I did. She is my grandma's friend," I rejoined.
"No way!" she responded in disbelief.

"Yeah, my grandma spent the day with her over at the hospital," I said.
"You know my daddy was over at the hospital too. But he never said who he went to see," she said undaunted.
"Oh, yeah?" I asked with an ominous tone.
"Yeah, he was there a good little while!" Andrea averred.
"What's yo daddy's name?" I dared ask, though I felt as though I already knew the answer.
"Billy Ray!" she indicated innocuously.
"Well, I be damn!"
"You know my daddy or something?" she asked innocently.
"Yeah, he is the one who put my grandma to the hospital," I said.
"Boy, quit lying! You mean to tell me that yo' grandma is the lady that he said he barely tapped on the hip, but she acted like he had run her down like a dog" she responded in disbelief.
"I swear! That's her. But wait, I thought you told me your last name was Lee," I recollected.
"My middle name is spelled L-e-i-g-h, like the white woman from Gone with the Wind! I go by that because Andrea Bonds just doesn't have a ring to it," she said, rather arrogantly. "*Ain't this just rich*! All this time, you knew my daddy! You better not tell him you know me, because he don't like me around boys. He ran off the last boyfriend I had. Daddy threatened to beat him like he stole something if he ever touched me. That boy was scared to hold my hand or even walk three feet close to me!"
"Well, yo' daddy is a scary man. He probably should have been a prison warden!" I quipped.
"Boy, you crazy! My daddy is a big old teddy bear," she replied.
"Umm… more like grizzly bear!" I retorted.
"He is the sweetest man on Earth. But when it comes to me and money, he don't play at all!" she cautioned.
"Well, I am already scared of him!" I said, as I jokingly moved away from her.
"You need to be scared of me!" she said, as she playfully began to punch me.

We tussled a minute until she fell on top of me. She looked into my eyes and we kissed. As if we were never going to see one another again. Her soft lips only paralleled her smooth skin. I associated her touch with what warm water was to an aching body. The way she made me feel when she kissed me was unlike no other feeling for which I had no frame of reference to describe. It was almost as if she and I had been separated by a time continuum, and brought together by the alluvial plains of the Mississippi Delta. We had been deposited back into our natural habitats by a universal intervention so implicit that it was not for anyone else to comprehend. Nothing else seemed to matter as long as she was around. *No Detroit. No Sidon. No Mama. No Huh. No nonentity.* Her essence oozed through her pores, and I inhaled it like oxygen. I longed for the time with her because it made me forget how unmentionably awful my life was. Somehow, she possessed the authority to make all my problems seem imaginary. She had become necessary to my survival. I required her. She was vitally obligatory and compulsory. It was evident to me at the time that without her entry into my, I probably would have lost all hope. But then there was her.

I suggested that we head to Lake Quinn. It was where people got Baptized, swam, fished, had BBQ's, and other family and community functions. There was a wharf off the levee where the people of Sidon and surrounding towns used to sit to catch fish. It squeaked when you walked on it, so you had to sit and wait a little while so the fish could forget that they heard noises above and scamper near it again. However, a new one was built on the other side of the lake, and the residents had all but abandoned it. The young Sidon residents would use it as a place to hang out; knowing no adults would be there to chastise them. I held Andrea's hand all the way there. She was my anchor.

During our time spent together, we talked about what it was like to grow up in Wichita and Detroit. She told me that she had broken her arm at the Sedgwick County Zoo while teasing the primates in their *unnatural* habitats. I told her how I'd broken my leg horse playing in the makeshift park in the middle of our project, and how it hurt like a son-of-a-bitch. She told me about the many class trips to Boeing and McConnell Air Force base during elementary, and I remarked about the numerous excursions I'd made to Motown Records and Ford Motor Company. It was amazing how similar our stories were, considering we were from two disparate locales; though we did share time a zone. We also shared stories of playing hide and seek, learning to ride a bike, getting sick from eating too many sweets, having chicken pox, watching cartoons on a Saturday morning, going to church, and getting *whoopin's* for silly stuff. Exchanging our stories was cathartic. We both shed a layer of tough skin and made ourselves vulnerable to one another.

When we arrived at the marina, we sat on the wharf. We sat listening to the sounds in nature while whiffing the odors fastened the landscape. The sun was being displaced by the advent of the evening as the trees bowed to its sovereignty. We were but lowly subjects under a majestic kaleidoscopic sky that looked down on a crestfallen, unkempt lake. It was amazing the see a naturally landscaped environment with another set of eyes. We found it therapeutic to simply absorb the ambient sounds of this ecosystem, the flora, and fauna, the muddy water off which light pirouetted in all its brilliance. We lay sprawled on the unstable wharf, closed our eyes, and just listened as night crept up on us like a bunny.

"You wanna take a swim?" Andrea asked.
"Get out of my head! I was gonna ask you the same thing," I said animatedly.
"Let's do it!" She exclaimed as she rose in excitement.
"Ok!" I followed.

We began disrobing and throwing our garments carelessly on to the wharf. I had stripped down to my undies in seconds, and she was down to her unmentionables. We looked at one another and in an instant, we were like Olympic swimmers as we canon balled into the lake; baptizing ourselves in the cloudy liquid. We swam with the clumsiness of reptiles, but with the stamina of fish. For the moments that we splashed around haphazardly, our aloofness seemed to wash away any griminess we may have felt bathing in the filth of the water. It was liberating and exhilarating to just let go and to just be.

I could hear no blues under the opaque waters. No bent notes. No chord progressions. There was only a peaceful refrain that had not been restricted by any particular cadence...melody...or aggrandizement. The notes were more graceful than a ballerina in an *en pointe* with her feet fully extended like a sylph. Its chorus was groovier than it had ever been. Andrea and I lie comfortably in those grooves as if they were bassinets. No matter how hard we were rocked we couldn't fall. We couldn't sink. Essentially, we thrived like underwater vegetation. Only unlike algae, we were capable of floating to the water's surface in an embrace. Holding hands and flapping our feet we seized an opportunity for a kiss. It was a musical. It was magical. It was palpable.

Chapter 14.5

Since I've Laid My Burdens Down

Dear Andrea,

Last night was the best night of my life. To take a swim in the lake with you felt so good. I have swum in that muddy water so many times, but it was really special doing it with you. This is already letter three and you don't know anything about the other two. I keep wondering if I should give them to you or not. My heart says I should but my head says, "don't be no fool." I am still learning to put the words together to tell you how I feel, not the right words, but just words from my heart. I just feel so stupid for writing and not allowing you to read them, but I can't stop now. It just makes to put these] thoughts and feelings I have on to paper and not keep them locked away. I don't think I have ever told anyone what I was truly feeling, even though in the past I may have thought I was. I could explain things pretty good, but in the end, it only sounded good to me. I guess that is all that matters. I don't know.

As you can see, I don't know much and a lot all at the same. One thing I do know today is that that swim with you and the kiss made me feel like I could fly. Here I go again, thinking I sound stupid. But flying is the only thing I can compare it to. It seems like when birds take flight, they don't care about what else is in the sky. They just spread their wings and go higher and higher. It's like they try to escape what's on the ground. I feel like that, too. I just want to escape and fly far away beyond the clouds to a world, unlike this one. See, I said all that and it only makes sense in my head. That's how I know I could never let you see these letters. I think you would think I was crazy or maybe you would want to join me. I am sure you, too, could imagine not living here in a place so limiting. I would love to share a place like that with you. We could be rulers of our own universe and leave behind this heavy world. I know you also think that we deserve to be free of all of hurt, pain, and suffering that this world offers. I know that of all the things that I have been through, I know I can look back to something you said or did that made me smile and it helps me. If you read this, you would probably think I'm giving you too much credit. But it's what I feel. I'm a boy and you are a girl, and the world says we can't be friends without messing it up by placing its judgments on us. You are my friend and possibly the only true friend I have ever had. Does that sound sad? Is there something wrong with me? I guess it doesn't matter. The fact is you have been good for me. You're not judgmental, and you are as straightforward as anyone I've ever met. You have kept our conversations so true and real. I have never had to guess if you were being honest with me. I'm laying across this bed of mine, and I feel whole knowing you can see the same sky that I admire which frames the same moon that I envy and the same stars that I wish upon. Just thinking about that gives me a good feeling all over. Knowing we can both breathe the same air has been helping me to sleep better at night because many nights I can't sleep. When I do sleep, I toss and turn while I have bad dreams but the dreams haven't been so bad since you showed up. I'm not as tired in the mornings, even though I don't want to get up and face the day. I do look forward to the chance to see you. Laying eyes on you makes the day just that much better. The summer is just about up, so school is starting soon and you will be gone. I will never forget what you have done for me. I have to stop here. I know I don't have much more to say. It's best to quit while I'm ahead. I'm gonna miss you. Take care of yourself and remember me.

Always,

Malachi

Chapter 15

No Mo' Weepin' and Wailin'

While Ms. Jane was still under psychiatric watch in the hospital, her children had given power of attorney to Miss Sally until they could take off work to tend to Ms. Jane and Old Man Jessie's affairs. They had even put Miss Sally over the funeral and burial arrangements. Everyone in town thought it all rather strange that they didn't want to handle it all themselves. Miss Sally had taken off work for a couple of weeks in order to handle everything. Uncle

Roosevelt and Huh had also helped Sally out tremendously. Of course, Miss Sally kept in contact with the children by relaying messages and getting feedback on major details. They had assured her that they would be there to tie up loose ends before the actual funeral. Miss Sally waited patiently. Not one of them showed up until the night before the funeral. It was the talk of the town. Miss Sally even had to be the one to get Ms. Jane discharged for the services. She had truly been an altruistic and resolute vessel in conducting business that should have been handled by Ms. Jane's next of kin. Not only did she not complain but she also didn't want any praises for what she had done. It was something not foreign to her since she'd done the same things for her husband years ago; only this time she hadn't been left bereft and bankrupt.

It was the day of the funeral, and Ms. Jane and Old Man Jessies' children, Jennifer, Louise, and Li'l Jessie all showed up decked out in extravagant clothing with faces as dry as bones. With their noses turned up, they looked like they were displeased with the way Sally had planned everything from the flowers to the respective casket and church selections. This made Sally really feel uncomfortable and unappreciated. She had doled out a great share of her time and even forsaken her income for a few days. Unc held her and told her not to worry, but she couldn't help but feel uneasy at the thought of Jane's children's dissatisfaction. As hard as she had tried to make sure everything was perfect, she felt that she had let Jane and her family down. Her facial expression told of her disappointment in herself.

"Look here Sally. You done did yo' best on this fune and ain't nobody gon' come up in here and make you feel bad 'bout it!" Huh said as loudly as possible so that Jane's children would be sure to overhear.

"Hattie, I ain't strong like you when it comes to people. My feelings get hurt easy. I don't want Jane's family to be mad wit' me!" Sally bemoaned.

"Well, hell, they shoulda come and done it all they self!" Huh said in an elevated tone.
"Hattie, they gon' hear you!" Sally whispered trying to shush Huh.
"So what? Ain't nobody gon' whoop my ass!" Huh pointed out matter-of-factly.
"Yeah, but they daddy just died, and I don't wanna cause no confusion," Sally replied humbly.
"Hell, they caused the confusion when they walked up in here like they got oil wells pumpin' in they backyards. Quiet as it kept, they should be mo' concerned wit' thanking you than upsettin' you. Look at 'em. All of got them big *dashboard* foreheads jes' like Jessie, don't they?" Huh whispered.

"Hattie, girl, you is a fool," Sally said as Huh statements evoked a much-needed chuckle.

"I jus' tell what God love to hear! The truth," Huh replied in that haughty way she had.

"Hattie hush wit' all that foolishness! You ought to be shame of yo'self!" Unc said as he laughed.

"Velt, you know I ain't stud'n them! Humph!" Huh retorted.

"Sally, have they said something to you?" Unc asked in concerned.

"Nah, they ain't said nothing. But the looks on they faces say it all," Sally returned.
"Well, don't let all that get to you. We got to go get Jane ready for the limousine ride!" Unc said.

"Why her damn children can't get her ready? Hell, they ain't handicapped!" Huh said disdainfully.
"Hattie, I don't mind. If they want to do it, then they'll tell me I guess!" Sally responded in kind.
"Sally, after all these years of hanging round me, you still handle shit like a white woman nah...better yet an Asian woman. Girl, you need to go tell them damned *motley face ass* children to make sho they mama get in the limo and into that church for the damn fune!" Huh said, demanding that Sally get a backbone and stand up for herself.
"I can't do that Hattie. I ain't like you. I gotta keep the peace!" Sally replied.

"Hell, me too. I keeps me a piece right in my pocketbook for bastards like them chirren!" she said as patted her purse and gathered it up under her arm.
"Hattie girl, I can always count on you for a good laugh even in a time as sad as this," Sally communicated.
"I'm jus' keepin' it real! Ain't no sense in you gettin' all stressed out 'bout all this. We love Jane and all, but this 'spose to be on her children shoulders, not yours!"

Sally, Uncle Roosevelt, and Huh retrieved Jane so that she wouldn't miss the limo ride to the church from the funeral home. Huh continued to talk trash about Jane's children to keep Sally's spirits up. Jane was still in a state of shock. She would only nod yes or no, for she still hadn't said a word since she stabbed Old Man Jessie to death. Sally and Unc had been her caretakers aside from the nurses and doctors for the entire week since. They made sure she got into the limo, and they were going to ride in Old Man Jessie's car, but Jane's children declined to ride with her, so Sally and Uncle Roosevelt rode with her. Billy Ray showed up with Andrea. My heart pounded like a jackhammer. I didn't even want him to suspect that I knew her, let alone liked her as much as I did. That man intimidated me more than any other person I had ever met and considering I was from Detroit that wasn't an easy feat. Just at the moment, I turned to walk away so as not to appear to be staring, Billy Ray motioned for me.
"*Shit!*" I thought as I paused before I crept over to see what he wanted. I looked directly up into his eyes because I didn't want my eyes to shift and look at Andrea.
"Yes, sir!" I said anxiously with an obvious lump in my throat.
"Malachi, you can calm down. I just wanted to introduce you to my daughter, Andrea. Andrea, this is Malachi, the young man I told you about," Billy Ray asserted.
"Nice to meet you, Malachi," Andrea voiced as she smiled at me.
"Nice to meet you, too," I replied as I swallowed hard and glanced quickly at her and back at him.

"Malachi, what's wrong with you boy? You act like you have seen a ghost or something!" Billy Ray said gruffly, and Andrea laughed.
I felt so embarrassed. The look on my face had clearly been of my obvious fear. My bladder started to fill up almost instantaneously. If I had had to stand there any longer, I would wet myself.
"Well, Mr. Bonds, I gotta go," I said as I pivoted.
"Okay, Malachi," said Billy Ray.
"Bye Malachi!" Andrea said as I scurried away like a frightened rodent.

I went into the bathroom of the church and I peed like one of those fountains in the middle of quadrangles. My embarrassment spewed out through my liquid waste. After that, I felt much better. Actually, I had gained a little bit of courage. I washed my hands, dashed my face with water, dried with a napkin, and I walked out of that bathroom with some semblance of dignity. I may have just been suffering from false bravado because as soon as I saw Andrea and Billy Ray again, my knees weakened.

Before the commencement of the funeral, the family had lined up outside the front of the church. This was one of the few times you saw a group of black people together and there wasn't a bunch of foolishness taking place. At funerals, black people wear their best Sunday black outfits. Most women usually wore one-piece dresses with big gaudy hats and veils, and the men mostly wore white shirts with black ties and black pants or black suits, some pin-striped. Both sexes would occasionally wear shades to mask the red eyes, which resulted from teeming amounts of crying. While most people tried to act as dignified as possible, at black funerals, traditionally, there'd always be those people who would cut up really badly in the way the showed their grief. There was a dense expanse of whooping, hollering, and hysterical crying when viewing the body. It was almost as capricious in nature as a circus but very customary. As the family walked in, I scanned the room to determine who would be the one to have an Oscar award-winning performance. I could not discern simply by looking who'd be the ones to show their Asses at Ms. Jane's funeral.

In my periphery, I could see Andrea sitting next to her dad, who ironically was sitting next to Huh. She waved at me inconspicuously and I smiled uncontrollably. I felt a little conflicted being that I was at a funeral for someone I cared about. There was just something about Andrea that made me unconventionally unlike myself, and I liked that feeling. I liked knowing that she liked me irrespective of my myriad of idiosyncrasies such as my inability to speak my mind, my reclusiveness, and my preoccupation with a cornfield. She grasped that about me, yet I had still been petrified to give her those letters for a fear of rejection. My instincts told me that she would not reject me, but my heart was unwilling to chance it.

This was only the third funeral I had ever been to. Something was a little off-kilter about this particular one. The atmosphere was disconcertingly strange. The order of service was similar, but there was something in the air. The soloist sang *Sooner Will Be Done* and there wasn't a dry eye in the place. Suddenly, everyone's eyes shot to Ms. Jane as she began weeping unyieldingly whereas she had been stoic before. The soloist was drowned out by the sobs. Her children, who were sitting beside her, tried to console her but were unsuccessful. She stood up and ran to the casket and draped herself over it. She screamed in a pitch so shrill I'm sure there were dogs somewhere whimpering. No one could peel her from the casket. The man with whom she had spent most of her life was lying in a coffin and she had put him there. There was no way to describe witnessing a grieving widow display such a huge amount of vulnerability in such a public arena. It was particularly troubling to watch and be helpless to do anything to comfort her.

"Oh, God! I killed him. I killed my husband! Take me, Lord. I don't deserve to live!"

Sally cried out much to our amazement, as she hadn't verbally communicated with anyone in the totality of that week. There was one deafening collective gasp from the congregation. As we all watched in perpendicular bewilderment, Miss Sally, seeing that Jane's children weren't going to intervene, stepped in. Sally went up to her and just held her. Jane turned around and fell into Sally's arms almost pulling her down. Uncle Roosevelt rushed to the front of the church to help hold both of them steady. He was such a true gentleman in that way, always running to the aid of the distressed without regard for himself.

"Sally, I killed him! I killed the only man I loved! I just wanna die!" Jane asserted in the recess of Ms. Sally's neck.
"Jane it's gon' be all right! I am here for you!" Sally consoled her as her children looked on with indifference.
"I can't live without him, Sally. Lord take me! Take me now!" Jane pleaded.
"Jane, don't talk like that now!" Sally admonished.
"I don't deserve to live!" Jane shouted as the tears drenched the neckline of Sally's dress.

Miss Sally slowly walked Ms. Jane out of the church and into the limousine. There Ms. Jane cried herself to sleep on Miss Sally's shoulder. She never woke up. Ms. Jane was believed to have died of a broken heart, which is conceivably the worst possible death a person could suffer. There's no closure. No warning. No prevention. Her soul was weary and her walk on the long arduous journey was over. Finally, she had found the tranquility for which she had yearned over the years. That night the moon sat over an unusually quiet Sidon and it bore down on the deafening silence that grief had injected into the souls of its denizens. There was no wind, no rain, just darkness from which more melancholy was pinched. Time was a marauder. A looter. A plunderer. The still of that night in the Delta was hypnotic. It was the stuff that gave birth to blues songs. The volatility of life. The irrevocability of death. But Ms. Jane's Blues had a farewell appearance. The swan had sung her song. *No mo' weepin' and wailin'...*

Chapter 16

Farther Along

A week later we buried Ms. Jane. Again, Sally had been the coordinator of all things for Ms. Jane. She worked tirelessly to help send Ms. Jane off in proper fashion. It was much easier considering she'd just done the very same things for Old Man Jessie. The services were bittersweet in that we all knew that Ms. Jane had died decades ago, so she finally got the rest of she needed in demise.

In a strange turn of events, her children left the house and Old Man Jessie's car to Miss Sally. They paid the taxes on the house for her and insured the car. Even though they hadn't publicized it very well, they had been exceedingly appreciative to Sally for helping their mother cope over the years. Sally was astounded by their gratitude. Unc assisted with her transition into the house, even staying there with her to help her become acclimatized before he left to return to Cleveland. Uncle Roosevelt left the day that Huh had her cast removed. She had insisted that he get back to his own affairs, as he had been so benevolent in assisting with the management of hers.

Huh had been free of cast for two days and was getting readjusted to walking, taking care of the household, and torturing me as she had hitherto. Andrea had only one week left before it was time for her to go back to Kansas, and I was becoming more and more distraught with the fact that I wouldn't be able to gaze upon her as I had become accustomed. My life was returning to its original dismal state. Just Huh and me.

"Malachi go outside and git me today's paper!" Huh demanded per usual.
"Yes, ma'am!" I replied just as traditionally as I made my way to the front door.

When I looked out of the screen door, I saw Billy Ray pulling up to the house. This time he had Andrea with him. I smiled wider than the Golden Gate Bridge. Not only because of Andrea, but Huh was in a better mood whenever Billy Ray came around. She had no longer abhorred the man who put her in the hospital.

"What you smilin' like a Chess cat fah?" Huh asked me gruffly.
"No reason!" I responded with a defeatedly.
"Knock knock!" Billy Ray spoke through the screen door.
"Come on in!" Huh shouted as she fixed her dress and hair to the best of her ability.

"How you feelin'?" Billy Ray inquired.
"Can't you look at me and tell?" she asked rhetorically with more arrogance than she had room.
Andrea snickered as she looked over at me."Hattie, I see you feelin' pretty ostentatious now that the cast is off," he teased.
"I don't know what no ostentatious is, but if it means beautiful. I will take it! Malachi, why don't you take Angel outside and play!" she articulated as if we were kindergarteners.
"Hattie, her name is Andrea!" Billy Ray corrected Huh.
"Well, hell, y'all know what I meant!" she replied.

It was all I needed to hear. I couldn't wait to be alone with Andrea. Considering she had been due to leave, I wanted to spend every second with her. As we walked outside, I longed to just smell her hair and touch her hand. It was those little things that meant so much to me and that I would miss once she left.

"How's it going now that your uncle is gone?" she inquired.
"Everything's cool. Things just kinda like they was before he came!" I lamented.
"Good or bad?" she probed.
"Well, let's just say I ain't dead!" I retorted.
"That's good because I wouldn't know what to do with myself if you were!" she said absolutely.
"Wow! Are you serious?" I asked stunned.
"Yeah, I am serious! You are a sweet guy and I am gonna miss you! You have really made my last few weeks here the best!" she asserted.
"And you have made my year! I couldn't have asked for a better treat than you," I said.

I wanted to kiss her so badly, but I knew Billy Ray would have had my head if I even thought about it, so I quelled my desire for the time being. Instead, I stared into her eyes, making love to them. I imagined us both in otherworldly space and time beyond the clouds where we'd rule the universe. Just in that instant when I started to daydream about my fantastical place, Huh came to disturb us.

"Malachi, y'all come on back up in here," she bellowed.
"Yes ma'am!" I called back. We got from where we sat in the front yard and proceeded to the screen door to reenter.
"Andrea, you ready to go baby?" Billy Ray questioned.
"Yeah, Daddy! It was good seeing you both again!" Andrea said dejectedly.
"You too, baby! Y'all have a good trip now!" Huh responded.
"Trip?!" I said impulsively without thinking.
"Yeah, Malachi, I was just telling your grandmother that Andrea and I had a wonderful time here in the Delta, but plans have changed and we have to go. We are going to spend the rest of the week in Memphis. I have some business there and I promised my brother we'd visit before we go back to Kansas!" Billy Ray expounded.

I knew that there was no way that Andrea knew of this new and unforeseen development or else she would have informed me to prevent the breaking of my spirit. My face sank in like a collapsed cave. It was as though he had extracted my heart from the chest cavity with his bare hands. I had no feeling in any part of my body. I don't know how I stood there without toppling over because my knees clearly weren't stable enough to give me any support. The world had stopped spinning and my head had started in its stead. I just hoped it was some nightmare from which I had been powerless to awake.

"Malachi, what the hell wrong wit' you boy. Yo' face jus' went white as a sheet!" Huh spoke out of turn.
"I'm okay!" I said with a duplicitous smirk on my face.
"Well, we are going to make a move. I don't want be on the road when it's dark! You be good for your grandmother, Malachi. Hattie, you take it easy and if it's really *easy*, take it again," Billy Ray quipped with more levity than I'd ever witnessed from him.

"Man, you *is* crazy. I will try. Y'all be safe," Huh cautioned them as they walked out of the door.
"Bye, Andrea!" I yelled without regard for my own safety.
"Boy, what's wrong wit' you yellin' in my house like a crazy man?" Huh remarked nastily as she jerked me by my collar.
"Leave me alone, old lady!" I shouted as I snatched away from her and ran into my room slamming the door.
"Billy Ray, y'all have a good trip! Let me go find out what the hell goin' on wit' this boy!" I heard her say snidely as she saw them off.
"Malachi, open this damn do'!" she bawled at me from the other side of the door.
"I said leave me alone!" I barked.
"Boy, you really done lost yo' mind up in *my* house! If you don't open this damn do', I'm gon' knock it down!" she threatened me.
I was numb to it. I didn't care what the consequences might have bee, besides, I knew she couldn't break down door made of oak.
"Do what you gotta do!" I returned.
"When I git my hands on you I am gon' beat you into next week!" Huh roared.
"Go away!" I squawked.

Finally, I heard her limp back to her room. I really thought she at least would pretend to try to kick the door in, but I remembered she was still recouping from the cast. I just lay in bed and looked up at the ceiling. My heart had been broken, and although I had never had the feeling before over a girl, it hurt like nothing else. To want something so badly and to be denied it felt like a living death. I had no other way to describe it. All of my organs were intact and my bodily functions were working properly, but my soul had been uprooted. I had always heard that the soul lives on after death, but that day I wasn't so sure about it. My anticipation was that I would at least have six more days with Andrea, but I was down to none and it just didn't seem fair. People that I loved just seemed to bolt hastily from my life. Suddenly, I knew how Ms. Jane felt the day we buried Old Man Jessie. She just didn't want to live if she couldn't be with him. My summer suddenly came to an abrupt end. Though it was still summer proper, I longed for summer's immediate return. I wished that I could have closed my eyes and magically awakened to it once more. By then she would be back. Although I knew it would never happen, it still brought me a sense of solace. My pain wouldn't end and that was more than I could say for my short time with Andrea.

There was no escaping the endless hold *My Delta Blues* had on me. I was doomed to be forever cloaked in a sadder song than I wanted. Fighting it was fruitless. The willful refrain badgered me like a kid brother. It followed me and emulated my worst habits. If only I could have outrun the notes, I would have fled the continuous barrage of measures full of lows and flats. I would much rather have composed and conducted my own score with melodies that soothed me instead of inflicting me. *O Blues thou art a cursed thing.*

Chapter 17

Short Bread

Virtually catatonic, I emerged from depression in search of empathy. It came to pass that I was walking the streets of Sidon shunning every fathomable form of recreation that boys my age craved, for none of them would vanquish my grief over Andrea. She was in my every thought. When I breathed, I could smell her. When a breeze would catch my face, I could feel her. There was no getting her out of my mind. I tried to think of anything that could have perhaps aided in a quick reclamation of my spirit, but nothing offered me comfort in the proportions that I required. I wandered about the awesomely flat land, which was the Delta like a nomad. No destination. No route. No mettle.

As I kicked dirt and rocks, I longed to be somewhere other than there. If only those clouds would open up and beam me into them, I just knew that there had to be a world for Andrea and me. As much as I wished that I had some magical power to will myself to a different time and place, where life would be easier for me, I knew it was never going to transpire. Ideally, if it were possible, it would have been some place where no one could ever leave me. That had become the only spot-on reality in my life. Someone would definitely make an exit. It all started with my dad. He had left before I could talk or even remember what he looked like. It seemed that everyone who should have been there to comfort me all bolted without so much as a goodbye. Andrea had joined them. Although, no fault of her own, it hurt even so.

Ironically, I found myself sitting glumly on the curb in front of Ms. Jane and Old Man Jessie's old house, now Sally's. I knew why I had gone, but I knew better why I had no business going there. I had returned to the one person with whom I'd become a man in the *biblical* sense. It was just a fucking bad idea. She was Unc's woman and I had already been insensitive to his romance with her. I had violated the unspoken code among men and family for that matter. I had gone rogue, so I decided to vacate the premises before I further exacerbated the situation. As I got up evacuate, I felt a hand on my shoulder. It was Sally. She stood over me, and I replayed the day we had been intimate. I wished I hadn't ever come back to the scene of the crime. My brain hadn't thought through what my penis had already contemplated. For now, it was the rock and Sally was the hard place.

"Malachi, you okay, baby?" she asked with sincerity.
"Yes, ma'am!"

I said with a tremble in my voice, as I had not really spoken to Sally since our encounter. She had had so much activity going in her life since discovering Ms. Jane's transgression, so there was just never an ideal time of which to do so.

"Now you know better than to call me ma'am. What you doing out here?" Sally continued.
"I don't know. Just sitting here thinking," I replied untruthfully.

Again, I knew unerringly why I had been there. I wanted to be inside of her in order to escape my misery. Though I knew it was wrong, it was my desire. I knew no other way to shift my gears. The one time we'd been together had cleared my mind in ways I had never acknowledged until that moment. If only for a few minutes, I needed that release as a distraction, for I was unquestionably about to combust emotionally.

"Child, I know love sickness when I see it!" Sally gloated as she placed her hand onto my back and guided me into her house.
"Sally, I just…" I started.
"You can tell me all about it inside," she affirmed.

I really didn't want to talk to Sally. I only craved to sleep with her and use her for her feminine parts. It was taciturn, but she had shepherded me out of her house after the first sexual tryst, so she had known that it was merely sex. Moreover, I felt like I was walking into a haunted house, so I was even less at ease than I had been on that day that Sally and I had intercourse. As soon as I entered, the fine hair on my arms and neck stood up because I recalled the last time that I had been there Jessie and Ms. Jane were both alive. The dilation of my pupils and the twiddling of my thumbs were sufficient enough for Sally to deduce my intrinsic fear of being inside this mausoleum of sorts. The evidence was clear, so I realized that that was why Sally continued to hold onto me until she detected that I was calmer.

"Come on, baby, sit down at the table. Let me get you some tea and some tea cakes," she said.

At this point I really started to calm down. Teacakes were my favorite. *You couldn't call a teacake a cookie*. It just wasn't the proper thing to do in the South, for it was more than a cookie. The teacake was a light, indulgent morsel of goodness whose recipe had been bequeathed through generations and shared in stories also handed down. It was a little piece of paradise that was much too blissful to be even considered earthly, literally. The Delta had its gems and this was surely one of which to boast. My belly hungered for the teacakes as I hadn't seen, much less eaten one in such a long time. A gluttonous spirit was upon me and I wasn't going to deny its or my satisfaction. Sally set a plate that *runneth over* in front of me, gave me a glass of tea, and I started in quick succession to devour them all. Eating the teacakes in all their epicurean glory was a welcomed temporary diversion. They filled a concrete void, as I hadn't eaten anything since I had been traumatized by the news of Andrea's departure.

"Thanks, Sally," I muttered with a mouth full of teacake.
"Think nothing of it, sweetie. I know Hattie probably ain't been able to get around to fixin' many of your favorite foods since she been sick," Sally said caringly.
"You talked to Unc Roosevelt lately?" I asked.
"Yeah, I talked to him just a while ago," she replied dryly.
"He say when he coming back?" I said trying to dodge being trampled by the elephant in the room.
"Just said soon! Now, why you duckin' what's really going on inside you?" she investigated.
"What you talking about?" I asked evasively.
"Boy, you just as love sick as you can be! It's written all over your face," she alleged.
"I…," I began.

"I, nothing honey! Who is she? And what she do to you?" she said, searching for answers that I really didn't want share, but I decided oblige.
"Her name is Andrea. She is Mr. Billy Ray's daughter. She didn't do nothing. They leave today for Memphis and then they go back to Kansas!" I replied sadly as I began to chew much more slowly.
"Yeah, I remember meeting her at the funeral. She is a pretty little thing and sweet, too. I never would have guessed Billy Ray would let you get near her," Sally injected.
"He didn't know about us," I said.
"Oh, I see. Well, how did you get around him knowing 'bout y'all?" Sally said, interrogating me much like an officer.
"Because we always met at our secret spot. No one knew about us. We liked it that way. Once I found out Billy Ray was her dad, we were careful to keep things hushed," I explained.
"You knew she would only be here for the summer though, right?" Sally asked.
"Yeah, I knew. I just thought we would have a few more days together," I said with a cracking voice.
"Aw, baby! I know that's gotta hurt. But you got to cheer up! You too young to be sad over some'n like this. School is about to start and some other little gals will be after you!"
"I don't want some other girl. I want her! She is just…! I can't explain it," I clarified emphatically.
"I understand what you saying. I wanted to leave my mama's house so, honey, let me tell you like my mama use to say: Yo' first love can be yo' best or yo' worst love, but don't let it be yo' last love," she said, proselytizing.
"What's that supposed to mean?"
"Well, baby, the first time we fall in love it is easy. We get all into the person and we love them in spite of themselves. From then on we tend to compare them to all other people we meet, and because they will never really ever compare, whether good or bad, we tend to miss out on some good folks," she preached.
"You saying I should just get over her?" I inquired.

“Naw, baby. Always keep her in your heart, just make room for others,” she prompted me.
“I guess I see what you mean, but for now it still don’t make me feel no better,” I responded.
“Sweetie, ain’t nothing gone make you feel better until you ready to feel better,” she said.
“I think you might be right!” I replied as she stood behind me and rubbed my shoulders.

I felt her hands moving closer to my neck. She massaged it ever so gently. The warm touch of her hand on my flesh made me much less tense than I had been during the extent of our talk. Though I longed for her hands to be Andrea’s hands, I was just glad there were hands. Her hand worked her way up to where she cupped my head and stroked my temples and began to kiss me on my neck. Instinctively, my eyes closed and my dick rose like a rooster crowing at 4.a.m. And in that instant, we were both startled by a loud voice.

“Sally, what in da the hell is you doin’ wit’ that boy?” Sophie roared as she busted through the screen door.
“Sophie!” Sally said with her mouth dropped open.
“Child, you done lost yo’ mine up in here kissin’ on this baby!” Sophie yelled.
“Miss Sophie!” I yelled.
“Don’t you ‘Miss Sophie’ me, I got a right mind to take a belt to yo’ ass! Care yo’ ass home right now!” she commanded.
“Miss Sophie, please don’t tell my grandma!” I pleaded.
“That’s fah me to decide, not you!” Sophie argued.
“Malachi, baby, go on home now!” Sally cajoled.

I looked back with my mouth fixed to beg her not to tell Huh, but the scornful look on her face revealed that my request would be falling upon deaf ears. I walked out of there now more dazed and confused than I been when I had been escorted in. I felt as though I had been tossed about in a cyclone, steadily spinning out of control. My head ached like my ears were throwing Double-Dutch ropes and my brain bounded up and down betwixt them.

Once again, after a rendezvous with Sally, I felt truncated. For a second time, I hadn't known how I would dig my way out this doleful state. The last thing I needed right then was for Huh to be on my case about Sally. I knew she was really going let me have it. She had already been evil with me for how I acted when Billy Ray and Andrea left. I really just wished to die because I didn't have the strength to deal with it all. There was no reason to live if I couldn't be with Andrea and have some semblance of peace in the place where I subsisted. I wanted to just end the unwarranted suffering. However, I knew something was keeping me alive and anguish was a means to an end.

My Delta Blues had become purple, the color of my bruised soul. My soul had never sung sadder songs theretofore. My heart had reached a bridgeless climax with no falling action or fortuitous denouement. Yet, the musicality of the pain was unrelenting. The drab bass line had arisen again to unsettle any security that I had mustered while Andrea and Uncle Roosevelt were constants in my life. I gleaned that my blues had to be significant of the fact that my life had been death incarnate.

There was no purpose to my living, no progress to my healing, and no sensitivity to my feeling. *My blues* would not sojourn. Its incessant molestation of my innocence left my spirit exposed. It was like standing naked in the middle of a room full of people there to point, stare, poke, and prod. No escape. My blues were never going to decrescendo and the agony would worsen as I continued to walk a path to nowhere, feeling nothing, having no one.

Chapter 17.5

Motherless Child

Dear Mama,

I hope that you are doing well. I decided I needed to write you this letter, even though you will never see it. I do this thing where I write to ease my mind about things. So far you are only the second person I am writing a letter to. I wrote some to this girl, Andrea, that I like. Before I tell you about her, there are some things I need to say to you. You are my mother and I love you with all my heart. I was so angry with you for leaving me when you got arrested. When I had to come to Mississippi without you and all my stuff, it was hard to deal. I was only twelve years old, and I felt like I was alone and nobody cared. In time, I was able to forgive you and get to my new situation. I know being in jail is not easy for you, so when you told me that you had found someone to love you, I was glad. I wanted to tell you when I talked to you last, but you had to go. If you are happy, I am happy for you. There is nothing I want more than for you to have someone to care for you.

The next thing I wanted to tell you was that I lied about grandma. I don't like being here. She cusses me out and hits me for no reason. I do everything I am supposed to do but it is never enough. She never says anything good about you and she always compares me to you. I respect her and I never talk back, but she still makes my life here with her really hard. Usually, I just lock myself up in my room after I eat, clean, and do homework. I don't have any friends and if I did, I think she would run them off. The lady is evil, and I hate her. I know that hate is a strong word, but it's the only word that fits. I see grandmothers on TV loving and spoiling their grandchildren, and I am left with the grandmother from hell. I don't want to be here with her anymore. She makes my life miserable, and I really just wish she was dead. As much as I hate to say that about your mama, it's a reality for me. We haven't said anything to each other since we had a big falling out, and it's fine with me. We never have to talk again. It don't make me no difference. Well, enough about her.

Finally, I want to tell you about Andrea. You are not the only one who found someone special. I met Andrea one day while I was out hanging at the Goal. She is the most beautiful girl I have ever met. She is here in Sidon with her dad visiting her grandmother. I wish you could be here to meet her. I know you would like her. There is no doubt in my mind about that. You always told me to find a smart girl and I did. She is not just smart; she is perceptive. She has this way of finding the good in me even when I don't see it myself, just like you. For weeks, we have been meeting up to talk and share our thoughts. She is a really fun girl who I love spending time with. The other day she and I read poetry by Langston Hughes and Angelina Grimke. I have read Hughes's

"Mother to Son" before, but when she read it to me, it had a new meaning, especially with you being away. It reminded me of all the advice you gave me over the years, and for me not to wallow just because things are hard. Her voice was so soothing to me. It was kind of like when you use to read to me when I was little. It made me feel real good. I read Grimke's "Two Eyes of my Regret" to her. Even though it's a sad poem about seeing and being reminded of your regret, it is beautiful. She wrote everything in that poem that I have felt, but sitting there reading it with Andrea was different. The sadness of the poem couldn't quite measure up to the beauty of the words. In the poem, she writes, how the eyes remind her of things from her past experiences; that line spoke differently to me as I read it to her because when I'm with her, I have no regrets. Looking back on that day now makes me sad because Andrea left to go back to Kansas. Now, I feel like there is no one left to physically care about me.

I am lost in a world of confusion and loneliness. Even at fifteen, I know that that is not a good way to feel. I will be honest with you; I just feel like lying down and dying. I want to get rid of this world before it gets rid of me. There is no reason to keep trying to fit into a place that doesn't want me in it. I have lost so

much: you, Detroit, Ms. Jane, Old Man Jessie, Uncle Roosevelt, and now Andrea. Having nobody in your corner in a place where you already feel out of place is hard. I know that this is hard to read, but I don't want you to worry about me. I think I will be fine after I get over Andrea being gone. It's just really fresh on my mind and heart.
Even though you are never going to read this letter, I'm glad I wrote it. Writing it down gets it off my mind and I always feel a little better. It helps me to sort things out. It's the only thing that keeps me sane sometimes. I know that sounds crazy, but it's true. Anyway, I love you and I hope you continue to be on your best behavior so that you can return to me.

Love always,
Malachi

Chapter 18

Since I Laid My Burdens Down

It had come to pass Huh was getting better, returning to her former self, save for the limp that the physical therapist informed her could be permanent. Sometimes she would use a cane to facilitate her mobility. The atmosphere of our domicile had slowly recaptured its traction as it had been prior to having Uncle Roosevelt bless us with his presence. The temporarily cozy household had recycled itself back into a cold place - *business as usual*. I had retreated back to my lowly place in serfdom with no foreseeable advancement to anything more or less as long as I resided in her *hell.* With Billy Ray and Uncle Roosevelt gone, certainly, there would no one to distract Huh from lashing out at me. I didn't care anymore anyway. She had not uttered a word about me disrespecting her the night that Billy Ray and Andrea left. In addition, I assumed that Sophie had not divulged what she had witnessed at Sally's, but still there remained a bevy of tirades in which he disparaged me: "*Didn't I tell you to fix yo' bed you black bastard," "Take off those muddy shoes off you cock sucking asshole," or "Git yo' nappy head ass off my couch and turn that TV off.*"

Days had passed and, Andrea, still a fixture in my teenage psyche, was becoming a memory. The cornfield had become my singular location for escape. I would take novels, nonfiction books, music books, a snack, and a flashlight down the rows with me just to get away from it all. I would let the words of the prose and poetry take me anywhere outside the limiting parameters of Sidon. I had read *Great Expectations*, *Roll of Thunder Hear My Cry*, *The Mis-Education of the Negro, The Souls of Black Folk,* and *Heart of Darkness* all within a three-day period. Sometimes I would imagine that the cornfield was my own kingdom. I was the ruler of all things. I considered it my practice for when I would be the ruler of the universe beyond the clouds. Suffice it to say, the eccentricity of it all kept me sane. I had retreated there so often that I had managed to circumvent the extemporaneousness of her verbal and physical abuse. While sitting in one of the neat cornrows with tall green stalks, I would dream, sleep, wish, and hope, although sleep was the only one of the aforementioned verbs a boy in Mississippi could actualize and see through to an end product. The others were like inaccessible orbs of gas in the heavens that were so far away that their evanescence shone more brightly than their luminescence.

No matter how much I sought refuge in that cornfield kingdom, the bitterness of the outside world seemed to invade me irrespectively. When I emerged from my place of solace, I was greeted by yet another slap to my face which drew a swoosh of saliva from my mouth and sent my books plummeting to the ground in respective booms. She stood there, leaning on her cane and looking like a witch prepared to cast a spell on me. Once more, she had succeeded in executing the notorious ability she had of blindsiding me.

"Why the hell you always up in that damn field? What the hell you been doin' in there! If I fine out you been in there smokin', I'm gon' try my best to fuck you up! You hear me?" Huh went on in a diatribe.
"Yes, ma'am!" I managed to utter through my numb face.
"Now, git yo' ass up to that house," she yelled as she slapped the back of my head.

I gathered my book and I plodded expediently back to the house devoid of further dialogue. I could hear Huh breathing like a bull as she meandered behind me. I didn't look back; if I had, something told me I would have needed a matador's cape and a picador's lance to help me put her down. However, I knew better than to look her in her eyes during these tense moments; moreover, I was no fan of blood sports, especially when my own blood may have been shed. Portentously, I had discerned that I had been in for far more than I had been prepared. I just knew how the witch operated. The kitchen was her cauldron. It's where she brewed meals and foolishness. As she finally walked in, I was standing there oblivious to the multifariousness of what was really going on. I knew it would be yet another entity whose sole purpose it was to obliterate to my already volatile existence.
"Set yo' ass down! What's this shit I hear 'bout you and Sally?" she barked.
"What you mean?" I asked trying to sound ignorant.
"Boy, I will come across yo' head wit' this here cane faster than you can blink! Now, what da hell is this 'bout Sophie catchin' Sally lickin' all up on you?" she asked.
"It was nothing!" I said.
"Don't sound like nothin' to me! Now, you listen here and you listen good. I am too damn old to be dealing wit' you whoremongerin'! This is a Christian house and it gon' stay

that way as long as *breaf* left in my body! I don't know what you and Sally got goin' on, but I don't won't you nowhere near her house no mo'," she growled.

It was clear that she didn't really believe what Sophie had seen, but also evident that she'd be dubious of Sally moving forward. Since Sally had acquired Ms. Jane's and Jessie's house and car, she hadn't been visiting or calling Huh. Since she had extra expenses in the wake of her acquisition, she took extra shifts at the hotel to supplement her former income. Considering all of the support she'd given Sally while she handled Ms. Jane's affairs, Huh took the apparent absence personally. Sophie's exposé of Sally and me had only reopened the wounds, so she continued to caution me.

"Now, yo uncle took up wit' her when he was here, but he grown and can do whatever he wants, but I don't want you nowhere 'round her. Do you hear me? If'n I catch yo' black ass over there again, you can give yo' heart to God, cause yo' ass belong to me!" she threatened.

Oddly enough, at that moment I surmised that she was actually showing that she cared about me. However warped her delivery, there was a slight acknowledgment of concern for my well being. In no way had I planned to be fooled and lulled into some false sense of security. I had been fully aware she was still as venomous as a viper in Vietnam. As I left the room, I heard someone knocking. It was Sophie. Oh, how I had come to loathe her and her obesity. Every time I saw her, I imagined the rawness of the inside of her thighs due to the constant friction as she toddled along. The edema in her ankles reminded me of full glass Blackburn Syrup jars. Her fat jowls gave the notion that there were no bones in her face. That trashy mouth of hers was the worst feature about her, if something edible wasn't going into it, something incredible was coming out of it. I hated that she was so slovenly and was always stirring up shit in an already shitty place. I went into my room where I could still hear them talking. I wished I could blink my eyes and transport myself to my oft dreamt of place in a galaxy far away. Since it was impossible, I lay on my bed listening to the foolishness she was about to utter.

"Hattie, did you talk to Malachi mannish ass?" she pried.
"Yeah, I done talked to him. He said it nothin' was goin' on," Huh responded.
"Nothin' my ass! If I didn't show up when I did, that boy woulda been all up inside Sally like a tampon. Now, Sally is my friend too, honey, but I am tellin' you, she had lust in her eyes fah Malachi! I ain't one to gossip, but I heard that that was not the first time he had been to Sally house and child, you know what that mean!" Sophie said speculating.
"Naw, I don't but I know you'll tell me," Huh returned.
"She probably done already got hold to him," she suggested.
"What you mean 'got hold to'?" Huh asked.
"Mean, she done give him some," Sophie ventured.
"Sophie, stop yo' foolishness! That boy ain't even been exposed to nothin' like that! Now, you done gone way too far. Sally mighta done kiss dis boy or some 'nother like that, but I know like hell she ain't laid down wit' Malachi! She might be a hoe, but she ain't crazy. I ain't gon' let you come up in here and bad mouth her no farther. All you do is go 'round spreadin' rumors about people, and that ain't the only thang you spreadin' look at yo' hips and ass," Huh said critically.
"Hattie!" Sophie gasped.
"Don't 'Hattie' me! Honey, it's time for you to go 'cause I am tired of talkin' to you!" Huh retorted.
"Hattie, you know I ain't mean no harm bout, Sally. I'm sorry," Sophie said as she backed off her accusatory tone.
"Don't be sorry. Be careful. You done to' yo' drawls wit' me. Do me a favor and stop eatin' and gossipin' so damn much. Turn a mirror on yo'self sometime… that's if you can find one that wide enough!" she remarked.
"I can't believe you sittin' here talkin' bout yo' best friend like that!" Sophie lamented.
"Child, if you is my best, I don't wanna see my worst! All this time I been 'round here helpin' yo' sour ass spread

rumors 'bout good people! I'm sick and tired of it and you! Now, git the hell out!" Huh said with a snarl.
"Hattie, you can't be serious!" Sophie responded.
"I am serious as a heartache, baby! Don't let da doorknob git stuck in yo' fat ass!" Huh quipped.

Sophie had had enough of the attacks, so she left, slamming the screen door behind her. Just hearing her leave made my day. At that moment, I wished I liked Huh and we could have high-fived to the way that she had handled Sophie. However, that was not the life we lived or the relationship that we had. We were two planets in the same galaxy but light-years apart. No moons. No stars. No oxygen. Each of us was as inconsequential to the other as vapor.

Later that night, after the fall out between Sophie and Huh and dinner, Huh had fallen asleep in the living room. Although I wouldn't have ordinarily, I placed a blanket over her as a gesture of appreciation for handing Sophie her ass on a platter. I went to bed, but I had been restless. Thinking about Andrea and wishing she were there took up an occupation in my mind. One lonely tear moistened my eye and rolled into my ear, as I lay there helplessly impecunious. The pleasures of life were dismally dismissive of me. I wanted so little. I had come to identify discontent whether my eyes were open or shut, so I often wondered had it been my fate to become a gelatinous entity stuck to Mississippi. I sought a change where I would be vindicated, loosed, and set forth into a world that would embrace me as a formidable citizen.

I also thought a great deal about Sally that night. I realized that like me Sally longed to be loved in a place where love didn't live. She didn't care from where or whom she received it, even if from an adolescent. I didn't have the desire to swim into the heart of her troubles, because I had already been submerged in my own. I had, by this time, backstroked into the soul of simple but complex lady. I was Sally. Our connection was kindred. What she required was what I required. What she needed was what I needed. What she longed for was what I longed for.

Sally and I were unstable and unassertive simultaneously. Neither of us had been equipped with the wherewithal to withstand the many blows to our self-esteem. I felt for her. I felt for us. I wanted to shield her from the pain that she would be sure to endure, but I had been unsuccessful in doing so on my own accord.

My Delta Blues and Miss Sally's blues had intertwined in a short-lived concert to an audience of two. The music was now our only common thread, as I had been forbidden to see her. Through the telepathy of blues, I willed her what little strength I could muster. If there was no music, there'd be no connection. There was a fading chorus sadder than a requiem. Our composition had been arranged by fate and performed by karma. Inspired by turmoil, the notes were expressly flattened much like our confidence levels. Our blues were unappealing because they were prohibited, taboo even, because she was an older woman and I was a child. I longed for the both of us to be on the other side of our discomfort. I pined for us to experience some pinks and yellows, any color other than the blues.

Chapter 19

Later Your God to Me

I woke up to Huh barking at me.
"Boy git yo' ass up so you can eat and clean up!"

Smells of coffee, bacon, toast, and eggs wafted down the hallway to my room. The aromas distracted me and afforded her an opportunity to yell at me all she wanted. Huh yelling was overpowered by the breakfast she'd prepared. It was particularly refreshing, as she hadn't cooked like that in months. Our basic breakfasts had recently consisted of toast and oatmeal or dry cereal. My mouth and stomach agreed undoubtedly upon consuming the culinary delights. I had almost forgotten to brush my teeth and wash my face before I ate. She would have punched me no sooner than I could think if I had not done so.

"Yes, ma'am!" I said as I smiled on my way to the bathroom. I relieved myself, washed my face, and brushed my teeth thinking of nothing but the feast that she had prepared for us.
"Shit!" she yelled from the kitchen. I finished up. I ran to see what was wrong.
"What happened?" I asked.
"Nothin', jus' had a sharp pain in my leg. It's alright now! Jus' sat down and eat," she commanded, and I started piling food on my plate as if I hadn't planned to eat ever again in my life.
"Boy, you ain't gotta eat it all at once. It's some mo' on the stove!" She made me feel greedy, so I backed off and dug in.

Thwack! The cane came across my left arm! She had hit me because I hadn't said my grace before I started eating. She didn't play about that. You had better not sit down and put your face in a plate without thanking her God for it. I didn't know what I was thinking or what i was thanking.
"Don't you ever, as long as you black, not thank God in heaven for the food you receiving! You hear me?" she demanded.
"Yes, ma'am!" I mumbled right before I said my grace.

I noticed that she kept instinctively clutching her leg. It was obvious that she was in some major agony. The limp had actually been exacerbated since she had had the cast removed. I wanted to ask if her leg was okay, but I knew she was either cuss me or hit me. Besides that wasn't how we communicated. We didn't show concern for one another. Our relationship was contemptuous and we both had become comfortable with that. Therefore, I sat there and I continued to eat doggedly, ignoring the fact that her leg was in pain. Moments ticked away, and I couldn't take it anymore. Just because she was inhumane didn't mean that I had to follow suit, as I had been wont to do.

"Do I need to call the doctor?" I broke down and asked.
"What fah?" she fired back.
"You keep grabbin' yo' leg," I pointed out.
"Boy, it's jus' a little pain. Nothin' I can't deal wit'," she winced in pain.
"You sure? Don't seem like just a little pain to me the way you keep frowning," I dared to say.
"Mind yo' own business, boy! I'm fine, I say! Hurr' up and eat so you kin clean up my kitchen," she asserted hardheartedly.
"Yes, ma'am!" I said as I took my final bites of food.

I began my mission to revive the kitchen to it former state of *next to godliness*. In our house, under Huh's iron fist, a kitchen wasn't considered clean unless bleach was employed into the dishwater, used on the counter tops, tables, floors, refrigerator, and stove. The floor had to be swept and mopped or you paid the piper, and Huh was the piper. A well-cleaned kitchen took approximately forty to forty-five minutes or even perhaps an hour, depending upon what had been cooked. That was just how things were. I had become so painstakingly meticulous and methodical that cleaning was like breathing, second-nature.

As I completed my chores, I overheard a series of expletives emitting from the living room. The pain in her leg was much more agonizing than she had been willing to admit to me previously. My first mind told me to call Uncle Roosevelt, but my first *ass* told me I better keep cleaning up and mind my business. Once I finished, I noticed that Huh was asleep on the sofa and her pain pills were on the coffee table. I went outside to think, conflicted about how to deal with this particular situation. I didn't consider myself a monster, but I knew in my heart I hated her, but did I hate her enough to watch her welter in pain? I thought more seriously again about calling Uncle Roosevelt. I knew we hadn't received any communication him in a couple of days, so I really just hoped that he would call and I wouldn't have to call him and risk Huh bucketing her wrath upon me. More so than anything, I wished she would call the damned doctor herself. Out of nowhere, a car materialized in our driveway. I hadn't heard or observed it. I shook my head in such a way to clear my blurred vision and much to my shock; it was Billy Ray and Andrea.

"Malachi!" Billy Ray resounded.
"Hey, Mr. Bonds!" I replied trying to regain my bearings.
"How have you been, son?" he asked energetically of me.
"I have been good. Thank you, sir!" I responded with jitters as I anticipated beholding Andrea's face.
"Hi, Malachi!" Andrea said, as she got out of the car in the most saintly voice I had ever had the pleasure of hearing.
"Hey, Andrea!" I responded hoping my elation over the fact that Andrea was back was not obvious.
"Malachi, is your grandmother home?" Billy Ray inquired sincerely.
"Yes, sir, but she is sleeping," I countered.
"I am going to go in and surprise her," he said, smiling.
"Help yourself," I said patronizingly, because Andrea was the only thing on my mind at that very moment.
"Why are you looking like you've seen a ghost?" Andrea teased, and then giggled.

She was more radiant than when I last saw her. Andrea's hair had been straightened and hung past her shoulders with a headband, keeping it out of her naturally fresh face. The rays of the sun made her skin shimmer and hair glisten. The white halter-top she wore revealed a taut midriff and the sky blue skirt, cinched at her waist, was just above her knees. Socks and shoes reminiscent of a Catholic schoolgirl adorned her long legs. My face was as vapid as dirt for her beauty and had been drained all of its color. She was just that mesmerizing.

"Feels like I did. I didn't think I would ever see you again to be honest. These few days with Huh…I mean, my grandma have been more like hell than ever 'cause I couldn't see and talk to you," I replied with no qualms.
"Boy, you almost sound like you love me or something!" she bantered.
"I do!" I said much more quickly than I could think not to. I hung my head in embarrassment and waited for her to discard me as refuse much life already had hitherto.
"You do? Whoa!" she said emphatically.
"Yeah, I mean, I don't know! I just know that I ain't never felt this way about nothing or nobody before, and I didn't like it when you left. Nothing mattered," I revealed unlike had I been wont to do.
"Wow! You almost sound like you meant that," Andrea said and laughed as I just poured my heart out to her.

I sighed and decided to walk away from her. Her reaction was indicated to me that she clearly didn't feel the same way. I felt like a complete fool for letting my heart speak for me and all she could do was laugh. She may as well have had spit in my face; maybe it would have lessened my humiliation. I had pined for this girl in her absence and she had returned only to make me feel like an idiot.
"Wait, Malachi! I wasn't trying to make you feel bad. It was not right of me to laugh at you. Truth is I care about you, too. I didn't want to get all mushy knowing I was leaving again. I thought if I blew it off, no harm," she lamented.
"Andrea, I ain't learned much in my life, but one thing my heart is saying to me is to stop hiding what I feel. Love is the only thing that don't want nothin' from me. It ain't try hurt me like people do. I ain't never loved no girl before. I don't know if I really love you, but I know I feel somethin' for you 'cause I'm changin.' I think differently and my heart beats differently. It don't just beat for me. It's strong enough to work for you, too. My dreams are different too - no more nightmares. I dream of places we can go rule our own universe. You help me sleep better at night. One

thing I learned living here in the Delta is that when it ain't no love, it ain't no life!" I harangued.
"Whoa! How did you get so smart so young?" She asked in admiration.

Even, I amazed myself by how I had sermonized to her. It had always been my experience to never have the right words as I had expressed to Uncle Roosevelt and in my letters. That day, the words found me.

"I wouldn't say I was smart, but I have had to grow up faster than I should've had to! Seen a lotta bad shit and been raising myself for the past few years. I ain't got no real relationships. Only connection I ever had was wit' my mama. I miss stuff like hugs and kisses. I know I am damn near grown, but it's been three years since I've seen my mama. So it's like when you came along, you made me remember feeling special to somebody," I quantified.
"I feel the same about you Malachi. You make me feel special, too. You are the only guy besides my daddy who just likes me for me, not what I look like. That is hard to find," Andrea acknowledged.

My heart pounded like a million sledgehammers in succession. My body temperature rose quicker than a brush fire. I wanted so badly to hold and kiss her, but I wasn't willing to risk Billy Ray walking out and catching me. He would invent more ways to skin me than one could a cat. But as I looked into her eyes, I knew I was looking into love. Just the idea of kissing her was fulfilling enough in that moment. I imagined our lips locked in an embrace so powerful it would ultimately propel us to that place I had dreamed about far beyond the clouds and the heavens. Perspiring, we met each other's gaze. The sun beat down upon us, but we hadn't even noticed the temperature. Our passion scorched us with much more intensity than the heat of the sun's rays.

"So what now Andrea? Where do we go from here?" I probed.
"I wish I knew," she said, sighing.

"I guess we gotta be creative to communicate while we are hundreds of miles apart!" I suggested.
"We can write," she advocated.
"That's a good idea. I would like knowing it was somethin' to look forward to," I agreed outwardly, but I thought of the letters I had already written her and how I had been afraid to give to her. Would I renege on my promise of letters? Again, I had been conflicted as my head and heart warred.
"You mean other than all the other barrels of fun here in the Delta?" Andrea said, teasingly.
"Ha! You think you funny, don't you?" I said as I smirked.
"I know I'm funny!" she said, laughing.

We shared a laugh just as tender as a kiss might have. In that moment, I was at peace again. I had Andrea back, and I had revealed my feelings. She hadn't rejected me; in fact, she had shared my feelings. I couldn't have asked for or written a better ending to our story. Feeling invincible, yet conflicted about our agreement to write, nothing could dismantle this moment, not even my internal conflict. I wouldn't allow anything or anyone to intrude upon my good spirits. Fearlessly, I marinated in the fact that she was here, and I did not dare think of the day that she'd be leaving because I could not let anything taint how I was feeling.
"So, Malachi, tell me more about this far off universe that we plan to rule one day," she instructed.
"Are you being funny?" I cut my eyes and grimaced.
"No, of course not. I really want to know where we'll be spending our eternity," she declared.
"The place is light-years away. It's called *Malachandrea*. We are gonnna travel there through telekinesis. If we look into each other's eyes and hearts, we spontaneously transport there. The universe is full of happiness and the only citizens are you and me. We will be rulers and we get to make up all laws of *Malachandrea*. It will be our way of escaping this world. We could be in love and be happy all the time. No grandmothers, no mamas, no daddies, no jails, no murder, no dying, no leaving for Cleveland or

Kansas, no sadness...." I articulated as gratuitously as I could.
"Malachi, that sounds like a perfectly magical place," Andrea said, marveling.
"Yes, and it will be all ours and we will colonize *Malachandrea* with our own DNA and it'll be the kind of place we wouldn't mind lettin' our kids grow up in," I continued.
"I like the sound of that because I do want my kids to have a mother and a father and to always be safe. One thing I'd like to see in *Malachandre*a is a statue of me. Can I get a statue?" Andrea requested.
"Yes, you can have anything you want my lady," I said proudly.
"Thanks my Liege!" she spoke in an English accent. We laughed.
I was smiling from ear to ear. She had quite the effect on me. I studied her as she pulled her legendary BlowPop out of the pocket of her skirt. Andrea unwrapped it customarily and slipped into her mouth as she held onto the stick. As always, I envied the lollipop's entry through Andrea's sweet lips. Just as I was being hypnotized by every delicate move she had made, Billy Ray came rushing outside.
"Hey, guys! I need you stay put! I have to take Hattie to the emergency room. The pain in her leg keeps getting worse!" Billy Ray ordered.
Having been enveloped in Andrea's quintessence, I had been remiss in my initial purpose for going outside. Seeing Andrea again induced me to forget that I had been struggling to figure out how to help Huh.
"Is she going to be okay?" Andrea asked concernedly.
"I don't know sweetie! Will you guys be okay alone?" Billy Ray asked.
"Yes, sir!" I replied intrepidly.
"I will call to update you soon," he promised.
"Okay, dad. Drive safe!" Andrea said as he hurried back Into our house to ready Huh for a wheelchair trip to the car to traverse back to the hospital she'd haunted just weeks prior.

"I knew something was going on with Huh. I asked her if she needed to call the doctor, but she told me to mind my own business!" I said.
"Why would she talk to you like that?" Andrea inquired.
"Umm, because she is old, bitter, and hateful!"
"That bad huh?" Andrea asked.
"Worse!" I replied.
"How so?" she probed.
"She has no sympathy. I am the least of things on her list of priorities. I mean, she makes sure I eat and go to school, but other than that, she wouldn't care if I fell off the face of the damn planet! Her world would keep right on spinnin'," I continued.
"I knew she was grouchy, but I didn't know she was a monster!" Andrea returned.
"That old lady done gave me more black eyes, bloody noses, and busted lips than most prizefighters give their opponents," I lamented.
"How do you deal?" she said, wonderingly.
"I don't deal. I suffer. I take the punches and I live through the pain," I said.
"That is terrible, Malachi. Does your Uncle Roosevelt know how she treats you?" she asked as she moved to sit down on the front steps.
"No, I tried to tell him, but I couldn't ruin his relationship wit' Huh. He still looks at her like his bothersome little sister that he gotta look after," I explained.
"So you just take on the world by yourself? Nobody in your corner?" she asked, interrogating me as she placed her hand on my thigh.
"Yes, that's about the size of it," I said.

The conversation ended with those syllables. We remained on the front steps until the sun went down and the stars came out waiting to hear from Billy Ray. Andrea put her left arm around my neck, grabbed my left hand, and tilted her head into my neck. The embrace was comforting. Staring into space I wondered what she had been thinking. We saw a falling star. I wished up on it, but I knew my wish would never come true. I had been wishing and waiting for years and never did a wish make good with me. Having Andrea was by my side was good enough. Being in that space with her gave me hope for the future eradication of an austere existence. She gave my life a salty sweetness that was far better than the bitter harshness I had known theretofore. I submerged myself in her aura. It cleansed my eroding spirit of all the toxins that had been implanted during my stopover in Mississippi.

The source of the greatest amount of my torment was lying in a hospital for the second time and I hardly cared. I didn't want her to be in pain, but another side of me felt that she had deserved it for inflicting so much pain upon me. I drifted into space wandering from universe to universe, dreaming of the world of Malachandrea that would liberate me from the awful truths that infiltrated my life as if they'd had right to. I daydreamed, as it was a mental escape of the uninvited demons that resided in my life. Longing to be free, I fell asleep on the porch. However, if I had never awakened, my only regret would have been not saying goodbye to Andrea.

An unfamiliar melody was delivered as the soundtrack to my dreams. While I slept, it penetrated my thoughts. Harps, flutes, and triangles provided the instrumentation. My Delta blues had been drowned out by the sugary notes of woodwinds, string instruments, and hand percussions. They were no matches for the new tune that played in my head even if in a dream. The blue notes paled in comparison to its minor notes. This melody had almost been symphonic, although tonally, it had no movements. It had become an overture, setting the mood for my extremely cinematic life.

Chapter 20

Trouble All My Days

Billy Ray had rushed Huh to the emergency room because the pain had intensified within the span of time of which she had left me to clean up the kitchen and when Billy Ray and Andrea showed up. The pain had become virtually unbearable for Huh, and she was still refusing to see a doctor. Billy Ray demanded that she go to the hospital and wouldn't take no for an answer. He had driven Huh and she'd moaned in agony for the duration of the ride.

No words were exchanged as Billy Ray sped through the very same part of town where he had first run into her, so to speak. His sole mission was to get her some help as soon as he could. His mind had been consumed with worst case scenarios and feeling responsible since he had been the catalyst of this pain through which she had been going. He tried to block that from his mind and just be concerned for Huh, but it was difficult for a man who was used to being in control. He couldn't shake the feeling that she might have waited too long to get examined. When they arrived at the hospital, Billy Ray wheeled her up to the reception area of the emergency room. The receptionists and nurses all summoned up memories of the hellish stint Huh had had there. The reluctance to assist Huh was etched in the wrinkles of their brows. She had left an indelibly bad impression that had fermented the staff.

"She needs to see someone urgently. She is in a lot of pain," Billy Ray insisted.
"Sir, are you related to the patient?" the receptionist asked.
"No, ma'am, I am here to assist her as she is immobile," he added.
"Do you have insurance, ma'am?" the receptionist inquired.
"Lady, you know me from last time and I got Medicare," Huh said in a growl.
"Ma'am, I have to ask as a formality," she returned.
"Look here, can't you jus' pull my record?" the old lady rumbled.
"You have to fill out new forms each time, ma'am," the receptionist replied annoyed.
"I'm in pain, and you want fah me to fill out some forms?" Huh asked just as irritated.
"Ma'am, can you just help her?" Billy Ray interjected.
"Well, will you be able to fill out these admittance and insurance forms for her?"
"I'll try. I just need for her to be able to see a doctor!" Billy Ray appealed.
"I don't need nobody to do nuthin' fah me! I can fill out my own damn forms!" she said in a listless voice, trying to catch her breath.
"Hattie, I can do this. We need to get you seen by a doctor!" Billy Ray said beseechingly.

"Billy Ray, I am a grown woman and been takin' care of myself fa almost fifty years!" she derided in a labored speech.
"Here you go, Mrs. Dixon!" The nurse said as she handed Huh the clipboard that included a throng of papers that needed to be filled out.

Huh started filling out the paperwork. Billy Ray had sat down adjacent to her tapping his leg irascibly. Sitting underneath his signature cowboy hat that he refused to remove when he entered any building, he watched Huh writhe in pain as she continued to write. He noticed her that the movement of her hand had become more prominently strenuous and her breaths more shallow. In a flash, she doubled over and the clipboard fell to the floor. He grabbed her and called for the nurse. A nurse ran over to her, checked Huh pulse and called for a gurney to take her to the ER. Billy Ray began to rant and rave about the service of this hospital. He even threatened to buy the relatively large county hospital and put all of the employees out of work.

"Sir, we are going to have to ask you to calm down or we will have to call security!" the receptionist cautioned.
"I don't give a damn about no security. I will wait on them and give them a choice set of words, too. People come to this hospital to be treated not surveyed. If you had just admitted her and not mandated that she complete the paperwork as a *formality*, she could have been diagnosed and treated. Instead, she had to keel over in a damn waiting room to be admitted. You country motherfuckers haven't heard the last of Billy Ray Bonds! I can *guaran-god-damn-tee* it!" Billy Ray ranted.
"Sir, you gon have to come with us!" said a burley black guy wearing a black and white security guard uniform, who was standing next to a paper thin white guy who looked on dressed in the identical get-up.
"I'll come with you to speak with your supervisor!" Billy Ray said with hostility.
"That can be arranged," said the guard.

As Billy Ray argued with security, they rushed Huh back to the emergency room. The color had left her body. She wasn't breathing. They ended up having to deliver a shot of epinephrine straight to her heart. She was revived and then they had to sedate her and put her on oxygen. The doctors ran tests to find that she had a blood clot in her leg and in her lung. Because she had dealt with the pain on her own and hadn't wanted to consult a doctor, the diagnosis had been inevitable. The blood clot in her lung had caused her to develop a pulmonary embolism. It was severe and her condition had become really volatile. Once security let Billy Ray go, he called Andrea and me. Our neighbor, Mr. Randle, gave us a ride to the hospital. Andrea stayed in the lobby and slept in three chairs. She was tired, as she had remained awake while I slept on the front steps. When I were finally able to see Huh, she was in ICU, heavily medicated and hooked up to plenty of monitors in addition to having IV's inserted. This was the most helpless I had ever seen her. Once again, my feelings were skewed by my scorn for her. I had no true emotion, except hate when it came to Huh. I was a blank page. There was nothing written across my face. My body language was untranslatable. I sat there in the hospital wishing I could muster some kind of care for a spiteful, old lady who couldn't give a sweet damn if I lived or died. Something was eating me on the inside like a cancer. I just couldn't shake it. Just in that moment, Billy Ray walked into her room in the middle of my contemplation. I welcomed the break for I had been on the precipice of a metacognitive collapse.

"Hey, son!" Billy Ray said.
"Hey, Mr. Bonds!" I said, returning the greeting.
"How's she doing?" he asked.
"The doctor said she is touch and go! I don't really know what that means!" I said.
"It's not too good son!" he replied.

In that instance, I felt bad for not feeling bad for her. I developed a lump in my throat that almost kept me from breathing. I had wanted her to die so many times before, but now that she really could die, I started to feel guilty yet indifferent.

"So she could die huh?" I asked.
"Yes, I am sorry to say!" Billy Ray consoled.
"Damn!" I said before I had time to think about it. "Excuse my language, Mr. Bonds!" I said.
"It's okay, son. I know you are upset about your grandmother," he said comfortingly.
"Actually, I'm not," I responded.
"What do you mean?" he inquired.
"I don't know how I feel right now, but I am not upset about her, because she don't give a damn about me!" I indicated.
"How can you say that?" he asked with dismay.
"Pardon me, Mr. Bonds, but that lady treats me like shit when ain't anybody around It's like I ain't even related to her. I get told what to do and when to do it and if I don't do it on time or right I get punched, hit with brooms, or whatever else will cause some damage. So no, I don't have no feelings about her at this moment!" I exclaimed fully aware that she was only a few feet away from me anesthetized.
"You are just overwhelmed by all of this! You will come around!" Billy Ray said.
"No! I won't! Why should I?" I cried.
"Because she is your grandmother. She has taken care of you for three years. You owe her enough respect to be concerned about her," Billy Ray expounded.
"Respect? Man, you gotta be kiddin' me! That lady wouldn't piss on me if I was on fire! And you wanna talk about respect. I take care of my damn self! The only reason I ain't packed up and ran away is because I am stupid enough to believe that my mama is getttin' outta jail one day and is gonna take me away from here!" I lamented.
"You watch your tone, young man!" Billy Ray chided.
"Why? You ain't my daddy!" I stood up and scowled.

"I might not be your daddy! But you will calm down and show me some respect! I am your elder! Besides your grandmother is lying over there fighting for her life," Billy Ray scolded me like no man had ever done.
"I am sorry, Mr. Bonds. It's just that you don't know what I go through in that house every day," I said apologetically as I returned to my seat.
"You are right. I have no idea. Son, but you need to always remember that the measure of a man is not what he goes through, it is what he learns as he is going through it! You say she is hostile towards you, well it must be contagious, because you seem pretty damn hostile yourself!" Billy Ray pontificated.
"I do get angry. I'm not happy here! Since I been in Mississippi, I just feel like I don't got nothin' to live for," I bemoaned.
"And that is Hattie's fault?" he asked.
"Mostly! You would feel the same way if all you heard is nappy head, no good, cock sucking motherfucker this and that every day of your breathing life!" I explained.
"Malachi! I am not saying you don't have a right to feel the way you do. However, your grandmother is very sick, and you need to find forgiveness for her or it will eat away at you like a tumor for the rest of your life!" he illustrated.
"Mr. Bonds, let's just be real. I am fifteen! I can only worry about today. How I will feel in years to come ain't important to me right now!" I clarified.
"Fair enough, son, but age doesn't have anything to do with forgiveness. It is a concept even a toddler can understand. I just think you are blinded by all the wrong that you have felt over the years. To an extent, I can understand it, but I know somewhere inside that fifteen year old soul you can find some compassion for a gravely ill woman," he said hauntingly. "I won't keep preaching to you son. I am sure in time you will make the best decision for you!" he finished.
"Thank you Mr. Bonds! " I said as Billy Ray got up to go check on Andrea.

I had a lot more thinking to do. This whole forgiveness thing sounded much easier to say than to do.

Three years had been a long time of living with the anguish I had been dealt under her rule. The cruelty to which I had been exposed was much too egregious for me to even consider forgiveness. However, what Billy Ray had said did make a lot of sense. I was willing to consider forgiving her on my own terms not Billy Ray's or Huh's.

Ms. Hattie's blues was a recurring theme that played in my empty soul. Just when Andrea had returned to me and I had a soupçon of peace, Huh's blues pissed it away. The chorus was the same and it reverberated in my ears, mocking me and the happiness Andrea had proffered. Huh's blues meant to make me as blue as azure, and it continued to haunt me like musical apparitions. As much as I rebuked the notes, they kept bending, becoming bluer than distant waters in which I'd longed to swim. *Huh* blues was the curse that I'd never be able to break and I had come to that realization in the hospital. I tuned out the tune but the bass line hummed in spite of me. Like *Huh*, her blues had beleaguered my spirit. I wished that I could float off into a distance and be unaffected by the melancholic melody that was *Ms. Hattie*.

Chapter 20.5

Ain't Nobody's Business

Dear Hattie,

I am sitting in your room with a pen and a paper towel that I am gonna use as paper to write you a letter. I am writing this letter because I need to say some things that I will probably never be able to say to your face. Writing is my new way of dealing with the stuff I've been keeping inside. This is good for me to do to clear my head. Right now you are in the hospital and the doctor says it ain't looking too good for you. He said you should have got some help sooner, and then you might not be lying in a hospital. I tried to get you to see somebody, but you told me to leave it and you alone. That's just the kind of relationship you and me have. I do what you say and no questions about it. I am used to that and the way you treat me. No sense in acting like we friends when that ain't the case. I am your bastard grandson who you don't like and don't mind showing me.

The time is right for me to get some stuff off my chest. I never wanted to come to live with you. It's just that I ain't have nowhere else to go. No daddy to take me in and nobody else. Just like it was not your plan, it was not mine either. It's just one of those things that we just got to deal with. When I used to visit you with my mama, you never had time for me. Just like now, you would feed me and that was it. It didn't really bother me then because I had my mama and I knew nobody else had to care. But when I came to live with you, I thought it would be different. I don't know why but I just thought you would have a little sympathy for a kid whose mama was in jail and had nobody else. Instead you made me feel like I was a beggar instead of your grandson.

At first, it hurt like hell to be mistreated and abused, and then I became numb to it. Although it still hurt physically, it no longer affected me emotionally. The hate for you that I had built up inside of me in some kind of way made me strong enough to push through the physical. I hated you to the point that I wished that you was dead so many times. I don't even feel bad for telling you because it's how I felt. The day you got hit by Billy Ray's car, I hoped for worse than what you got. Now that you are lying in hospital room and I don't know which way your life is going, I kind of feel bad for the thoughts on one hand and right on the other. I just can't think for the life of me why a grandmother would treat her grandson, a boy of her own flesh and blood like you did. I kept blaming myself for the abuse and telling myself to be better and you would be better. The better I got, the worse you got. The open hand slaps, the punches, the kicks, the brooms, and the canes were all weapons against a boy who couldn't or wouldn't defend himself. Basically I shouldn't have needed to defend myself against a woman who should love me instead of loathe him. I read all these books and see movies and TV shows with all these goody two shoe grandmothers and I wondered why I got a witch for one. You were a rotten excuse for a grandmother and I still hate you for that. I don't know if I still want you to die though because that would make me like you and I know I am not that evil. Besides if you died that would make a few people like my mama and Uncle Roosevelt sad and I do care about they feelings. I know you ain't never gonna read this letter because when I am done I'm gonna put it in my pocket and when I get home I'll put it safe place where I put my other ones. Getting all of this off my mind felt good. I hope you don't die, not my sake but for Mama's and Unc's; they love you and I love them. I can't say I love you because I just don't know if I do. Wake up and live your life. Hopefully, you can do a better job at that than you had been doing.

Malachi

Chapter 21

Hard Time in the Old Town Tonight

After I penned that letter to Huh, I fell asleep in the chair in the hospital room. Billy Ray and Andrea had left earlier so they could wash up and put on fresh clothes. They would be back to retrieve me so that I could do the same. Miss Sophie and Miss Sally both visited. Sophie wasn't going to take any chances of feeling Huh's wrath anymore. She had come as soon as she heard this time. Although at odds, Sally had also been a first responder. There was no way she would let her fear of the consequence of our encounter hinder her from being there for Huh. We all had sat around her bed quietly talking and praying. Well, at least they prayed; I listened more so than anything. I didn't believe in their God. He'd jilted me at the altar long ago and I was good with that. The ladies had come and gone, still I sat dangling between there and nowhere. My soul wearily searched for a balance in the midst of instability. I longed for peace within, but a battle between my conscience and my feelings had been waged and I was a casualty of war.

Sitting parallel to the person who had broken my spirits, my consciences continued to be tested. I was in a drab hospital room watching my antagonist suffer. Still very apathetic, my mind wouldn't stop chewing over this forgiveness of which Bill Ray had spoken. As I observed, I saw Huh move. My eyes protruded of my sockets like golf balls. Her hair was matted to the pillow. She surveyed and inspected her location. She appeared dazed and perplexed as she attempted to raise herself up; however, the many monitor wires and IV needles had prevented her.

"Come here Malachi," she whispered.
"Yes, ma'am!" I replied as I made my way over to her bed vigilantly.
"Get me some water," she said, barely audible.
"Ok," I acquiesced.

I walked around to the other side of the bed to fetch the water pitcher and cup. It seemed like the longest walk I'd ever made. Longer than the walk home when my bike had been stolen, longer than the walk from the bus station to the bus, and much longer than the walk through Sidon after Andrea had left. As I poured the water, I thought to myself how ironic it had been that even with limited mobility, she was still ordering me around. Reluctantly, I held the cup and straw up to her mouth. I looked away as she drank. I couldn't stand to look at her for two reasons: one, I hated her and two, I didn't want to feel sorry for someone who had never had any sympathy for me.
"Thank you baby," she managed to speak.

I turned my head sharply towards her in shock as she had recited words I had never heard exit her lips as long as I had had the discontentment of knowing the old lady. I began to think that I must have misheard her. If I had, I really wanted to know what she had really meant to say.

"You're...welcome," I responded reluctantly, and I placed the cup back onto the tray next to her bed.
"You here by yo'self?" she investigated.
"Yes, ma'am!" I replied.
"Malachi, you a sweet boy," she said as I stood stunned.

I had been transfixed on her mouth to see if her lips matched the utterances that had emitted from them. My mind was incapable of wrapping itself around what was transpiring right before my eyes. Huh was actually sounding like what a good grandmother was supposed to sound like. Something was askew. I had clearly entered an alternate universe. Then I thought to myself that it had to be the strength of the pain medications that had simulated the fallacy.

"Come a little closer, Malachi, so I can talk to you," she beckoned.
"Yes, ma'am," I replied as I moved closer guardedly.
"I don't know if you know or not, but yo' grandmamma might not make it. The doctor ain't said nothin' to me, but I know it in my spirit. It's okay, 'cause I done made peace wit' God. Now, I need to make peace wit' you. I know I ain't been too good to you, but I didn't mean no harm. I jus' wanted you to be tough. You gotta be tough to make it in this here world. See, I didn't raise yo' mama good enough. I was too easy on her. She had you too young, and then she went up there to Detroit and followed the wrong crowd. Now, the peoples got her and I can't do nothin' to git her back. And I know you miss her 'cause I do, too. If I could have one wish fah you, it's to be back wit' yo mama," she lamented.

Tears started to well up in my eyes like water behind a dam, and like a dam my eyelids would not let them pass through. The tears were not for Huh; they were for my mother. I did miss her and I wished that I could be back with her, too. I had become overwrought with sadness because I knew it wasn't likely to happen.

"It's alright to cry if you need to Malachi! I know these years wit' me ain't been the best, but all I know is what I know and I know I love you. I know you can't say you love me, because I was awful terrible to you. I was intendin' to help you be a man, but, somehow, I think I broke you. If I did, Malachi, I'm sorry. I jus' didn't want you to turn out like yo' mama. I wanted you to be strong enough to reject the thangs that got her put away. I jus' mighta gone 'bout it the wrong way," she said apologetically.
"How do I know this ain't just your medication that's talkin' now?" I probed.
"Baby, it jus' might be the medicine, but it's my heart that's talkin'," she said surrenderingly.

"I wanna believe that you love me, but you never told me before. If I would have just heard it one time, then the other stuff I could forgive and forget. Now, it just sounds like you tryin' to get into heaven. And if that is the case, don't use me as a one-way ticket," I said in a reprimand.
"Malachi, you got ev'ry right to feel the way you do, but trust me baby, I am bein' as real as a dying, old woman can be," she explained.
"Well, now you let me be real! You have treated me like a nobody for a long time. You have beat me, talked down to me, and humiliated me way too many times to count! I got to admit I wished you was dead plenty of days. When I came to the hospital this time, and I saw you layin' in that bed, I hoped you would take your last breath and I would be free. How could you treat your own grandson like you treated me? No better than a dog!" I explained.
"It ain't no excuse for it, no matter how much good I thought I was doin," she said repentantly.
"What kind of good did you think was gonna come out of it?" I inquired.
"I was tryin' to make you into a better man than yo' own no account daddy," she replied.
"You didn't even know my daddy! How did you think you could make me better than him?" I questioned her motives.
"I know he was never there fah you. I don't know no *good man* that's not gon' be there fah his son," she said.
"So you tried to beat his *no goodness* out of me?" I asked..
"Malachi, I can't say enough how sorry I am. I was jus' plain wrong. Ain't other way to put it. Dead wrong," she sighed.
"You damn right it wasn't!" I swore, unconcerned for my disrespect to her.
"I dreamed about yo' mama and how I failed her as a mama. All she wanted me to do was take care of her baby and I failed at that too. I also saw Jane in the dream. Her and Deacon Jessie was back together and happy. She said to me in the dream, 'Hattie you got to make peace before you leave Earth. It ain't way to die wit' hell in you.' So when I woke up and there you was, I knew the peace she was talkin' 'bout was wit' you. I know you ain't gon'

believe me, but I been proud of you over these years. You keep that house clean, you always respectful, and done good in school. Yo' mama was the same way, too, but she ended up on the wrong side of thangs. You such a good looking young man. You gon' be a good man, in spite of my foolish ways and me. I know that and I can leave this world believin' that."

"Who are you? Where is Hattie Lee Dixon? The cold-hearted old lady who made me sit outside in the freezing cold because I left the iron on, the woman who pushed me into the wall and left a dent, or the woman who busted my lip because I dropped a sock?"

"She right here," Huh said as she hung her head in shame. "Much as I try, I can't deny my faults. Got too many of 'em to keep hidin'. You right, I'm an old foolish woman who can't even piss on her own right now, but I hope you fine it in yo' heart to forgive yo' old grandmama even though she don't deserve it," she said as she drifted back into unconsciousness.

I had been too nonplussed to think clearly. I was an abyss, a vacuous soul. The confusion with which I had experienced during our discourse jimmied any spirit I had left in my body. I didn't know how to feel. I found myself walking down the hospital corridors wandering like a nomad. Nowhere to go, but everywhere to roam. There was no oasis. I came up empty and devastatingly devoid of strength. Desiring clarity, none quenched my thirst. The light in the hospital seemed to flicker like a candle coming to the end of its wick. The serenity of the building suddenly seemed to morph into a stir. There was quiet pandemonium, and it was driving me insane. My mouth was a dry as lint. And because my eyes had been in a watery blur, I couldn't find my way to a fountain to satiate the dryness.

Finally, I could see nothing. My mind collapsed and soon my body followed. As I lay there unconscious, blurred images boogied in my head. I hadn't known what drunkenness felt like, but I had been certain it was a comparable feeling. Although I couldn't make out the visions, I could hear a male voice that sounded vaguely

familiar. It whispered, "Your grandmother is very sick and you need to find forgiveness for her or it will eat away at you like a tumor for the rest of your life." After the voice dissipated, I felt someone slapping me on my face. It was Billy Ray.
"Son, are you okay?" he said fretfully.
"Yeah, I'm okay!" I replied still in a daze.
"Come on, Malachi. Let me help you up," Billy Ray offered.

When I got up, Andrea's face came into focus. Suddenly, there was calm in my spirit. Billy Ray gave me several cups of coffee and water. A nurse had come to check my vitals. She found that I had passed out from dehydration. The confoundedness had faded and I had a revelation. I did love Huh, but I hated her more. Although I loved her more than I had been willing to admit, that didn't negate my detestation of her. She had been the only person in my life for a long time. Yes, the experience had been an unpleasant one, but I survived. She had revealed that her intent was to make me strong. In many ways, I was stronger for having endured the injury that she had inflicted in my life. Andrea kneeled in front of me, and she looked into my eyes. Her eyes spoke to my soul and although empty, my soul attended. She took me by the hand and led me back to Huh's room. It had outdistanced my former longest walk. I took a deep breath. Andrea let go of my hand. She walked back to the waiting room to rejoin Billy Ray as I entered the room. Huh lay there as still as a stone. Outwardly, she appeared peaceful, but she was restless within. I knew I had to try to wake her.

"Grandmama?" I uttered for the first time in my whole life.
"Malachi, that you?" she said in scarcely a whisper.
"Yes, ma'am, it's me!" I replied.
"I been waitin' on you to come," she murmured.
"I forgive you," I said as Uncle Roosevelt walked into the room. He placed his hands on my shoulder as he looked upon his weak, little sister.
"Malachi, baby, thank you, I love you," she said as she slipped into a coma.

I didn't say it back. Better yet, I couldn't say it back. To forgive her was difficult enough, but to admit that I loved her was asking more of me than I had been willing to do. Uncle Roosevelt gripped her hand and squeezed it as tears fell from his eyes. He had felt as if he'd stayed in Sidon, her health would not have waned. Billy Ray had called him and he had arrived as soon as he could. The doctor had forewarned us of the precariousness of her life, so Unc realized that there was the possibility of not having much time left. Ms. Sally, Sophie, Andrea, Billy Ray, and Pastor Nelson all entered the room with special permission from the doctor. He had said we needed to gather around her in support in her time of need. I battled with my tear ducts in a fight I had lost. Water trickled down my face like stream down the sides of mountains.

Suddenly, I remembered a few good times. They had been intricately buried underneath the rubbish of all the harshness. I remember the first Easter that I had been there. She made me a white short suit. She tailored it just for my prepubescent body. Although I was much too old to wear it, I was proud of the suit because it was sewn very well and mostly by hand. The jacket was long sleeved and double-breasted, with six buttons down the front in two columns of three, but only three of them were functional. The shorts were about four inches above my knee, adorned with sateen strips down the out seam. I wore yellow socks, a yellow shirt, a white bow tie, and white dress shoes. Looking like a toddler, I walked around like a peacock.

Then there was my thirteenth birthday. She cooked my favorite foods: spaghetti, fried catfish, garlic bread, and lemon cake with cream cheese icing. Even though she never said happy birthday, it was implied through all of the fuss that she had made in the kitchen. She hadn't required me to clean up the kitchen that day and she had put $20 under my pillow that night. It was a welcomed diversion from her normal coarse conduct towards me. I hadn't had to say thank you, because that was not a requirement for either of us. That was just the way things were between Huh and me.

As we all sat around her bed, thinking of how he doctors had said that they had done all that they could do. We watched as if she were a work of art of whose meaning we were attempting to discern. Suddenly, there was a tremor in her body. She moved and stopped. Horrified, we called the nurse. The nurse ran in to check her vitals. The tremors stopped. She began to move again and she seized. The nurse let go of her in order to allow the seizure to take its course. We looked on in panic. Again, the movement stopped, and then she started breathing erratically. Her monitor began to beep slower than it had been. Beep. Beep. Beep. Beep. Flatline. She was gone.

Sally collapsed into Uncle Roosevelt's arms as she wailed in agony at the loss of yet another friend. He held her tightly as tears cascaded from both their eyes. Sophie buckled at the knees and started screaming for her God, asking him to have mercy, and why. Billy Ray clutched Huh's hand, and Andrea gripped my hand as I stood stunned. What I had dreamed once upon a time had happened, but it hadn't felt nearly as good as I once thought it might. The reality smashed into me like the natural coldness of a wrecking ball. Reverend Nelson moved in closer to Huh opposite Billy Ray to offer conciliatory words to Huh.

"Peace I leave with you; my peace I give unto you, not as the world giveth. Let not your heart be troubled, neither let it be afraid," Reverend Nelson said, reading from the Bible. "Mark the perfect man, and behold the upright, for the end of that man is peace."

She lay in front of us, yet she had vanished. A soulless cadaver replaced her. I buried my face into Andrea's neck and I let out every emotion that I had kept bottled up for years. I was simultaneously angry, sad, and confused. The world seemed more wrong than right. There were no more blues. An earsplitting quietness took their place. As much as my blues had haunted me, I would have gladly welcomed their return to have Huh back. The irony had its own music, only I was not an audience to it.

Chapter 21

Hold On

Dear Father,

It sounds funny saying that to somebody. Ain't nobody my father. I only have a mother. She was the only person who was ever there for me. Mama was the only person who showed me she loved me. She kissed me, hugged me, read to me, tucked me in, and made me feel safe. My mama might not be the best mama but she is far from the worst. So ain't no daddy for me. I guess I really should refer to you as my DNA donor. You really the person who helped make me. You ran away from her and me. What a coward! Anyway, it really doesn't matter because you will never see this letter. This letter is for me. I needed to write this for me. For fifteen years, I wondered why you never rescued me from the shit I went through. Where was you at? I waited. Someday I thought you would ride in on a horse and save the day, and we would go far away. You never came. I never left. It hurt. Over the years, I stopped caring. I just finally realized you didn't give a damn and with time I didn't either. I needed to believe in something else other than a fairy tale, daddy. I put all my trust in me. I was really all I had. Don't get me wrong, my mama loves me, but like you she ain't around now. The two people that brought me in this world are both absent. She locked up and you, with no face, are locked away in a memory. I hated you. No, I still hate you. I hate you even more now, because my grandmama tried to beat the "you" out me. She thought you was a sorry excuse and didn't want me to be like you. For three years she tortured me because of your sorry ass. I lived in fear of a lady who supposed to love me. She ain't showed me she love me, but right before she died she told me she loved me. I hated her for a long time but now I hate that she gone. That's how fucked up my life is. I blame you for how she treated me. You was the one that drove her to hurt me. Wherever you at, I know not one thought of yours is about me. I know you knew about me. You had to know. You chose not to know me. You chose not love me. You chose to live a life without me and I was forced to live one without you. The sad part is knowing you have a whole family out there that don't even know or care you exist. That is something I can't get out my mind. I can never forgive you for what you left behind for me. The pain, the abuse, and the rejection. Your freedom from me caged me. I'm still in that cage just like my mama. You are the warden. Thanks so much *fucking* much for the X Chromosome.

Your bastard,

Malachi

Chapter 22

You Got to Die

Writing that letter to my father was very therapeutic. Although jostled, I was fortifying myself through my reading and writing. Nothing was right with the world but nothing was really wrong either. Uncle Roosevelt had found Grandmama's last will and testament in the nightstand next to her bed. From that day forward, I no longer referred to her as *Huh* I finally acknowledged our kinship. As a result, I fight lighter. The world was no longer on my teenage shoulders. I was finding that homeostasis I had sought so desperately. The grey areas had harvested some color. Days and nights no longer bled into one another. There was clearer distinction. A line of demarcation. A brand new horizon. Although Grandmama had left her body, her spirit lingered with us. There was always a Hattie story, full of antics, thrown about to lighten the mood.

Uncle Roosevelt and Sally handled the arrangements, although there was not much to do. After seeing the mess that Sally had endured preparing for Old Man Jessie and Ms. Janes' funerals, Grandmama had organized everything prior to her death. Uncle Roosevelt set out to execute Grandmama's wishes while he grieved. It all too much reminded me of the mother from *Imitation of Life*. Just like hers, the will and plans were laid out extremely detailed. She outlined how she had wanted things to be controlled. Shockingly, she wanted to be cremated followed by a memorial service. Unc and Sally also collaborated with Billy Ray to get everything prepared exactly how Grandmama wanted it. Billy Ray had even tried to pull some strings with some government officials he had known to have my mother released to attend the funeral. However, due to federal regulations moving her across states lines was prohibited. She had been allowed more phone time to call us. The conversations had been very upsetting and unfortunate. We couldn't know the pain it was for her to lose her own mother while behind bars. Sometimes she was barely able to speak, so the prison staff had permitted Rocky to call for her to relay messages. Rocky was actually a nice lady. Her love for my mother was clearly evident in the way she spoke about her and through her vast knowledge of all of us. In those many conversations she was able to inform us that she had had no children, but she had raised her sister's children because her sister had died of breast cancer. Rocky had always been attracted to women, and she'd known early in life she never wanted to be penetrated let alone be impregnated. They were both remorseful that my mother had not been able to be in attendance.

The memorial service was beautiful and very brief. Practically everyone in town attended the memorial clad in white instead of black as she had requested. Sophie sang a surprisingly on pitch perfect rendition of *To God Be the Glory*. In all the years I had known Sophie, I never knew she could sing. It shouldn't have surprised me as her mouth was big enough to be able to round out those vibrato notes she belted in her soulful contralto voice. She had brought the house down and there wasn't a dry eye in the whole of the place. Reverend Nelson eulogized her in a true Southern style of sermonizing.

"*Sister Dixon lived a long life full of joy and pain, yet she fought the uphill battle to become a better Christian. She, as we all do, fell short of God's grace, but she never gave up. Even in the end, she realized that she needed God's mercy and His forgiveness as well as the forgiveness of others before she could leave the physical. Knowing this was paramount to her entering the gates of heaven to receive her crown and long, white robe. While there is nothing that we can do for Sister Dixon as she is settling in her to her new place in Eternity, we can change those things about ourselves that are not pleasing to God. Let us grieve not only for Sister Dixon, but for the state of our own lives,*" Reverend Nelson proclaimed as he seemed to soak in the realness of his own words

.

Most Southern preachers had that same way of straying from the topic of the deceased. They usurp an opportunity to pontificate to the crowd, instead of honoring the life of the deceased. Many of them jump at the chance to preach at a funeral because they know that there are many people in attendance who are *not* regular churchgoers. Therefore, they relegate the deceased to two or three sentences and devote the rest of the time trying to force people to get right with the Lord while they can. It was all bullshit to me. The Lord had no authority. *This was a man's world*. Man made the Bible, *sin*, and choices. There was no long, blonde haired, blue eyed, dress and sandal wearing Jew going to drop out of the sky and rescue anybody. Faith was a name not a fundamental of proselytization. As far as I was concerned, once people realized that the *moment* and *free will* were the only things that they truly owned in this world, the better off they'd be.

After the service, there was a repast at the town community center. The funny thing about a repast in Mississippi was that it was no different than a Thanksgiving or Christmas dinner. There was more food than there was usually room to serve it. The dinner was set-up included several entrees, sides, breads, and deserts, with friends and church people serving. Most people left repasts as full as ticks carrying numerous *to go* plates for those spouses and children who were not in attendance. Although it was highly inappropriate, most Mississippians had no concept of how gauche certain behaviors were. It was these same behaviors that others thought to be primitive in many ways. However, it was also the staunch nature of Mississippi's inhabitants to not give a shit about what others thought.

It had been a long, draining day. After the repast, everyone went to their respective addresses, except Billy Ray and Andrea came by our house afterwards since they would be leaving the next day. Billy Ray had been extremely magnanimous in his contribution of time to Grandmama's final wishes. Andrea and I sat in my room and we conversed about nothing and everything for what seemed like hours. Our relationship had grown stronger by the day.

The night before the memorial service, we both sneaked out of the house to reunite at the Goal. It was late, so no one was out there but us. We stood in the same spot where we'd met. The faint breeze picked up individual strands of her hair as if was a stylist. Lollipop in tow, she smelled of a sweetness that was like a marriage of honeydew melon and honeysuckle. We found a patch of grass and we sat Indian style facing one another. She taught me two of the sweetest things: an Eskimo kiss and butterfly kiss. She leaned into me and placed the tip of her nose onto the tip of my nose. She moved her head from side to side as if saying no while bumping my nose ever so tenderly. It was the sweetest thing I had ever experienced until she leaned in and placed her right cheek onto mine lining up our eyelashes. She whispered, "Blink."

I did and it was the most erotic, non-erotic event that I had known theretofore. Andrea was great in that way; I never knew one person could have so much inside of herself to give to someone else. I was thankful that I'd met her.

Billy Ray and Unc were in the kitchen having coffee. The conversation was fairly quiet so Andrea and I could only hear murmurings of what they had been saying. They had been unobtrusively discussing what men their age discussed, well at least what I had gathered. All of a sudden, we heard shouting. Andrea and I ran into the kitchen where the two of them persistently attempted to best one another. There was so much fuss; we could hardly decipher what they were actually saying to one another.

"Unc, what's goin' on?" I interrupted.
"Not a goddamn thang. Billy Ray and his daughter was just leavin'," Uncle Roosevelt asserted.
"Dad, what's the matter?" Andrea probed frantically.
"Nothing sweetheart. Roosevelt and I were just having a slight disagreement," Billy rejoined.
"It sounded like more than that, dad. So what's going on?" she pleaded with Billy Ray.
"Tell her, Billy Ray. Tell her what you just told me," Unc demanded.
"Andrea, sweetie, let's go!" Billy Ray sighed.
"Mr. Bonds, what the hell is going on?" I asked.
"Malachi, watch your tongue! You know better," Billy Ray said, volleying.
"He ain't got to watch shit. Damnit, be a man and tell'em what's going on," Unc reprimanded.
"I will pretend that I didn't hear that. Let's go, baby," Billy Ray urged.
"You can pretend all the hell you want. Ain't gon' change nothin'," Unc yelled at Billy Ray and Andrea as they exited.
"Unc, what was all that about?" I investigated.
"Billy Ray got the damn nerve to tell me that he wants you to go live with him and Andrea in Kansas. He say I am too old to raise you!" Unc despaired.
"Why would he say that? And why would I go to Kansas?" I asked very intrigued by the idea of living in the same house as Andrea.
"That's what I asked, too, and that's when thangs got heated up in here. He done ran my blood pressure up. Now, I am too old for that!" Unc and I both chuckled and I was glad to see him lighten up.
"Well, I do want to come live wit' you Unc, if you will have me," I declared.

"Son, you know I will. You can keep going to school here, 'cause guess what? I'm moving in. How 'bout that?" Unc asked.
"That'd be good, but I want to do what is best for you," I returned.
"I know your mama and Hattie would want you to stay here, so that's what we gon' do," he stated.

Unc grabbed a hold of me and squeezed me tighter than a belt. It was almost as if he was trying to squeeze all of the worry out of me. If it were his objective, then it worked because I never felt safer. Thanks to Grandmama's arrangements, Uncle Roosevelt would be my legal guardian until such time as my mother was released. However, the truth of the matter was that it was highly unlikely that she would be getting out before I graduated from high school. Nevertheless, it didn't preclude me from believing that she would get out earlier on that good behavior she'd promised me.

Through the entire clamor of the past few months, life was starting to finally get simpler for me. I just regretted not being able to get to know Grandmama the way Uncle Roosevelt had known her. There was new music. There was a symphonic band playing a brisk march in my mind. It was rhythmic and upbeat and fully aligned with the trajectory of my new found peace of mind. My life was in a processional, and I was the grand marshal of my own parade. The time signature changed and alternated between cut time and 6/8 time. My heart could now keep up because it was no longer burdened. Although Andrea had to leave abruptly, because of the turmoil between Billy Ray and Unc, it didn't affect me as much as it might have formerly. I knew we'd come together at some point before her departure. My music quashed the sadness. The optimism inside me was as ceremonial as the march. Thirty-two measures of robust and balanced percussive beats drumming away the entire affliction I had known hitherto.

Chapter 23

I'm Satisfied

The days passed since the fight between Billy Ray and Uncle Roosevelt. Although they hadn't really resolved anything, they remained cordial to one another. Andrea and I had an extended period of time to get to spend with one another as Billy Ray had decided to stay around just a bit longer. This allowed Andrea and me to meet up at our usual spot as well as our inaugural spot. Some nights we would play basketball at the goal, and I'd let her win, but I guarded her really closely in order to be able to smell her Shea butter lotion. It was refreshing to watch her lackluster jump shot and even her uninspiring free throws; nevertheless, she was a hustler on the court. I had to admit that as great as I had been on the court, she made an athletically concerted effort to *break my ankles*. She wasn't afraid to sweat and that made her even sexier to me. That was the most fun I had ever had at the Goal.

Other nights in our spot, Andrea would sit between my legs and lie back with her head resting in my abdominals. She'd rub my legs and calf muscles as she suckled her BlowPop. We played hide and seek in the dark. I always found her, but she never found me, as I had become really skillful at hiding. Life made it easy. The hours we spent seemed more like days, as we savored the sweet moments, tender kisses, and ephemeral embraces. We had definitely fallen in love, although we never admitted it to one another. It was comparable to me not having to tell my grandmother thank you. It was understood just like the "you" in imperative sentences.

We soaked up every second we could steal. We drowned in one another; however, we knew it was keenly transitory. School was to start next week in the county. I wasn't ready to face another dry, uneventful school year. My sophomore year at Amanda Elzy High School could wait as far as I was concerned, but I was abundantly aware that it wouldn't. I had been fated to return to being in the company of a bunch of country bastards who cared as much about geography and Spanish as they did about the wax in their ears. School was an absolute bounty of misfits and nonentities. Being there was like being in the midst of a tornado and I was debris. The prospect of school was offset by Uncle Roosevelt's presence.

Uncle Roosevelt had sold his house, moved in, and began some major renovations on our old shack of a house. It had finally started to look like a home in its appearance. Every now and then, he let me help with the projects. He put replaced the carpet with hardwood flooring. He put in storm windows, crown molding, and new sinks in the kitchen and bathroom. The work he put into the house was indicative of Uncle Roosevelt attempt to give a fresh façade to a place where I had experienced tumult. It was his way of righting a wrong of which had been unbeknownst to him. I appreciated his effort to provide comfort in a once uncomfortable place. It made me feel contented to have a father figure in the house. It was the kind of feeling that that no words could build sentences to explain. I didn't even think I wanted to be able to explain it. Unfortunately, having a father still had been an anomaly to me. However, I was glad that the universe, as I had known it, saw fit to bless me with Uncle Roosevelt. Yet, in all my happiness, there was something eating away at me like a malignancy. As much as I tried to discern from whence this feeling was coming, I was powerless to its bizarre enormity. Just as Andrea was walking up to the door, it all became crystal clear. The love of my life would be leaving.

"Hey, Malachi. Hey, Mr. Lipsey," she spoke as she entered the house.
"Hey, baby! How you today?" Unc replied in his usual good-humored manner.
"I am fine. Thanks," she declared.
"Come on in and have a seat. Lemme grab you a some'n to drank 'cause it's hot as fish grease out there! Malachi, I'm going back to the hardware store. I'll be back in 'bout an hour" Unc said as he handed Andrea a soda.
"Okay, Unc!" I replied.

Butterflies flitted around in my stomach so madly that I became more nervous than a kindergartener on the first day of school. I hadn't been alone with Andrea since a few nights prior; I would often forget how easily she sent me into anxiety. Trying my best to keep it together, I pretended to be cool by walking over to the refrigerator to grab me a coke, and without fail, I had fallen on my face. Andrea laughed herself to tears as she rushed over to help me up. As embarrassed as I had been, I still managed to laugh at myself. It was good to see and hear her laugh, although I hadn't wanted to eat the floor, I was glad to be the source of her cheerfulness.

"Hmmm... laughing at a man when he is down?" I got up still giggling heartily as well.
"That was funny how you tried to walk over there all smooth then you landed on your face. That's what you get. If I didn't know better, I would think you was still trying to impress me!"
"Impress you for what? You have been impressed since you met me. You took one look at all this right here and fell as hard as I just did!"

I said arrogantly as I cupped my face parenthetically and smiled really widely.

"Is that right?" she said as she stood up and moved closer to me poking me in the chest with her index finger.

The closer she had gotten, fragrances scaled up my nose and hypnotized me. Her hair smelled like cocoa. She was chewing the gum from the BlowPop and her perfume was made of vanilla. The mixture of scents made for an aromatic medley that stimulated my erogenous zones. As we were millimeters apart, she stopped poking me, lay her head on my chest and put her arms around my neck. I, in turn, put my arms around her waist. For as many times as we had embraced, this by far, had been the most poignant. We both had known what the other was thinking, that it would probably be our last time holding one another and we cherished it in that instant.

"Now, what were you saying?" I asked.
"Well…" she started.
"Exactly! Just as I thought." I replied.

In that instant she looked up at me. My eyes met a gaze that I had only seen in Miss Sally's eyes. Immediately, I became nervous. Beads of sweat formed across my brow. However, I calmed myself down and I moved in to kiss her. Her lips tasted like Coke and strawberries and I became instantly aroused me. I grabbed her head and I held it firmly as I kissed her more passionately. She tightened her grip on me as she intuitively surrendered to me. We moved slowly, still in our embrace, into the living room. We fell onto the sofa. She was on top of me as our lips remained in an exasperatingly sensual lock.

Anxiously, she rose up and took off her shirt. I wrapped my hands around her waist. Her body was sinewy, and just to touch it had been my greatest reward. I had known no other softness of which to compare her skin. We continued undressing one another as if we had been unwrapping gifts of nakedness. Naturally, we explored one another's bodies, kissing and touching one another, like there was no way of separating. We made love. Although we knew our youth should have precluded us from the forbidden activity, our souls wanted and needed it.

We lay there in post lovemaking breathing deeply, smiling at one another. Before we could catch our breaths, we realized that we needed to get up and get dressed before Uncle Roosevelt returned. I noticed blood spotting. I guess this was from the storied *popping of the cherry* or *breaking the hymen*. We washed up and we got dressed.

"Was that your first time?" she investigated.

However, I hadn't known it was because it had been really good or terribly bad, although hoping for the former as opposed to the latter. I had to bear in mind that since I wasn't privy to the origin of her question, I wasn't quite know whether to be honest.

"Well, I guess, kinda!" I said self-consciously.
"What's that supposed to mean?" she asked attentively.
"It's the first time I have ever made love to a *girl*,".

I replied only to make the distinction because my only other experience had been a woman. Surely, I hadn't wanted her to probe any more as I didn't want to reveal that that woman had been Sally.

"Oh, okay, I won't ask any more questions. Well, it was my first time. But for some reason it seemed like you knew exactly what to do, when to do it, and how to do it. I was very impressed," she sustained.

Even though I was very brown, I blushed and my faced reddened. I was gratified to know that after what we had experienced together, I had been impressive. I had taken extremes amounts of joy in knowing that I had pleased her to a point worthy of praise. For that, I had had to give Sally credit. If it were not for her tutelage, I would have been as bumbling as I had been grabbing the Coke from the fridge.

"Thanks, that really means a lot to me."
"No! I should be thanking you, Mr. Dixon," she said and we both laughed. "Well, Malachi, dad says we are leaving tomorrow. That's why I showed up with no warning. I had to see you. I knew I wouldn't be able to sneak out tonight. We are leaving at like four in the morning. I know I'm going to miss you," she lamented.
"I understand. These past few weeks been very hectic for me, but the one thing that kept me goin' was your smile. I will miss you more than I even wanna think about right now," I said as I grieved internally.
"I wonder why they say 'All good things must come to an end'," she pondered.
"I don't know. But right now in this moment it sounds more stupid than poetic," I remarked.

I pulled her close to me, resting my hands around her waist. She looked into my eyes as if they were the skies and she longed for a place in them. Once again, we said nothing but our hearts understood every unspoken syllable. The chemistry was so undeniably organic; we were giving off sparks capable of igniting wildfires. Just as we moved in for a kiss to seal our fate, we heard the doorknob rattle.

"Hey, y'all, I'm back," Uncle Roosevelt yelled through the house as he arrived.
"Hey Unc!" I called back as I ran into the kitchen.
"I got a lot of stuff out in the car. Malachi, come gimme a hand," he directed.
"Mr. Lipsey, I can help, too," Andrea said as she entered.
"Nah, baby. Malachi and me can handle it. Besides you too pretty for manual labor," he complimented.
"No, she ain't. She can help," I said playfully, followed by a slap on my head by Andrea.
"Don't play with me boy," she said, and we all laughed.

"I don't play. I threw away my radio because it played too much," I responded.
"You are not funny. Now, go on out there and help your uncle!" she instructed.

Andrea and I teased one another as I helped Uncle Roosevelt unload the car. We always had so much fun together. She knew how to make me smile, and I knew just how to push her buttons. To know that it would all be over made me recoil at the thought of not being able to touch, taste, or smell her. Writing letters would not be sufficient, but it was a reality that I had to accept if I wanted to remain in contact with her. I had taken the last of things from the car to the house.

Uncle Roosevelt was outside prepping some materials to be used to build a picket fence around our front yard. We were inside at the kitchen table playing her favorite card game: Speed. In the game of Speed, each player is dealt five cards face down to form his hand and another five cards face down, and remain face down to serve as replacements as each card is played. The rest of the cards are dealt to form two parallel stacks face down with enough space in between for two face up cards that will serve as the foundation for playing upon. When each player picks up his first five cards, he may arrange them strategically in his hand. On the count of three, both players turn over the first card of the face down stacks corresponding to his right hand into the space between the stacks. Once the cards are face up, the game is in play. The players can only have five cards at a time while playing. He may replenish with the other five cards face down. The object of the game is to dish a card on top of another card either one card higher than said card or one card lower than said card. When neither player can play with the cards left in his hands, the player must turn over new cards from the stacks between them. This all must be done as fast as possible in order to rid yourself of all ten cards in your possession. Andrea usually beat me more than I had been able to beat her. Basketball was my game, even though I let her beat me, she wasn't as munificent about letting me win in Speed. She was ruthlessly competitive and she relished in defeating me as many times as she had.

"Andrea, baby, yo' daddy is out here!" Unc yelled in from outside.

"Okay!" she replied.

Although he had not known the extent of our relationship, Billy Ray knew we had become good friends since such time as Jane's funeral, so he didn't mind letting Andrea visit, as he had felt unthreatened by my seemingly unassuming nature.

The moment seemed to go in slow motion. Still sitting, I reached out to grab her hand as she got up to walk over to the door. She looked down at my hand as I could tell she had not the will to force herself to look at me. One single tear rolled down her face, so being that the mood had grown lugubriously quiet, we could almost hear it splash onto the floor. Never looking up, she loosed my hand and exited without as much as a whisper. I, too, was speechless. My heart had a lot to say, but my mouth could think of so little. Goodbye had silently spoken for us both. The music had finally concluded.

Chapter 24

All Night Long

I couldn't sleep after she had left me that night. Again my mind would not allow me to rest as it had numerous times before. My eyes would not allow me to cry, so there was no release of this feeling inside. Never had I dreamed that Andrea would come to mean so much to me. Our last day together replayed over and over in my head as if it had its own rewind apparatus. The more it replayed, the more the guttural pains beleaguered me, sort of my own version of Braxton Hicks. It was a rhythmically cyclical hurting that was simply indescribably unbearable. If only there were some natural epidural, I could have taken it but there wasn't.

For as numb as my heart had been, the discomfort tottered between feeling and unfeeling. I stayed up writing my thoughts about the events of the summer. Everything that had happened that summer had affected me in some way and had changed me in other ways. I had risen and fallen in a three-month span of time.

I grew up.
I regressed.
I progressed.
I digressed.
I pressed on.
I loved.
I lost.

The stresses of life had worn me extraordinarily thin. I was a ghost of my previous self. With Andrea leaving, I had to try to will myself to pull it together. By any means necessary, I knew I had to be able forge a pathway through the dim desolation of the Delta.

The next morning after having absolutely no sleep, The smell of sausages awakened my senses. Unc was in the kitchen cooking breakfast. I got up and showered. Then I wandered into the kitchen. Much to my chagrin, Billy Ray was sitting at the table. The look in his eye was really strange. The look on his face was very ominous, and it made me feel uncomfortably awkward. With a furl in my brow, I looked from him to Uncle Roosevelt and back to him. They had seemed more than cordial in this space which for me had diminished in size, due to my being confounded by Billy Ray's presence.

"Come on in and get you some'n to eat, Malachi," Uncle Roosevelt instructed.

"How's it going, Malachi?" Billy Ray inquired.

"Good. You?" I responded inertly.

"Going well, thank you," he answered.

"Well, Malachi, I am going to the store. Billy Ray wants to talk to you. I will be back in a few. You need anything while I am out?" Uncle Roosevelt asked, appearing miffed.

"No, sir. Thank you," I replied.

"Alright, I'll be back," he said dolefully. I knew that his disposition was off duet to whatever he and Billy Ray had discussed before I came in to the kitchen. Whatever it was, I didn't like the smell of things.

"Okay, Unc," I called.

I began to scoop the grits onto my plate, and I could tell that Billy Ray didn't quite have the words for what he wanted to say. His eyes were uneasy and his body was as tense as a horse that sleeps while standing. His hands shook nervously, and he mouth was clearly dry even though he had been drinking coffee. He kept opening his mouth but no words escaped his lips. I finished piling on eggs, sausages, and toast. Reluctantly, I decided to break the ice.

"So what did you want to talk about?" I asked as I stuffed my face with morsels of Southern comfort food.

"Malachi, I want you to know that this is the hardest that thing I ever attempted to do."

"I don't mean no harm, Mr. Bonds, but how could talking to *me* so hard for you? You are a grown man," I said, and I ate more as I waited for his response.

"If it were only that simple," he said.

"It should be," I said nonchalantly with a mouth full of food.

"Well, son, I just want you to know that I never meant to deceive you or intentionally hurt you. There are some things that you need to know. I am not who you think I am. I mean, I am who you know me to be, but I am just more."

"You talking like you a spy or a murderer or somethin'," I said, laughingly.

"No, that would be much easier," he said rather peculiarly.

"Mr. Bonds, my goodness, can you just say it? You are startin' to creep me out!" I exclaimed in mid chew.

"I am sorry, Malachi, there is just no easy way to say this," Billy Ray said..

"Just say it!" I cried.

"Okay! Malachi, calm down. Well, son, I'm your father," he sustained.

"Mr. Bonds, wit' all due respect, you are good guy and all, but you ain't my daddy. You are nothing like what my mama described to me! So what is this really about?" I demanded.

"Son, I know that this is not the best time in your life to find out about me, but it is true. I really am your father," he maintained.

"Is this a joke, man? If it is, this shit is not funny at all!" I shouted as I dropped my fork onto the tabletop.

"Malachi!" he growled.

"Excuse my language, Mr. Bonds, but I do not appreciate being messed wit'!"
"I am not messing with you! I met your mother, Celeste…," he began.
"Don't you say her name. You don't got that right," I barked.

It had disturbed me to actually hear him say her name. No one really said her name anymore. She had become this anomaly with different monikers such as mama, your mother, yo' mammy, my daughter, and most wounding of all, jailbird.

"Fair enough. I met her when she was 18 years old. I used to do contract work for the Leflore County School District, and the day I saw your mother on campus, although, I was significantly older than she was, I fell for her," he said, narrating her story.
"You gon' really sit up here and keep this foolishness up!"
By this time I had stood up with a stern look on my face and an even more venomous look in my eye. This conversation with Billy Ray was only making my condition worse as it had intensified my fragility. Not being able to fathom why Billy Ray had wanted to hurt me, my anger towards him heightened as he continued to talk.
"My marriage was a mess. We did nothing but fight, and we had basically become roommates. We were in our thirties and still had no children. I always wanted children, but she didn't want any. This placed a huge strain on the both of us," he continued.
"You are serious about this," I said as I sat back down bemused.
"I wish there were some other way to be about this, but I am very serious. Your mother and I shared a strong bond, but it had been forbidden. She had gotten pregnant, and I was the happiest man in the world. Your mother and I had discussed my divorcing my wife and getting married and raising you. Two months into the pregnancy, your mother had a change of heart, and she had lied to me saying that she had miscarried. I was completely heartbroken. She distanced herself from me, and I had no choice but to let

her go. Before today, with you right now, letting her go was the most difficult thing I'd done. My whole life had been shaken up and tossed about. However, my wife discovered the relationship, but she decided to give us another chance. She said she'd reconsider having a child with me if I would leave your mother alone completely. I let your mother go, even though I loved her, to work on my marriage and to raise a family. Eventually, we moved to Kansas. I had learned to live without your mother, and I had fallen back in love with my wife. We had Andrea a few months after you were supposed to have been born. My wife died minutes afterwards. I had no idea until a few months ago that your mother had actually given birth to my son," he bemoaned.

"So after hearing this story am I supposed to feel sorry for you? 'Cause I don't believe yo' wicked ass," I said as I rose to exit.

"Wait, son, I know this is a lot, but it is all true," he pleaded.

"Don't call me 'son,' 'cause ain't nobody earned that right," I yelled in fury. If it had been possible, steam would have emitted from my body; I was just that incensed.

"Duly noted. Malachi, you have every right to be mad, but that won't change the truth about your mother and me," Billy Ray explained.

"And don't sit here and talk about my mama like you know her. If this is true, that was years ago, and you don't know her life. So if I was to believe you, just how did you find out about me?" I investigated.

"Your mama called me from jail," he replied.

"What the hell? How'd she get your number?" I asked incredulously.

"She said she had her public defender track me down. I didn't really care. I was just glad she had finally given me an opportunity to make things right with you," Billy Ray declared.

"Make things right? You can't just come up in here and sing nursery rhymes and think everything gonna be right. It don't work like that," I exclaimed.

"I didn't mean it like that," he said apologetically.

"How did you mean it?" I inquired.

"I meant that I could get to know you and try to make up for lost time. Time we can't get back, but we can make the most of what is left," he expounded.
"So this is why you told my uncle you wanted me to come live wit' you. Man, you are a piece of work."
"That was wrong of me. I thought if he would, agree then it would be no need to tell you about who I really was," he explicated as he took off his hat. Sweat dripped down his forehead like rain on a windshield. He took out his handkerchief to rid himself of it.
"So, does Uncle Roosevelt know now?" I questioned.
"Yes, I told him before you came out of your room. He wanted to tell you himself, but I begged him to allow me to do it. I didn't want to distort your thoughts about your uncle, he's a good man," he confessed.
"I knew something was different about him before he left. You could never make me feel no kinda way about my uncle. I don't need you to tell me how good of a man he is. He shows me every day," I shot off.
"Look, I know you....!" Billy Ray began.
"You know I am what? 'Cause you don't know me at all," I said.
"I know you have had a hard time of it here with your grandmother. You told me as much at the hospital. I wanted so badly to tell you when you said I wasn't your daddy, but the timing was not right. I knew you needed to make peace with your grandmother before she passed," he elucidated.
"So what? That don't mean nothin'. You don't know my story," I said reminding him.
"I want a chance to hear your story. I would love nothing more from you, son," he contended.
"I am not your son!" I yelled.
"Take it easy, Malachi. I know you are frustrated, and I am not making things better," he went on.
"You dead right about that. You ain't making nothin' better for me. I really wish you would just get in your car and go on back to Kansas and leave me alone. That's how you can *make things right*."
"Listen, Malachi," he bellowed.

"No, you listen. Ain't shit been right around here since you rode into town. If you didn't hit her wit' your car... You know what? It don't even matter. I don't need you trying to mess my life up more than you already have," I said guardedly.
"I am not trying to do anything of the sort. But I know I do I have to let you take the time you need for this to sink in."
"You ain't got to let me do a goddamn thing, but I will *let* you out!" I exclaimed.
"I hope you can understand one day..." he started as he walked towards the door.
"What I don't understand is why you felt like you had to tell me. I ain't never had no daddy, and I damn sure don't need one now," I yelled and slammed the door behind him.

He left, and I sat there in the living room even more depressed and confused than I had been before he showed up. The world around me kept constantly changing. Nothing was black or white. Nothing was right or wrong. Life had no purpose. I had no purpose. I was just a shell. My mother was in jail. My grandmother was dead. My girl was leaving. My DNA donor had returned. The worst revelation was the fact that my girl was not my girl but actually my sister. My soul sadly sank into sorrow. It was like drowning in quicksand. I couldn't breathe. Everything had been so muddled. All I could see was darkness. I blacked out there on the sofa.

"Malachi! Wake up! Malachi?" Unc yelled as he slapped my face several times.

I slowly opened my eyes and saw Uncle Roosevelt with an alarmed look on his face. I wondered how long I had been out, but more so I wondered why I had awakened. My mind went back to all those Sundays in church when Pastor Nelson would preach about how God only takes you off the earth after you had fulfilled your purpose. I didn't believe their God, so why had he seen fit to spare me? I wasn't one of his pawns who went to church willingly and faithfully. I didn't thump a Bible and I was definitely no holy rolling Jesus freak. To me, *Jesus* was a Mexican who sold quesadillas and margaritas.

"I am okay Unc," I acknowledged.
"How long you been out?" he asked.
"I don't know," I responded.
"You need some water. Wait right here," he instructed.
"Okay," I rejoined.
"I guess Billy Ray told you, huh?" he asked as he passed me the mayonnaise jar of water.
"Yeah," I said after I had taken two gulps of the water.
"I wanted to tell you myself, Malachi," he lamented.
"You believe him Unc?" I queried.
"He was right on as far as dates and everything. Had to be some truth," Uncle Roosevelt admitted.
"Why now?" I wondered.
"He said he just found out after all these years," Unc said.
"Unc, this just ain't right," I maintained.
"Why not?" he asked.
"If he is my daddy Unc, then that makes Andrea my sister," I explained.
"What's wrong wit' that?" Uncle Roosevelt interrogated.
"Unc, Andrea ain't just my friend."
"How you mean, son?" he posed.
"I like her as a girlfriend. We have kissed and stuff," I confessed.
"Oh! Damn, Malachi. I can see why this is so hard to take on," he said understandingly.
"Hard ain't the word Unc. It's killin' me. My world won't just settle down. It keeps upchuckin' up on me. Just when things goin' good somethin' always seems to come mess it up. It's a wonder I can keep standing. I been holdin' it together pretty good, but I wanted to give up so many times before. But Unc I don't know if I can do it this time. It's crushing me," I expounded.
"Malachi, I can't tell you how to feel. I can't imagine how you feeling, but I can offer you one piece of advice. Pray 'bout it. God'll reveal an answer. I know you ain't never really heard me speakin' of God and all, but I know the true power. He can bring you from low places to high places, if

you have a mustard seed faith. I know you young, but you can benefit from his might! All you got to do is trust in him," he advocated.
"I really don't have no faith in God," I admitted."
"That's alright, son. I will have enough faith for both us. Feel how you need to feel," Unc said empathetically as he hugged me in that tight embrace as only he could.

I appreciated his compassion. He had the biggest heart of anyone I had ever known, and it had enough room for me and all my woes. Unfortunately, this time his hug just hadn't been enough to withstand my suffering. Defeated and exhausted, I reunited with my Delta blues. The blues were colder than before. There was the same rhythm and instrumentation, just a different day. The notes bent around my neck and squeezed the rhythm out of my heart. Unlike previously, I welcomed my blues. Although the blues had been my nemesis, at least the bass line was consistent, dissimilar to the happenings of my life. I swaddled myself in my blues, and I realized that after all this time, they had been my one true comfort in a comfortless space.

Chapter 24.5

What Have You Done?

Dear Mama,

I don't even know where to start. The world ain't been no oyster for me. Any time I would find a pearl; somebody came and snatched it away. I'm alone in a world with nothing to call my own, except my pain. That's mine. I own it lock, stock, and barrel. The last time I wrote a letter to you things was different. I gave you my blessings on finding love in a loveless place, and I told you about my girl. It was a happier time, not much more but happier anyway. Grandmama was alive then. I also told you about our relationship. Well, you would be glad to know that we made peace before she died; I never told you that in the phone conversations we had after she died. I know you was too sad to even think about that, but it's okay. Andrea is really leaving this time. We said, or at least didn't say, our last goodbyes, but said them without saying them. It was hard to see her go. Uncle Roosevelt and Sally probably gonna be getting married soon. They got real close lately. I am happy for them. Ms. Sally got a promotion at her job, and they see each other when they can. She is thinking about renting out her house to move in here with us. I think that'll be good for Unc. Miss Sophie left town to go visit with her sister in Texas. She couldn't take all the stuff that's been going on here. I won't miss her. I thought that nothing could top my broken heart until earlier today. I know you know what I'm gonna say. How could you, mama? How could you lie to your little boy all those years ago? I wanted a daddy so badly, and you told me he was no good and didn't deserve a sweet son like me. You also told me he was a high school boyfriend who moved away after graduation, and you never heard from him again. I lived that lie. I live your lie mama. All I had was you and your word. I lived and breathed by your word. I ain't have no reason to believe that you lied. You always did what you said and said what you meant. You were the only person in the world that I could trust. For fifteen years, I told myself I didn't need no daddy because I was special without one. I learned how to be a man from you, TV, and Miss Sally. Since you ain't gonna never read this letter, it don't matter how Sally taught me, but I'm guessing you could figure that out. Mama your little boy is broken. Billy Ray Bonds came into my life at a rotten time. With your help, he shattered the few things in my life that was okay. Now, ain't nothing okay. Even my relationship with Uncle Roosevelt is different. Mama, the girl that I was telling you about in the letter is Billy Ray's daughter, so if he is my daddy, then she is my sister. I made love to her, so you got to see how messed up this is. Mama, you caused this. It's your fault. I have to be real with you as much as it would hurt you if you read this; I got to get this out. You are the reason my whole world is spinning out of control. I don't have anything to grab ahold of. It's like being in a speeding car driving with no brakes; I can't stop until I crash. Mama, I'm crashing, and I ain't got on no seat belt and I have no airbags. I just wish you have told me the truth about Billy Ray, and, right now, I wouldn't be losing what little mind I got left. I remember when I was ten, and I told you that I wished you would get married so that I could have a daddy, and you told me that that was never gonna happen, because you would always be my *mama* and *daddy*. I laughed, but I took pride in that because to me that meant you would love me as much as two people could. I felt secure that that was the case because my daddy was a loser. Now, I find out that you deceived him and me. Him I can understand, but I can't find a bone in my body to understand why me. What did I do so wrong to deserve being lied to? I was always a good son through the drugs, the drinking, the boyfriends, and the jail time. I stood by you through it all, and all I wanted was to be loved and not to be lied to. I don't think that was too much to ask from your mama. But I don't hate you, but I'm very disappointed, because I thought the bond we had was tighter. Now, I see that I was a fatality of the wreck that is your life. I am sorry if that hurt, but I am hurting, too. I'm alone and scared, and all I want is a hug and kiss and the truth from my mama, not some man who missed fifteen years of my life. I hope I can make it out of this storm because right now I don't see any help in sight.

Love Always

Malachi

Chapter 25

Trouble in Mind

I woke up to a new day. Although I felt a little bit better after drafting that letter to my mother, Andrea was on my mind heavily. I wanted to see her. I wanted to talk to her. I just wanted to be able to know that she was okay. However, I knew she couldn't be okay. I knew Billy Ray had to have already informed her. I knew that the way that we felt about one another would not be easy for her to be able to lock away just as it had not been easy for me. Still, I wanted to know how she was coping. She was tough but on the inside she was brittle.

As I lay in bed, I wondered now that my life had been shaken up once again, if I would I be able to get it back on track somehow. The assurance I needed did not come quickly enough. This faith of which Uncle Roosevelt had spoken was seemingly not my ally. There weren't any mustard seeds in my garden. I lay there looking up at the ceiling as I had done so many times before, longing for that place beyond the clouds, I once childishly called it Malachandrea, for I wanted to dwell there with Andrea where we would be at ease. That wasn't going to be possible, because the girl I wanted to whisk away to an enchanted land was my sister. There had to be change of plans; I was going to have to fly solo. There had to be a place for a boy like me who was *basically* good, gentle-natured, streetwise, compassionate, and lovable. My Achilles heel had been that I was a magnet for strife. It was this magnet that kept drawing me closer to the edge, but something kept me from jumping off that cliff into an even more hellacious abyss. I just hadn't ascertained what that I had been.

Somehow, I rallied the strength to shower and dress myself. My appetite was nonexistent, so I mostly drank water. Uncle Roosevelt felt dearly for me. Even he didn't have the words to help me feel better, but I remembered that he had told me, "Sometimes silence is good for you. Words can't always express what you feel in yo' soul." Not a truer word had ever been spoken.
I moped about, wishing for a speedy recovery, but I knew that was like wishing for icicles in an oven; it was never going to happen. As I walked through the house, I noticed that Unc was gone. He hadn't fixed any breakfast or left a note. It had been unpromisingly odd, but I also knew that he was seriously making resolute efforts to complete the renovations on our house. Therefore, I assumed that he had gone out to the hardware store or lumberyard for more supplies and had been unintentionally negligent in informing me.

I went outside and stood on front porch. I looked out over the vastness of the Delta. The greenest of grass lay before me and its virility astounded me as the wind tickled the blades. I saw trees full of branches that seemed to paint the skies bluer than any sea in which I would ever swim. Animals scavenged about unafraid, because the Delta was their home and its inhabitants were their brethren. It was in that moment that I came to the realization that I was unsuited, and because I was unsuited, I couldn't be pollinated and germinated like the roses of the Delta; however, I knew their thorns would forever prick me. I was that fish out of water. I couldn't breathe in this awkwardly beautiful landscaped region where simple was too much and too much was simply overbearing. There was no medium. No balance. I had been thrust into this lush expanse without the proper tools of survival. Being born here was plainly insufficient to maintain a sustainable existence.

I looked to the east, and in the distance I saw Unc driving up. He seemed to be driving unusually slowly. The closer he drew, the more menacing my thoughts became.

Once he pulled into the driveway, he sat in the car a while before he vacated it. This did not bode well for me at all. My head filled with uncomfortable thoughts and butterflies filled my stomach, and Unc exited the car and unto the porch. He grabbed me by my back and led me into the house without saying a word.
"Sit down, son," he directed.
"Why Unc? I think I'll keep standin'," I countered.
"Malachi, please sit down!" Unc pleaded with me.
"Unc, just tell me what it is," I begged.
"Malachi, ain't no easy way say this," he continued.
"Just say it," I commanded.
"Billy Ray woke up this morning to find Andrea dead."
"What?" I exclaimed.
"Malachi, please sit down," Uncle Roosevelt pleaded.
"What hap…," I began, but grief overtook me, and I began sobbing wildly.
"She overdosed on some pills that belonged to her grandmamma," he explained.
"No!" I screamed.
"She couldn't take it when Billy Ray told her that you were his son. It was way too much for her," Unc clarified.

I hit the floor beating it and cursing it. I took out every frustration on the newly laid hardwood floors. My hands became raw. Unc tried to pry me away from the floor, but he gave up when he realized that there was no use. He had known that I had had all that I could take. He just rubbed my back as I cursed my life and my existence, as it was the very reason Andrea had taken her own life.

"Unc, I didn't do nothin' to deserve this," I bawled.
"I know, son," he comforted me.
"I am a good person, and this *GOD* y'all keep telling me to have faith in can't exist. If he do, he got it out for me. I am tired of fightin' Unc. This world don't want me, and I don't want it! Your God can have it!" I lambasted.
"Malachi, don't talk like that. With life, comes tests and trials. I must admit you done had yo' share, but don't git to talkin' crazy now. You can beat this just like you done beat

the rest of the hell you been through. I didn't get to be this old by being stupid, so I know a thang or two. You tell that devil that's ridin' yo back to get behind you. You be patient hear? God ain't through wit' you yet!" Uncle Roosevelt professed.

"That's fine 'cause I am through with him. You can keep yo' *God*. He took my mama, he never gave me a daddy, he took Grandmama, he took Ms. Jane and Jessie, and now Andrea. I guess you want me to wait around until he take me and you huh?" I asked.

"Son, we all got to leave this here earth one day," Unc reminded.

"Well, why in the hell did he bring us here?" I questioned.

"Some thangs jus' is Malachi and you ain't supposed to question 'em. Like I told you befo' God is mighty. Can't fight his against his might," he cautioned.

"Can't fight against somethin' I don't believe in! I just don't want nothing and nobody messin' wit' me," I said in opposition.

"He ain't messin' wit' you son, jus' testin' you. If you jus' hold on, you can pass this test just like you been doin'. Don't give up. Keep goin'," he said.

"I ain't got nothin' left. I can hardly breathe," I lamented.

All of a sudden, the room grew so silent that we could hear the house settling. Unc's face was so full of grief; he aged right before my eyes. He tried as hard as he could to quell my feelings of self-deprecation and denunciation for his God. Unc knew that there was nothing more that he could say to make me see things his way. He sighed helplessly trying to look as supportive as he could. While I appreciated his support, it just wasn't enough.

Ms. Jane's dirge had long pursued me. It found and subjugated me. I had been ensnared in its moroseness. There was no escape. I was being dragged along the endless measures of low solemn notes in common time signature. Their reverberation left me desolately bereft, as did Andrea's death. The dual death had a difficult dichotomy: I grieved for my girl, and I had sorrow for my sister. A cowbell occupied my head. It kept ringing in my ears played only by the air that had remained in my body. My ears were the only appendages, which had any function, everything else had shut down. The emptiness fueled my loneliness. The loneliness resurrected my lowliness. I was hopeless. All of the optimism had opted out as all positivity potted and posited itself nowhere. *The story of my life.*

Chapter 26

No One's Safe

The cornfield. It was where I went to hold hands with the universe. It was my sanctuary in the guilelessness of the Mississippi Delta. I would walk out of our back door. My bare feet glided over the dirt and through the temperate grass to dwell in the middle of its awesome wonder. The tall fading corn stalks swaddled me in a comfort like a manger. When the wind would whip through and find me hulled up, it spoke to me in foreign languages, but somehow I understood, for when the universe is involved, comprehension is boundless. Sitting on the ground in the majesty of nature was like sleeping in the clouds. Therefore, I sat there as often as I could in order to feel some semblance of comfort of which my world had been barren.

No one had ever known of my safe haven, with the exception of my grandmother and Andrea, as I knew it would be incomprehensible to the average person. Even at the tender age of twelve, I was wise enough to know that some secrets are best kept and kept in solitude. If I'd ever had any friends, I wouldn't have disclosed it to them, because friends were dispensable. They were just a means to eventual disappointment. Once hope, faith, and trust were put into people, human condition and human fallibility ultimately proved more powerful. When it's all said and done, friends amount to invitations to funerals, both proper and proverbial. It certainly wasn't my wish to be clad in black around a gathering of sobbing, remorseful people and I didn't want it after my own demise. This discernment was the reason that I maintained my refuge as long as the farmers neglected their jobs.

The cornfield was my safe space in the midst of turmoil, hurt, and confusion of which the Mississippi Delta was comprised. It was my calm in the eye of the storm that was my life. I was unchartered island. My soul was a peninsula that bathed in the waters that had cooled the bodies of slaves and quenched the thirst of slave babies. There was a distinct musicality that existed here. The sky was the blank paper on which many scores were written. The stratus clouds were the notes that filled the measures, and the heartbeat of the flat rolling land provided the rhythm with which the birds used to croon and coax the worms out of the dry ground. The subtle breezes were reminiscent of the timbre of a finely tuned viola. It brought with it a warm coolness that caused my eyes to tear up as the blades of the stalks danced wildly in what appeared to be choreographed sequences. The hum of the bees served up a perfect pitch that made my eyes water, because its beauty was too much to contain. The bark of the old Labrador retriever in the distance was an unknowing metronome by which time was kept. There was a virtual, perpetual symphony orchestra around me. I loved this kind of music far more than I loved food, water, or even breath. In many ways it was more nutritious than grains and more sustaining than air itself. It always made me cry, and methodically I wiped away the residual tears that dampened my shirt. Then I would clap uncontrollably and give a standing ovation to what only I seemed to know subsisted here in this wasteland, this my harbor of happiness, my microcosm of paradise.

I knew that this was the closest thing on earth that I'd get to that universe beyond the clouds. When I was there, I knew peace. I knew perfection. I knew passion. The cracks in the ground that I sat upon grew deeper and deeper since the rains were usually few and far between by midsummer. But I deduced that the cracks did not crave water, because after a rain, even the cracks knew that they would thirst again.

I knew life was no chance encounter. Just as sure as the seasons changed like clockwork, the universe remained the same opening itself up to reveal its offerings to every creature and creation. Hidden away in my lush retreat, I basked in the corn's freshness as I perspired in the Delta's oppressive temperatures. All around me, life was taking place, but I wanted nothing to do with the anything or anyone outside. I did not want to be contaminated by the toxicity of the dark spirits that dwelled inside the souls of the people. I'd rather have grasshoppers leap over my lap and dragonflies murmur in my ear, for those nuisances made for much better company than the confused individuals that traipsed the Mississippi Delta landscape seeking the next best thing since a slice of light bread. Drinking their syrupy sweet tea and smacking on their Doublemint gum both of which the sugar ate away at their tooth enamel as well as destroyed their kidneys. Smoking their Kool Filter King cigarettes and homegrown reefer filling their lungs with tar and formaldehyde, they walked about either ignorant or indifferent to nicotine's carcinogenesis.

I became content to let their problems be theirs as long as my place of safety was mine. It was the quintessential balance of things as I had come to know it, so I lived detached from the Delta dwellers while I was in my own space. Mainly because I knew the freshness of waters from which they would *never* sip. I knew skies bluer than blue. I experienced an existence that I never could imagine outside of the cornfield. Being there in the middle of *their* nowhere and in the pleasure of *my* somewhere gave me a slight sense of conceit, but I still knew I could never escape the life of degradation and eternal damnation I'd come to know. However, it was there that I tried to press forward and to leave things behind me in the past. Each day as the sunset and the mosquitoes busied about to draw my blood without anything as technical as a tourniquet, I dreaded to depart from the solace that this place once brought, but I had to relinquish my grip on it and its grip on me.

Walking away, I marveled at the violets, oranges, and azures that painted the neck of the sky. I could literally see the footprints left by the sun as it exited to prepare the Earth for the shift from light to darkness. It was breathtaking. So much so, tears fell, as I understood that this time when I left the cornfield I was crying because I knew I would never return. I no longer felt safe. I had flown on the wings of what little strength I had for far too long. There was nothing left. I walked gingerly back to the house, a bird shitted on me as I meandered through. Life continued to fuck with me and the universe seemed to assist. My jitters felt like mini earthquakes rumbling inside me. The sun laughed at me. The closer I got to the door, my soul's colors started to change from a purple to deep mahogany. The sun's laugher melted my face into sadness and an ominous wind began to whistle through the green thicket and followed me inside house where no one loved, lived, or survived.

Inside, I was uneasy. My world has been rocked like an ark on treacherous waters brought about by a flood. There had been no way to prepare myself for life's entire arsenal of mass devastation. As I lay my eyes upon the site that was once my escape from worldly nothingness and my means to spiritual fullness, all I saw was a cornfield. No soundtrack remained.

Chapter 27

Payday

I lost the will to eat…to taste food. To be nourished. Deserting the cornfield made me conclude to no appetite would henceforth be my lot in life. I refused to talk to Uncle Roosevelt, because as bad as I should have felt mistreating him, his feelings were of no consequence to me. Nights passed, but my eyes never closed. With each blink, a tear fell. I lay awake wanting to disappear, wanting to float out of my mind, out of my body, out of this world, out of this life. Nothing could tear my thoughts away from Andrea, even though she was gone. The walls began to close in on me, so I decided to get out of the house. Still clad in my previous day's attire, I left the house unkempt. Vagabond was too much of a euphemism. Piss and sweaty funk smells arose from my pubic area. Armpits smelled of rotten onions and my breath reeked of bile; I cared not. Good hygiene was not a prerequisite for those of us who have lost. Roosevelt had given up on begging me to shower. So had I.

I trod the road that led to that abandoned marina off of the levee of Lake Quinn where Andrea and I had swum so clumsily, yet gracefully. As I neared the rickety deck, I smelled death. Fish. Birds. Dogs. Etc. Eerily, I was not affected. I was quite calm and at ease in the midst of all of the extinction. I walked to the end of the fishing wharf as if I were easily an Olympic diver. I sat down and intently stared out over the still brown water and watched the sun illuminate its deep murkiness. I frowned at its attempt to blind me.

I looked over the waters and through grasses and noticed the dirt. I hoped for answers to all of the questions that had gone unanswered within me. If I could just make sense of things, maybe I could regain an ounce of clear-headedness. I yearned for some kind of intervention that would assist me in salvaging this senseless life of mine. I sat there wishing for the peace that I had only known scarcely, but I found none. My head was unable to rationalize, and my heart couldn't find comfort. The clouds about my head stirred around, aloofly playing hide and seek as the sun prepared to make its departure. The lavender kissed auburn horizon was a beauteous sight, but in my haze, it had gone unnoticed, although the warmth of the colors did remind me of Andrea...my girl Andrea, not my sister Andrea. I was in love with the former; I had never met the latter, and that made me feel damaged. Spoiled. Ruined.

Before I knew it, the dark night sky was hovering above me like a bumblebee. The stars twinkled like tiny candles in the distance. Mosquitoes swarmed around me in aggressive attempts to draw my blood. They clearly had no respect of persons, for if they did my tainted veins would not have made their short list. Needless to say, I bothered not to swat them away, as I had neither the energy nor the will to do so. Eventually, I became innocuously oblivious to the pinch of the bites. I listened as the orchestra of crickets, which played an all too familiar refrain that deepened my depression, as it reminded me of my displacement. It was at that moment that I no longer cared to know the *whys*. I no longer cared to know how I could rebound. I just wanted to live free of all the pain and hurt. Looking out over the gloomy waters, the lake seemed to beckon for me. *To call my name. To need my physicality*. Even though I wasn't a trained swimmer, I could hold my own, so I stood up on the deck and I leapt into the muddy lake fully clothed.

Surprisingly, I was moving about naturally in the polluted water. I swam so well that a smile almost adorned my face. But agony wouldn't allow my lips to spread and reveal my teeth. It blocked the smile, and my despair continued to run much deeper than the water in which I swam. After swimming for so long, I had become tired. It was a weariness that I had never felt before. It was far worse than not wanting to get up for school after only an hour or two of sleep. I didn't know how to assess this sudden feeling; I just knew that I wanted to alleviate this tired feeling that was obviously overwhelmed me. I declined a natural inclination to tread water as I felt myself getting heavier and heavier. I closed my eyes as I sank. I held my breath. The warmth of the water felt like being inside Sally the day she had stolen my innocence or when I fucked her. Who was at fault? She for gaping open her mouth and letting me ejaculate in it or I for allowing myself to come inside of a full-grown woman? What a thing to think about at this moment. It was too late to make sense of nonsense at a time like this.

Their God would forgive Sally. She was a believer, but there was no absolution for me. I accepted that right then and there, so I set Sally free, not that I had that power, but because I knew she'd be fine. Right there under a crescent moon and a sky full of stars, I fell asleep in the lake that was walking distance from what was supposed to be my home. Water easily filled my lungs as if they were two pails. I didn't fight the liquid. I let it run its course. I had given it the permission it required, to do whatever it willed. My oasis had become my grave as watery as broth, but with much more flavor. As I drank my last mouthful, my soul floated out of my body.

Even in death my Delta blues continued. There was no heaven or hell. No angels. No devil. No long white robe. No pitchforks. All of the things I'd been told about dying were fictitious. The bible lied. The preacher fibbed. The church prevaricated.

If only I could be the messenger to spread the gospel that there was no line in which to stand and await judgment. *That there was no God and no Satan was waiting either.* Death was not a destination vacation. It was just a stop, like a period that ends a sentence. No, it was more definitive than that. An exclamation point! There was just a fleeting, soulless voice with nothing to which to

cling. So all of the tithes paid and offering given could have saved you from foreclosure, repossession, or disconnection. Jesus is not the savior. He wasn't born in a manger in Bethlehem and hadn't died on a cross for sins. I had travelled from Detroit to Sidon to nowhere and there was no Jesus to usher me in either transition. He had been painted into our lives by conspirators to brainwash us, no whitewash into believing in the necessity of deities.
As my soul dissipates, my body still lay in the depths of waters with my eyes open and my orifices filled, alone in death much like I had been in life even when people were around. The music didn't stop. And trying to escape it only made my bass line stronger and deeper. The lyrics remained the same and only the melody had changed. Finally, my guitar was broken, and I had no wordly attachment or accompaniment. Just…

Souls Collide

In this passage from life to death, I didn't see what I had been promised. Land of milk and honey. Crowns and mansions. Just darkness. Loneliness. Emptiness. No Andrea. My reality was in a sarcophagus. And my sarcophagus was like a pressure cooker quickly preparing me as worm's meat. I was to be given back to the Earth from which I came, from which I was derived. There was no fanfare. Where's that Heaven everyone promised me? Fuck that! Where was Hell? Weren't they my either/or? My coordinating conjunctions… Death was more disappointing than life, especially since I'd known it so many times. It was like welcoming a bully to your home when no one was there to protect you. Perpetual punishment. It no longer mattered, but death didn't halt my grief. My bereavement. I grieved for Andrea. How did I get sweet sister and a tender lover, as a prepackaged deal? Disturbing… Rules applied. Because the rules worked against us, our fate was sealed, like the fictitious Jesus Christ licked the seal himself. My Andrea was gone and all because she met me, her brother. The taker of her virginity... What a burdensome load to bear knowing you had a soul mate that is also your kinsman. For me it was heavy, but I had built up muscle to withstand the weight. Andrea was way too fragile. Her immune system had been compromised by the wicked Delta and for that reason; she perished in its enormity and its treachery. She was yet another innocent slaughtered for her humanity like a pig for its bacon. Inhumanely. No empathetically. I couldn't go on living knowing that I was the cause and cure of her pathology. I had to stop breathing the freshness of the Mississippi air that had enslaved me with its stale dogma and invisibility and false sense of security. It snatched the one truly good thing I ever had the pleasure to know. Andrea. My love. Not my sister. But…my only reason for living…

THE END

The White Privilege Club

A NOVEL BY

abidemi omowale kayode

9 minutes

The feverishly barefoot woman gulped the aged scotch like sweet tea as tiny sweat droplets beaded across her brow. She threw her head back and the liquor washed over her pickled tongue and crashed the back of her throat like oil on cylinder walls. She sought hope in the bottom of the bottle. Then brought her head down chin level with the bottom of the framed obligatory family portrait behind her. Squinting, her lips were a thin line. The woman extended her reach to set the glass on the counter. She made no sound. She stood stoic and contemplative. What would she do next? She wiped her mouth with the sleeve of her nightgown like a man ready for a bar room fight, she took one long toke on the cigarette. As it crackled from the pull, the ash precariously clung to the end of wishing for the same unfound hope. The woman never blinked. She stared illogically in one direction. In a daze, the she stubbed the cigarette out on the table. The shellac sizzled like bacon on the oaken antique. The act was remarkably iniquitous given that the woman had inherited the coveted piece from her great grandmother. It had been in her family

and its finish had been uninterrupted for decades. The table was like one of her children only she may have treated the table a trifle better, up until now at least. Smoke wafted from the table. She respired smoke through her nostrils and then she balled up her fists.

Engineers couldn't have constructed buildings as formidable as the rage that had built up inside of her. Her eyes, like cherry tomatoes, met the back of the oblivious woman in the kitchen. The more she surveyed her, the more steam rose from her shoulders, neck, and hair enshrouding her in a haze of hatred. Boiling water dribbled onto the stove as she narrowed in on her housekeeper.

The housekeeper stood in front of the stove. Per usual, she maneuvered around the kitchen that wasn't hers rather rigorously and rhythmically. Innocently and obliviously, she removed spaghetti from the box breaking the handfuls of spaghetti pasta into the pot. It was one of the housekeeper's habits that the woman loathed. It was incomprehensible as to why her housekeeper insisted on breaking the spaghetti in half before immersing it. This infuriated the woman to no end, but she'd endured it for years. This day would be profoundly different.

The woman glanced furtively at the clock, noticed the time, but cursorily returned her eyes to the housekeeper's back silhouette. She walked toward the housekeeper planting her feet unobtrusively into the hardwood floors as her enmity bloomed even more for the housekeeper.

As she approached her, the irate woman instinctively extended the reach of her arm, opened her fists, and snatched the housekeeper's hair. Then she pushed her head into the erupting, hot water, which contained the pasta. The housekeeper dropped the pasta box spilling the remainder of the raw spaghetti onto the wooden floor. With flailing arms, she rearranged the items on the stove. The housekeeper hastily pushed the pot off the burning ire so as to decrease the impending damage to her face. She gasped for air and on a dime turned around and met the gaze of her attacker. Her eyes bulged when she realized it was her employer. Alarmed, the housekeeper noted that the enraged woman's face was as red as a beet. Before the housekeeper could form let alone utter words, the woman seized the housekeeper by the neck and drove her head into the cabinet above the kitchen counter. Her head was met with a crackle from the wood as the housekeeper frantically tried to loosen the woman's grip. The housekeeper did a quick twist and managed to catch one good wind. She disengaged herself from her employer barely but successfully. Grabbing the back of her throbbing head, the housekeeper doubled over in agony, but the woman charged at her again.

She yanked the housekeeper by her garments and flung her into the refrigerator door. Upon bone to metal contact, the housekeeper plummeted to the floor face first. Just as her fleshy body slapped the ground, the woman jumped on her back and began to pummel the housekeeper with her fists repeatedly. The housekeeper protected her face with her hands and considered her next move. She begged the woman to stop through muffled pleas, but the woman was relentless and the housekeeper had to think swiftly in order to save herself. Through her fingers she spied the bar stool near, so hastily and in one quick-thinking move, the housekeeper grabbed the stool by a leg and managed to pull it on top of the woman. The wood seat of the stool cracked the woman in the crown of her head allowing the housekeeper to free and to upright herself. She attempted an escape, but the dazed woman saw clearly enough to grab her by the ankle. The housekeeper stumbled, but kicked loose. The agile woman erected herself, grabbed a knife and charged at the housekeeper with her forearm sandwiching her body between her and the wall by the refrigerator.

She pressed hard against the housekeeper's throat. The housekeeper grimaced and winced in pain. She tried to plead for her life.

"Please let me go!"

"Shut the fuck up or I will slit your goddamn throat!"

"Why are you doing this?", the housekeeper said in duress.

"I haven't done shit yet," the scarlet-faced woman said between her teeth.

"Please...", the housekeeper begged.

"Didn't I say shut the fuck up, bitch," she blasted.

"Okay...okay", she muttered.

"Are you fucking my husband?"

"No", the housekeeper replied.

"Don't lie to me or I will cut you six ways to Sunday. So you better make a wise choice," the woman admonished.

"I'm not lying," the housekeeper said as the woman put more pressure on her neck."

"Are you going to stand here and tell a bold faced lie even when there is a knife in my hand and I can gut you like a fish?" She said as she brandished the knife across the housekeeper's face.

"I'm not lying," she whimpered as she tried to pant for air.

"Then I guess I will have to slit your throat," the woman concluded.

"I would never. You know me." she implored.

"I thought I knew you. I thought you were my friend, not just the woman who cooked and cleaned up this goddamned house. But to find out that you've been fucking my husband is a total betrayal of trust. I know he has had a few whores, but to know you are one of them," she paused.

"No ma'am", she began.

"Don't no ma'am me. All these years in my house, right under my nose, and probably in my bed. You and him! The dishonesty, the disloyalty," she lamented.

"I promise," the housekeeper beseeched.

"Your promises mean nothing. Stand here right now and tell me that my husband isn't your daughter's father," she scolded.

"Oh my God, it's not what you think," the woman supplicated.

"Not what I think? So it's true?" she inquired.

"Yes, but..." the housekeeper responded as the incensed woman lowered the knife and stuck it into the housekeeper's flesh and pushed it up.

"Ain't no buts, bitch!" the woman stated as she drove the knife into her housekeeper over and over.

Blood rushed from her abdomen like mini geysers, but the fuming woman kept poking the housekeeper like a pincushion. The stabs were intimate. She penetrated her in a sadistically sexual manner in extremely close proximity to the housekeeper's vagina. The woman kept stabbing her until her housekeeper coughed up blood over her shoulder. Finally, the housekeeper collapsed. The woman yanked out the knife and held it in her hand. She wheezed. She tried to stabilize her breath as blood pooled in middle of the kitchen underneath the weight of the housekeeper. Then suddenly there she was standing in deafening silence, grueling regret, and a puddle of blood.

It was the calm after the storm. The woman was dazed and confused, but she felt vindicated. She felt emboldened. She had taken back her power. Stoically blank faced, the woman traipsed across the wet, messy floor leaving bloody footprints. Soaked in blood, she pulled the wooden chair from underneath the table. She plopped into the chair still wielding the knife. She then placed the weapon on the table near the stubbed cigarette butt. The woman reached under the table where she kept a stash of Marlboro Lights and matches. With bloodstained fingers but steady hands, she tapped the top of the box three times onto her left wrist.

After she lifted the top on the box and pulled out one. She tossed the sullied box onto the table. She dangled the cigarette from her dry, ashen lips. After she slid open the matchbox, she drew one match. Against the side of the box she struck the red head of the match and a flame materialized. The woman cocked her head to the left and lit her cigarette and tossed her damp hair to the right. She took a long toke and filled her lungs with smoke. Then she lobbed the matchbox to the table. She breathed in and sighed. The smoke relaxed her. It sent orgasmic spasms down her spine as she scissored her forefinger and middle finger together to extract the cigarette from her mouth. The woman held the cigarette five inches to the right of her face. With her left hand she clutched the recess of her inner right elbow and then she released more smoke through both her nostrils. Through her nose, her demons had been exorcised. She released her guilt into the universe as she emancipated the balance of the smoke through her thin lips. Smoke filled the emptiness of the room.

Though her mind raced, her body was stationary and tranquil. Her existence was static but her emotions were dynamic. In an instant, she became unbothered. The murderous woman took another leisurely drag of the stick of tobacco as her eyes squinted narrowly upon intake of the smoke. Her eyes like freshly glazed donuts fixated on the clock again. She'd thought that she had been engaged in battle with her housekeeper for an infinite amount of time. Just how long had it taken to slay the dragon? It seemed like a lifetime, but in actuality, it had only taken moments to mercilessly stab and to murder. *To commit homicide*. 9 minutes. The clock now read 2:58, just one hour before school ended. She realized she had to think fast.

Chapter One

Heart of the Delta

Living here was like singing in a United Methodist Church choir. Bland, meaningless words of hymns sung from an ancient hymnal that only ministered to the souls of the woefully insipid, exceedingly superficial, and the progressively unenlightened. Monotonous songs, which had neither a melody nor a rhythm, and they made no sense in the way that things were *supposed* to make sense. Sense had no purpose and purpose just made no sense. If any of that makes sense. The people were like scattered notes on the measures of scores written by people who possessed neither musical ability nor classical training. Musicality, be damned.

The town of Greenville, Mississippi was no more than a spatter of ink on a map, a chunky, haphazard shape among other awkward, arbitrary shapes. Its existence equates to a working prostitute in a convent. Obstreperous. While Greenville is the home of many notables and such, none of them compare to the *broads who brunch. The ladies who lunch. The dames who dine on their husbands' dimes.*

Yes, this coalition of conservative housewives who had been bequeathed certain immoderation by birthright or by matrimony, had nothing but *time* on their hands. They were known to sip spiked juices in the mornings, mint juleps in the afternoons, vodka tonics in the evenings and neat Scotches for nightcaps. While their livers pickled in the ferment of alcohol, they planned capricious church functions, fundraisers, charity balls, cotillions, pageants, and fashion shows. These ladies existed; rather, they exist and are no figment of the collective imagination, though they are not much more peculiar than what the mind could imagine, as they were relics of antiquity still perpetuating their relevance in modernity. However, they are as real as it gets. *Women as tough as concrete and as concrete as gargoyles. Matriarchs of the status quo*.

They propagate a reality for which the faint of heart has neither the penchant nor the appreciation. These ladies have a long legacy in the heart of the Delta. Quiet as it's kept, one might argue that this group of women, in fact, is the *heart of the Delta*, because the very heartbeat of the town started within their wombs. Simply having the ability to be impregnated and birth a certain refinement and *culture* into the universe made them particularly unique and an unequivocal force of nature.

Without them, their spouses may have been important, but with them, their spouses were *impotent*. They are the kind of women that have been married so long that sex was as indistinguishable as spring cleaning or paying bills or running errands. Fucking their husbands had the tendency to become a once a year, tedious, time-consuming occurrence. And because of the imminent infrequency of sexual relations, it is customary for the wife to sanction her Delta husband a concubine or two as long as he neither flaunted it for her or the world to take notice, though that wasn't fool-proof, nor could he bring home some sexually transmitted disease or better yet some bastard child looking for his cut of a possible inheritance. Some of the unspoken rules of which these housewives set almost as frequently as those dainty little timepieces that adorned their delicate wrists.

Oh goodness...the Delta. Rolling, flat alluvial plains that stretch just north of Jackson, Mississippi and just shy of Memphis, Tennessee, scenery so unconventionally picturesque that only a Southerner, a true Southerner that is, could value and comprehend enough to describe. Depending on the seasons one could picture...

Withering fields of crops.

Towering branchless trees.

Inconsequential flocks of grackle.

Freshly tilled soil.

Rusty bridges.

Kudzu.

The Delta's terrestrial expanse is known for its fertile soil. The ground is storied to be much more generative than its abovementioned women. The soil is said to have soaked up more *black blood* than hospital gauze and because of that Negro hemoglobin, "shit" just grows better in Delta. *Cotton. Soybeans. Corn.* The men in the Delta farmed that sanguineous soil, not just any men though. There were the traditional, big corn-fed ex Ole Miss or Mississippi State football players or frat boy *trust fund babies*. The ones who would never make it into professional sports, but were sufficient enough in college to make *mommy* and *daddy* proud enough to drive to Oxford or Starkville or to wherever the away games whisked them off.

These are the chickens who'd come home to roost after they'd received their "B.S." degrees with their wives who had opted for "M.R.S." licenses versus M.A.'s, M.S.'s, or M.B.A.'s. It was no secret that some women only went to college to literally find a Tom, *Dick*, or Harry with which to join in *holy* matrimony, forsaking all education thereafter. These were the kinds of girls who wore stylish headbands to match their outfits from Cato and tortoise-rimmed glasses to feign intellect. They wore their dresses and skirts just short enough to garner the attention of men but to leave something to the imagination for those who sat in judgment. There were girls with names like Mary Lou, or Betty Sue, or some cute nickname like Bitsy or Kitty. To the unassuming eye, she was the sweet and innocent, but she was definitely cutthroat enough to obtain the man for whom she pined and she would stop short of *nothing* to wed and keep him. These girls had been wired from birth, reared if you will in the ways of predation. They were not outwardly savage, just elegantly so. The Phi Delta Thetas, Sig Eps, and SAE's were the most sought-after, prime prey, the crème de la crème, so these ladies be damned if they were to come up empty handed. That wasn't how their mothers or their mothers' mothers had coached them. The early bird *always* got the worm but if she were to awaken a tad bit earlier, she could get the *snake*.

It was quite the common thing to see debutantes turned wives of the former frat boys affect just as much importance, correction: more importance than their husbands specifically if they'd born more than two children. To these women, they had earned the right to share the spotlight because having children made them gain weight, and sometimes more pounds than they had been as a young Delta Gammas, Tri Delts, or Chi O's. Weight was not an inconsequential matter, because they would so often reminisce on their more eclipsing, *skinny* days, some even battling bulimia or anorexia, while still having rousing discourse about frivolous things like the celebrated Fall Rush, petty Pancake Breakfasts, and humdrum Sorority/Fraternity mixers.

They'd habitually talk about their illimitable contention with how the likes of Millie Sue Haughton even became eligible to apply to a sorority let alone rush one. Decades later these women still assert that she was "only" permitted to *entrance* into Tri Delta because her boyfriend Jim Stovall's mother worked in the Dean of Students' office. Otherwise there was no way, barring an act of Congress, that the sorority would have accepted a bucktooth dilettante with no connection to Ole Miss prior to her enrollment. Or how Judy Walker secretly dated best friends, Howard McWhorter and George Thomas, but she chose George because he had been accepted into Ole Miss Law school, and Howard *only* gained conditional admission into Millsaps College's MBA program. Their pettiness was as reserved as their unremitting memories of yesteryear. They longed for do-overs and repurposed shots at youth of which they knew they would never be granted. No genies would come to their rescue. Unrequited hopes didn't bother or hinder these women.

These Delta dwelling women were blue-blooded, purebred socialites who possessed the refined lineage to prove their necessity in any community they were implanted. They didn't have to prove themselves to people, as a matter of fact; one might aver that people had to prove *themselves* to these women.

They are like Chihuahuas to their men and children all bark no bite as husbands were dispensable and children were means to an end. They are like German Shepherds guarding against their personal images, because image was everything and they'd guard theirs with their lives. They are like Pit Bulls regarding their money; they would just as soon as sink their canines into any violator and commence to mince them to shreds. Like this breed of dogs, these ladies have a prodigious sense of gameness, agility, strength, level of intelligence, trainability, and obedience. However, when it comes to their parents and in-laws they were Labrador Retrievers, there was no limit to the lengths they'd go to be loved and petted for being *good* girls. Like Retrievers, these women were nimble, great *runners*, and immensely loyal to the bloodline of the family.

Odd darlings, they are. Spindly little things like Wilma Flintstone, medium sized like Marilyn Monroe, or even a little corpulent much like an aging Liz Taylor, they all clamor for attention. And if there were awards for their performances in life, these opportunistic ingénues would spare neither expense nor dignity to outdo the next matron all for the *accolades*.

Only a keenly discerning eye could detect a true *bitch*. The word bitch had no pejorative existence in the Delta, in fact it had been transformed into a term for intimidating respect. These women wore the label like a pageant sash. It was a point of pride to be called a bitch, because not many real *bitches* existed in Greenville. Amidst the sophisticates, there was a bevy of actresses who could at best contrive the attributes of a *bitch* rather than be true thoroughbred *bitches*. Among the throngs of civic organizations of which to belong like the Revolutionary Daughters, Junior Auxiliary, Arts Council, and the Serenity Lodge for Women, there were two *real* bitches in Greenville, Jean-Marie Percy-Tiller and Lucretia Ann Unger-Simmons.

When Jean-Marie was young growing up in Greenwood, her name was pronounced *Jean* like the clothing garment *jeans.* As she matriculated into the upper middle class, she fancied being called "John-Marie". Though she spoke no other language than her Southern dialectical English, she'd always say "It's John-Marie, like the French. Jean-Marie came from a long line of nutcrackers, so *bitchiness* was the second chain of her DNA, and even though it was fused intricately with hydrogen bonds like everyone else's physiological make up, one might deduce that some deficiencies existed somewhere, maybe in the *cytosine* or *guanine*.

Lucretia Ann was raised to be a bitch; she knew it from the tender age of three when she was tutored on how to *bust the balls* of her stuffed animals. She was taught to neither take shit nor to allow people believe that she ever *takes a shit*. These two ladies had been irrigated by the uncommonly brown Delta water, seasoned by the brusque Delta air, and baked in the exasperatingly sweltering Delta sun, so neither of the two cared much about the Delta's opinion, because in their minds, they had the only opinions that mattered. Jean-Marie and Lucretia Ann had become the matriarchs supreme, by default of their age, of their own *bitches' coven,* if you will.

The Delta had been long defined by its Confederate roots, but nothing-mattered more than a Delta's woman's denotation of it. The Delta was her oasis. Her oyster. Her treasure. And no two women embodied that more than Lucretia Ann and Jean-Marie. Their reign proved to be more menacing and enduring than the flood of 1927, and everyone in Greenville evoked considerable emotion as it related to the flood. Even those who were neither born nor thought of were even impacted by the story of heavy rainfall, that was neither theretofore heard of nor fathomable for that matter. Torrential storms befell the city and its inhabitants with an inexplicable vigor. Levees breached and the river was high enough to misplace men over 6 feet tall. Rooftops were barely visible. Accompanied by thunder and lighting, the rains dispirited the townspeople.

Oh but, even the historicity of floods, the Civil War, and the Yellow Fever outbreak paled in comparison to the stories of the women in Greenville. Neither Greeks nor Romans could mythologize the sins, exploits, mischiefs, and capers experienced by the ladies of the Delta. Their unusual plights in the densely populated South were flanked and marred by their social ranking. There was a certain implicit hierarchical system or manner of doing things that was just the way of life for them, but anyone with even modicum clairvoyance could see through it. One could detect a woman's worth, her value, and even her wealth in something as minuscule as her choice in *maids.* The Help.

The Delta woman who preferred to hire a white woman as her wait staff was the wealthiest of the lot. This dame, because of either her inheritance or her husband's salary, could afford to pay a woman who looked like her to wash her windows, clean her toilets, cook her food, care for her children, and hand wash her unmentionables. Even though the white maid was more likely to pillage and plunder, it was a risk she was willing to take because she treasured the space where she laid her head at night. Then there was the lady who hired a black maid in order to display her status across the tapestry so richly steeped in antiquity. Hiring a woman who had more subservience helped this type of Mississippi Delta woman feel more inclined to bask in her opulence. A sense of importance was a requisite for a *semblance of significance and self worth*. She gave her black maid grueling, grimy work like cleaning floorboards, degreasing ovens, washing windows, and the like. This Delta woman had become painfully aware that the men in her life lives mattered more to society than hers. Having a black housekeeper gave her an authority she'd otherwise not established which bolstered her feminist pride. It gave her pleasure to toss her unwanted garbs onto the floor and admonish her black maid to pick them up, take them or give them to her underprivileged family members. It was as charitable as she had been required to be.

The Delta woman who hired a Hispanic, Latina, or Mexican woman as her housekeeper was only concerned with services of her maid. She had no desire to get to know her *help* other than (1) her name, which by the way, she still never quite got right, and (2) how long it would take to complete the tasks she was to perform. The less English she knew the better. For this housewife wanted to teach her maid the words she deemed most essential in the English language such as commands and depreciatory words in order to instill fear in her, because usually *Maria* and *Ana* were undocumented. Since deportation was conceivable, they endured the cruelty and maltreatment. In turn, the *help* was more acquiescent than any of the four types. They uttered "Si, Señora" at least 100 times per day while dignity oozed out of their pores like sweat.

The Southern belle who employed Asian maids was mostly less well off. Asian maids worked fast, furiously, yet haphazardly. They didn't keep house as well as the main three types of help, but they made up for their paucities in speed and fastidiousness. The food they prepared was bland, the beds were never amply made, the ring around the tub was still slightly observable, and children didn't respect them at all. They maintained employment because they were slight in stature. This made them easier to order them around. They were the perfect candidates for being seen and never heard. The most appealing quality about these maids was their unattractiveness to husbands and inability to speak English literately. There was just something highly unappetizing about slit eyes and pitch-black hair. Though these wives couldn't explain it, they didn't care as long as it was a clear and palpable truth.

The type of residence in the Delta disclosed the kind of woman who resided there. It took a different kind of wife to coerce her husband into building or purchasing the right home. The woman who could own a three-story home, two floors, and a basement that she could furnish as an extra floor, had her husband by the balls. She was terribly pretty, equally smart, and usually was a lawyer, doctor, or an MBA also, but she no longer practiced, because her *man* had to be the principal breadwinner, as he wouldn't have been as well respected had his wife excelled in a like career or otherwise. The home was plantation style and was replete with 8 bedrooms, 5 and half bathrooms, a sunroom, a guesthouse, and a green house. This wife would find ways to hold shit against her husband so that if his parents or the community ever discovered, it would ruin him. It was usually something like cross-dressing, impotence, or a predilection for young girls and on the occasion, *young boys*. If she lived in a two-story home with 6 bedrooms and four full bathrooms, she was usually insanely beautiful and was able to maintain a particularly fit, svelte body. Her husband saw her as a trophy and would dare not do anything to drive her away, because his penis was usually small, but she didn't mind as long as his bank accounts were not. The woman whose husband bought or built her a flat with 5 bedrooms, 3 bathrooms and an attic was usually his second choice for a wife. This man couldn't attract the woman that he truly desired and he settled for this woman, who was brutally submissive as she knew all too well that if her husband had his druthers she wouldn't be his Mrs. The last of these women was only able to finagle a flat 3 bedroom home or condo with 2 bathrooms, but her perk was a swimming pool. The pool gave her leverage, as it was usually the go-to place for gatherings in the spring and the summer. She wasn't as attractive as others may have liked, but she just as haughty in her demeanor because her husband was still well off enough to buy her the car of her choosing and still send her on shopping sprees with the other ladies.

Speaking of cars, the most regal of these ladies had to drive a Mercedes. This car gave her status, style, and bespoke a certain class. She drove around with her nose in the air as she pronounced it MER-SUH-DEEZ to all her friends and family. Her husband bought her the newest model each year so for her these cars were like tissues she discarded after one use. The only other vehicle she drove was her minivan in which she drove the kids around to feign some motherly instinct of which she had none. Hell, she hadn't the foggiest of idea which sports or activities her kids were involved in. She dressed appropriately for whichever event her maid reminded her.

The woman who drove the BMW was as rich but was more classist. She had a driver. Her driver was usually a black man whom she bossed around like a child. His only response was, "yes ma'am and no ma'am". Complaining wasn't an option for him because he was compensated well enough to put his grandchildren through college. She too knew the importance of her cash payments to *Rufus* or *Sylvester* and she used this knowledge to her advantage. Driving her car and making sure it was spotless inside and out were his principal duties. He wasn't allowed to speak unless spoken to. This lady reassured him with her forked tongue that they were neither friends nor equals. It was an odd pairing because on occasion she'd ask him for advice. He'd oblige her with sensible counsel that often made her question his 6th grade education. Although she leaned on him for advice, he knew that her gleaming, black BMW was the barrier between the two of them.

If she drove a SAAB, she was cunning and conspiratorial. She wore sunglasses at night and for that none of the women trusted her so they kept her close. The other women invited to all of the social gatherings in order that she could be watched and observed in an atmosphere of which she really didn't belong. Her car was her broomstick in which she flagellated through the neighborhoods of her *frenemies* to witness their affairs when she was not in their presence. Her adversaries usually scoped out her surveillance of them. They found her clandestine acts to be immature and foolish, yet surreptitiously vile. She very rarely caught them slipping, but when she did, it was awfully and horribly egregious. They looked down on her SAAB because her frugal husband would never have bought it brand new. He would purchase the car that was primarily used for test-driving purposes. It was how he saved money, but his wife knew that there was no way to save face other than putting on airs, which this wife did well much to the irritation of her contemporaries.

The last breed of white woman raced through town like a bat out of hell in her Volvo wagon. Her husband too was parsimonious in regards to his wife and children, but spendthrift in regards to himself, vintage cars and golf clubs and such. As a result, she had constant road rage even on the two meager highways in Greenville. On the occasion that she did pick up her kids from private school and was running late, she'd cut people off, flip the bird, and even use a few choice obscenities and epithets. Her Volvo was a lease, so she too got a new one each year or every 25,000 miles, but nonetheless this housewife was often the butt of jokes. It was joked that this type of woman's husband really wanted to trade her in lieu of the car because she too had reached her mileage limits.

This smorgasbord of white women luxuriated in white privilege with their fancy homes fit for the pages of *Home and Garden* but their lives made for perfect fodder for books written by Jackie Collins. They lived lives devoid of any knowledge of what went on across town. These housewives wandered about inconsiderately soaking in their insipidness, relishing in their wateriness, and rocking in their blandness all of which served as bulwarks to the real world and its outliers. For them, there was no poverty line. They were too far above it to even be concerned with its ability to exist. It has been said that rich women are not concerned with whether there *is* food like the poor, or if there is *enough* of it like the middle class, they are only concerned with how it's *presented*. Presentation is everything. So is it with these women's lives. Presentation is key to preserve one's prominence, one's rank, and one's clout. Food was of no consequence, for there was usually more of it thrown away then eaten. Like food, racism, too was ubiquitous. It was as invisible and as dangerous as carbon monoxide. It too, like their privilege, was denied more than bastard children. This undeclared "club" of women existed everywhere, but none existed in more rare or raw form than in the Mississippi Delta.